D0056120

YA

C-1

BOOMERANG

HELENE DUNBAR

DISCARDED

STAUNTON PUBLIC LIBRARY

Sky Pony Press
New York

Copyright © 2018 by Helene Dunbar

Excerpt from "Poem" (You do not always seem able to decide) from *Poems Retrieved* by Frank O'Hara, Copyright © 2013 by the Estate of Frank O'Hara. Reprinted by permission of City Lights Books.

All rights reserved. No part of this book may be reproduced in any manner without the express written consent of the publisher, except in the case of brief excerpts in critical reviews and articles. All inquiries should be addressed to Sky Pony Press, 307 West 36th Street, 11th Floor, New York, NY 10018.

First Edition

This is a work of fiction. Names, characters, places, and incidents are from the authors' imaginations, and used fictitiously.

Sky Pony Press books may be purchased in bulk at special discounts for sales promotion, corporate gifts, fund-raising, or educational purposes. Special editions can also be created to specifications. For details, contact the Special Sales Department, Sky Pony Press, 307 West 36th Street, 11th Floor, New York, NY 10018 or info@skyhorsepublishing.com.

Sky Pony® is a registered trademark of Skyhorse Publishing, Inc.®, a Delaware corporation.

Visit our website at www.skyponypress.com.

www.helenedunbar.com

10 9 8 7 6 5 4 3 2 1

Library of Congress Cataloging-in-Publication Data available on file.

Cover photo: iStock
Cover design by Kate Gartner

Hardcover ISBN: 978-1-5107-1321-5
Ebook ISBN: 978-1-5107-1322-2

Printed in the United States of America

To Beth Hull,

who held on to my rope when I was at the end of it.

And to Brent Taylor,

who broke my fall.

You do not always seem to be able to decide
that it is all right, that you are doing what you're doing
and yet there is always that complicity in your smile
that it is we, not you, who are doing it
which is one of the things that makes me love you
—Frank O'Hara ("Poem")

To know the road ahead, ask those coming back.
—Chinese Proverb

ONE

I wasn't sleeping and I wasn't thinking about sleeping, which was sometimes all I could do when my mind was racing with thoughts of everything I should be doing and everything I shouldn't have done and everything I needed to figure out but couldn't.

Instead of sleeping, I was lying in the oversized tree house in McKuen Park like a homeless person. Appropriate, since I was between homes.

Instead of sleeping, I was pressing my nose against the wood and closing my eyes and letting the faint smell of cedar remind me of another tree house an hour away. I was thinking about the things I'd done there. And about the things that had been done to me. And about the things I'd wanted to do, but hadn't been brave enough to try.

I was wondering why threats that hung over your head felt sharper than the blade of an ax, and why caring about people made you responsible for them in ways you hadn't intended.

I was watching the sun rise through the wooden slats and reminding myself it was the same sun that rose over that other tree house in Barlowe. And I was considering the different ways that you could leave a place by running away from it or by running toward something else; and the different ways that you could come back, by choice or by force.

I was thinking about how everyone assumed I was forced to leave and came back by choice.

And how much they would hate me when they learned they were wrong.

The flashing red and blue police lights danced against my eyelids while my head throbbed in time to the screaming sirens.

To their credit, the time it took for Millway's police department to get here had to be some sort of local record. Still, they didn't need to show up with all of their toys turned to high. It wasn't like I was going to make a run for it.

I stuffed my blanket into my backpack and stood up, stretching my muscles, which had gotten stiff and cramped from the cold. I ran my palms over the wooden face carved into the roof of the park's tree house—the logo of Woodhouse

Houses—one last time. If anything felt like home in Millway, it was this small carving.

My best friend, Trip, said I should call the cops on the emergency "direct-line-to-the-police-in-case-your-cell-is-dead" phone as soon as I got to the park. But I'd needed time. Time to convince myself that I wasn't making the biggest mistake of my life. Time to get used to the idea of being back in freaking Millway. Time to wrestle with my anger. Time to miss him. The past couple of hours hadn't been enough to process any of those emotions.

The blaring sirens stopped and a fifty-something police officer headed my way, flashlight drawn, casting shadows as he walked through the park and up the wooden ramp to the tree house in the uncertain darkness of early morning.

On second thought, maybe Millway hadn't changed that much. I would have thought most towns would spare at least two cops for the return of a missing kid.

"Michael Sterling?" he asked, looking me over from head to toe. The name sounded strange, kind of like hearing your favorite bedtime story long after you thought you'd forgotten the words.

With one hand, I shaded my eyes against the bright flashlight beam. I wrapped my other tight around the small wooden boomerang Trip had carved for me. As it had for the last two years, the charm hung from a leather cord around my neck like a talisman. Without Trip, I felt small, insubstantial.

Without his voice in my ear, our desperate plan seemed like nothing more than smoke and mirrors.

The officer was still waiting for an answer.

"My name is Sean Woodhouse," I mumbled, both because of the cold and because it was easy to tell that my answer wouldn't thrill him.

A shadow crossed his face as he lowered the flashlight.

"But, yes," I admitted through chattering teeth. "I used to be Michael Sterling."

I was still bleary when Police Chief Perkins walked me to his car. I reached for the handle on the back door, but he quickly opened the front one for me. With a cautious smile I didn't deserve, he said, "You aren't a prisoner, son."

I got in and waited for him to close the door. Then I shut my eyes, letting my head rest against the window.

"Your mom is going to meet us at the hospital later," he continued as he climbed into the car and started the engine. "I know you're eager to see her, but I think you can understand why we need to take you to the station and verify it's really you first, right?"

I nodded, even though *eager* wasn't the word I would have chosen.

"She's been on pins and needles ever since you left that

message on our hotline. You could have just called the precinct or 911, you know. We would have sent a car right out."

I opened my mouth and then closed it. He didn't want to know that Trip had been the one to leave the message, not me. He didn't want to know how pissed I was about being blindsided by the whole plan that brought me back.

Perkins drove off. The movement of the car made me start to zone out, but I kept getting pulled back by a wave of adrenaline-fueled fear. I wasn't afraid of seeing my mother, although *that* wasn't high on the list of things I was looking forward to. It was more that I kept picturing Trip confusing left and right like he did, and crashing the truck on his way home after dropping me off at the park. That fear poked into me like pine needles. It didn't matter how angry I was with him for almost single-handedly forcing my return and putting Maggie and himself—everyone I cared about—at risk. Every time I closed my eyes, I imagined his body crumpled by the side of the road, bruises stalking his skin in the early morning light.

I swallowed the urge to tell the officer to slow down. To lie and say that I'd never met, much less *been*, Michael Sterling. I wanted to be back in the cottage in Barlowe, making sure that Maggie took her medication on time and hopelessly trying to help Trip with his math homework. I wanted that life back so badly that I had to link my fingers together to keep from throwing open the door of the squad car and running away. Again.

The radio crackled and whistled like an orchestra gone mad. I entertained myself with the idea that Millway had become some hub of criminal activity. But I quickly dismissed the idea and turned my attention back to the window. With a thin coating of snow over everything, the town looked like Pompeii frozen in time under a blanket of ash. Main Street was still filled with tiny stores under striped awnings: ice cream parlors and coffee shops, book- and pet stores, and a shop that sold candles and charms to those who had nothing better to do with their money.

Perkins drove us through town at a good clip. We cruised past the high school, its parking lot dominated by a million-year-old GO MUSKETEERS sign, to the police station, a building still stuck in the 1950s. Single-level. Red brick. Desperately in need of a paint job.

Before he opened his door, Perkins said, "We have your fingerprints on file from Frost's school registration day. That's been a good program for us. After you . . ." He stopped, clearly remembering who he was talking to. "Well, we're just going to run them now and match them up, and then we'll get going."

I pushed my way out of the car and stumbled, one black sneaker over the other. I took a deep breath, mumbled an apology, and tried to pull my head together. Getting out of this car was the easiest thing I was going to do all day.

When we walked into the station, the few officers in the room turned and watched with wide eyes, like I was some ghost back from the dead. The weight of their stares was unnerving after I'd spent the last five years trying not to be seen, working to never stand out. Did they see a seventeen-year-old kid with dark shaggy hair who'd rather be in a million other places? Or were they remembering some picture flashed on the evening news five years before?

I had an urge to stick out my tongue or give them the finger, but didn't want to end up on the other side of those bars. Instead, I focused on the gun bouncing in Perkins's holster as I followed him, and wondered if he'd ever needed to fire it in Millway.

He sat down at a metal desk, then gestured for me to take a seat on the other side. Remnants of a half-eaten breakfast littered the surface: milky coffee that was starting to separate and a half-gnawed bagel with speckled cream cheese. If it had looked remotely appetizing, the fact that I hadn't eaten in what felt like days might have mattered. As it was, the leftovers made me vaguely sick.

I pushed my bangs off my forehead and clenched my surprisingly sweaty hands.

"You okay, Michael?"

I dried my palms on my jeans. I'd only been back a few hours and I was already falling apart.

"Sean," I demanded, and then caught myself. I needed this guy on my side. Pissing him off wasn't part of the plan. "Can you call me Sean?" I asked as nicely as I could manage.

Chief Perkins lifted an eyebrow like he was already tired of the whole ordeal. He pulled an electronic pad out of a side drawer and held his hand out for my own. Then he cleaned my fingertips with an alcohol wipe and rolled them one by one, pressing them down onto the pad. The whorls and valleys of my fingertips were captured in black images on the screen. For a minute, I prayed that the record would come up empty—*This boy doesn't exist*—and I could walk out.

I wondered if the machine could tell the cops anything aside from my identity. Could it read the sickening feeling in the pit of my stomach? Would it betray the fact that the details surrounding my leaving and coming back weren't what everyone thought? Or would those whorls still have cells from Trip's skin embedded in them?

I wrapped my arms around my stomach. I couldn't look away from the monitor. Neither could the police chief. We both inhaled, our eyes fixed on the screen.

"Here we go," he said and pushed a button.

The machine hummed ominously and then beeped. I dragged my eyes away from the screen to look at Perkins. When he turned back to me, his eyes were shining. Everything about him had softened, like ice cream melting in the sun.

"Well, I'll be damned," he said. He cleared his throat, and for a minute I thought that the search had come up empty, that I'd gotten my wish. Then he reached over the desk to squeeze my arm. "Welcome home, Michael."

This time, I didn't bother to correct him.

There was a buzz in the police station. A feeling of celebration for a job well done, although they seemed to forget that no one had actually *done* anything.

My return had zero to do with them. I would have pointed that out had they not seemed so damned proud of themselves. I didn't want to be the one to bring everyone back down to earth. That would happen soon enough.

The cops who were staring at me earlier came to the desk under the guise of grabbing paperwork or dropping off files. One by one, they gave me some complicated kind of smile and clasped me on the shoulder. No doubt, each assumed I'd been through years of torture and was about to start the happiest part of my life.

For a moment, I wished they were right. That I'd spent every night of the last five years dreaming of coming back to Millway.

I waited while Perkins conferred with some officers and then collected an armload of files. The amount of paper lying around was enough to make me wonder if the police department's computer was just for show.

"We're heading to the hospital," Perkins explained as he led me back to his car. "Your mom will meet us there with the department's social worker. It's just a formality. Nothing to worry about."

I got in the front seat without prompting, and listened to Perkins carry on a conversation with himself. My head kept hitting the window from exhaustion, but I got the subject matter of his monologue: Millway's new ice rink, the connection to the freeway, how other police forces around the country were studying the town's methods for collecting data on children to keep them safe.

Then he started talking about my mother. *That* subject kept slipping in and out of my mind.

He seemed to know a lot about her, but I knew better than to ask the questions that had bugged me even from the safety of Maggie and Wilson Woodhouse's home in Barlowe.

I wanted to know whether my mother had gotten a job that didn't involve sweaty dark rooms and leering men. I wanted to know what sort of carnage I was going back to. And if I was allowed a bonus question, I wanted to know if she'd drunk her way through the trust fund my "damned grandparents" had set up for me. They'd wanted to make sure I had a future, even if their own daughter didn't.

It was clear that none of those questions would please Chief Perkins and there was nothing to be gained by pissing off a cop, so I kept quiet and watched the trees go by. Each one made me feel more on edge, as if the rustling of their snow-tinged branches was an accusation. I wasn't sure what they would think my biggest crime was: going away or coming back. They'd probably have had a good argument either way.

By the time we pulled into the hospital parking lot, I was sweaty and full of nervous energy. My fingers tapped a rhythm on my jeans, and it made me nuts that I couldn't figure out what song they were playing.

Perkins gripped my shoulder, a strangely comforting gesture. "You have nothing to worry about, Michael," he said. "Your mom never gave up hope that you'd come home. Hell, no one in Millway did. Today is going to be the best day of her life. Of both your lives."

The sincerity of his expression made my stomach lurch. Throwing up in a cop car wasn't going to win me any friends, though.

I pushed hard against the door and puked outside until I had nothing left.

TWO

In my memories, my mother is taller than I am, dressed in a dirty pair of jeans and a ripped T-shirt with dull hair pulled back in a messy blonde ponytail and nails bitten to the quick.

It took me years of being away to remember any of the good things about her. How sometimes she'd try: staying home to cook me dinner, paying the bills often enough to keep the lights on, looking over my homework like it was something she cared about. Then she'd be gone for a couple days—or she'd be so drunk or hungover it didn't even matter—and I'd run out of packs of ramen and clean clothes for school.

It took Trip's dickhead uncle to teach me that my mother's dance with oblivion and neglect had nothing to do with me. Even though, maybe, it should have. Even though having a kid should have been more important to her.

But standing here now in the hospital hallway with its shiny walls that reeked of antiseptic, the first thing I realized was that I was taller than her. It surprised me more than it probably should have.

Next, I took in her blue dress, necklace, and matching earrings. I'd bet most people wouldn't fixate on jewelry when they were seeing their mother for the first time in years. But to me it stood out. It was something she hadn't bothered with before, and it made her look different, like maybe the mother in my head had a pulled-together twin I'd never met.

Chief Perkins pushed me forward as my mother's watering eyes passed over me like she was trying to commit every inch of me to memory.

I wrapped my hand around the boomerang that hung from my neck and took a deep breath. It was almost physically painful, but I forced myself to look straight at her. For a minute, I was worried she'd rush up and grab me. Instead, she held back, linking her fingers together in front of her like a little girl in a store full of expensive, but useless, glass figurines.

Perkins cleared his throat. "It's okay, Amy," he said. "It's really him. He's back."

She nodded like she didn't quite believe his words, then returned my stare with gold-flecked brown eyes that mirrored my own.

She took a step and reached up slowly toward my hair. I was sure she was going to ask how my natural blond got to be the color of midnight, but she didn't. Her hand stopped before it touched me, and I was relieved when she drew it back.

I inhaled, expecting the sharp smell of vodka and sweat, but there was nothing except a whiff of drugstore perfume—floral. It reminded me of the lilies that grew on the border between the Woodhouse property and the state park behind it.

My mother and I stared at each other like little kids trying not to blink. It wasn't until Perkins pushed me forward and said "Hug your mom, son" in a voice that left no room for argument, that I raised my arms and we touched for the first time in five years.

There were, apparently, manuals for these things. Kids went missing all the time—typical police business. Tracking. Interviews. Reconnaissance. Search-and-rescue. Search-and-recovery.

The police knew what to do when things ended badly. They were given courses in how to comfort grieving parents, and all of that.

But in the cases where the kids were found, things got more complicated. Apparently too complicated for local police forces to deal with themselves. After the doctor gave me the once-over, we waited for everyone to figure out what they were supposed to be doing. Perkins told me that a few years back, the FBI published a bunch of manuals to help. I couldn't stop thinking of the sex ed pamphlets Trip brought back from school—pamphlets we'd cracked up over with titles like "Love or Infatuation?" and "Sex Makes Babies." What would these ones say? "Victim or Runaway?" "Leaving Breaks Hearts"?

I wasn't sure why Perkins decided to share that no one in Millway had ever cracked open the "returned kids" book. I thought he was apologizing, but it was hard to tell.

He told me they'd question me. And after, if my mother wanted, we could follow one of those pamphlet bullet points and meet with some social workers to "learn to communicate" and "rebuild our relationship." I hoped she wouldn't think that was necessary.

I closed my eyes and pictured the police officers frantically searching the station for the right guidebooks:

Damn, where did the manual go? We didn't think he was going to be found. Do you have it, Ron? Oh, wait. Here it is under a box of donuts.

I didn't know what was actually in those books, and I was both unprepared and terrified to find out. There would be questions I didn't want to answer. And probably a bunch I couldn't. I had no intention of lying to the police, not that I could anyway. Trip always called me "pathologically honest." I was incapable of lying under pressure.

But just because I was going to tell the truth, that didn't mean the answers I had to give would make anyone happy.

I wanted to feel like I was coming home, like I was taking charge. Instead, it felt suspiciously like I was giving up. The problem was, I didn't know how to give up the woods with their rustling trees or the family I'd chosen to be a part of in Barlowe or the dusky nights I'd spent crashing into Trip, never with a plan, but always in a kind of raw and desperate frenzy.

Perkins had another officer drop us at the house to escape the chaos of the hospital. My mother and I sat quietly in the back of the police car looking out our respective windows, a flurry of questions hanging between us like a curtain. *Why? What? How?*

When we got to the house, the cop of the moment held back a bunch of reporters clutching microphones like sabers, and ushered us to the front door. My mother's house looked like every other one on the block. I'd forgotten how fussy and manicured the area was and how the neighbors used to complain when my mother would leave two weeks' worth of trash out and always on the wrong day. How she'd never rake, telling me it was Maine and eventually it would snow and cover the dead leaves, so why bother?

Now, I kind of got her point. I searched for a wildflower, a bent tree, something unique, but it seemed like the only way people here showed any kind of individuality was by painting their front door a different color.

Walking through the blue door (the neighboring houses were red on one side and green on the other) made me feel like I was waking up from a dream, no idea where I was. As the fog cleared, everything came into soft focus: splashes of color, the angle of a chair, the expression on the face in a picture on the wall. Every tiny element jabbed somewhere deep in my brain like it didn't want to be completely forgotten.

My mother reached up and touched my shoulder with a light, birdlike hand. Tentative, as if she wasn't sure how I'd react. My shoulders tensed, but I didn't pull away.

"If there's anything you need, let me know." She sounded like the hostess of a party or a flight attendant making the rounds.

I closed my eyes and took a step farther into the room. *It's just a table. Just a chair. Just air in the room,* I repeated to myself as I moved to the flowered couch and sat on the edge.

Being here felt wrong.

"Can I get you something?" My mother headed to the kitchen. I knew she meant a soda or something to eat, but suddenly everything I needed was far away, wrapped in the safety of the trees of Barlowe State Park.

I didn't trust myself to speak so I shook my head.

"You're so . . ." Her voice cracked and we stared at each other. I wasn't sure whether to wish this awkwardness away. Without it, we'd have to talk, really talk, and there was no way I was ready for that.

It suddenly felt like the air in the house—or maybe all of Millway—was too thin. Sweat trickled down the back of my neck. I didn't need to touch the wooden charm to feel it resting against my chest, rising and falling with every breath, pulling me back.

My mother swallowed the rest of her sentence and started a new one. “We have a couple of minutes until Chief Perkins comes by,” she said as she straightened her skirt again. Her face was open and expectant. She looked younger than I remembered, like I'd been growing up and she'd been aging down. Maybe she had a painting in the attic, like *Dorian Gray*.

“That's fine,” I said, because I needed to say something. Only it wasn't fine. In fact, there was only one possible good thing about being back—the plan Trip and I had come up with when we were thirteen. Someday, we figured, I'd come back to Millway, get control of my grandparents' trust fund, and then leave again. That was the day I could save Trip from his uncle, Leon. We'd take off and see the world. Eventually I'd go to college and Trip would start his own woodworking business and we'd have the life we'd always wanted.

I'd never thought about what coming back would feel like. I never thought Trip would be the one to set the plan, prematurely, in motion. I never thought I could hate him for it. And I never thought that my own fear of the darkness lurking in his uncle would become something so tangible that it was Leon's face I saw when I closed my eyes and his voice I heard ringing in my ears, telling Trip he was worthless.

I shook my head, trying to clear the sound away. “Everything's fine.”

The clock was ticking impossibly slowly. Did anyone use ticking clocks anymore? Weren't they all digital?

I ran my thumb over the grooves in the wood of the

boomerang and imagined Trip out behind the house, an ax raised over his head. "You're dangerous," I told him once. He could chop up a log in no time. I think I was hoping he'd believe me and use the ax the next time his uncle came after him. Instead, he'd made some crack about it turning me on and I'd gone inside and sulked for the rest of the day.

"Is it? I mean, is everything really fine?" She sat and wrapped her arms around herself. "I don't even know the right questions to ask. Were you hurt? Did you . . . I mean the police will ask all of those questions I guess, but . . ."

I stared at her. *Yes, I'm hurt*, I wanted to say. Wouldn't you be hurt if your best friend betrayed you? But I knew that wasn't what she was asking, and I knew she wouldn't understand even if I could bring myself to tell her everything.

After a pause, my mother cleared her throat. "I don't know that much has changed in the house, but I can show you around, if you want. I didn't move, in case you came back. I wanted you to be able to find me."

I was pretty sure this woman was an alien. My real mother wouldn't even have stayed home for a whole evening so that I could find her.

"Do you want to see your room?"

I tried to remember what my room here looked like. All I saw in my head was my room in Barlowe. The blue walls with scrolling quotes painted on them. The wooden star carvings that hung from the ceiling and cast shadows all around the room. The kinetic sculpture made up of a dizzying array of intersecting circles that Trip made from an oak tree that had been struck by lightning.

I blinked the picture away and saw my mother waiting. Following her, I stopped to look at the photos lining the stairway. My mother as a teenager staring out from the frame with so much focus it was as if she could've taken a step and ended up in the room next to me. A little boy who must have been me—blond with a forced smile, sitting in a field of sunflowers the same color as his hair.

There were no pictures of a man. I never knew who my father was. It didn't matter how drunk she'd gotten, my mother would never tell me. I wasn't even sure if she knew. I'd stopped caring about getting an answer years ago.

These photos should have made me feel some sort of connection. Instead I felt detached. Intellectually, I knew it was me on the wall reading a book, kicking a soccer ball. The problem was I couldn't tap into what being Michael *felt* like. All I knew, all I felt, was Sean.

My mother opened the door and waited for me to catch up. The room was a time capsule, a child's room with a patchwork quilt on the single bed and slightly faded posters of baseball players on the wall. MICHAEL was scratched into the desk. The room felt desolate and unused, as if it were holding its breath, waiting for someone to come back.

There was an eerie lack of dust. How often did my mother come in here?

Her eyes crinkled as she pointed to a stack of wrapped

boxes in the corner. "I bought you presents every year for your birthday and Christmas. Of course, it's silly now," she said, almost to herself. "I mean, you'll have outgrown most of it. But I wanted you to know I didn't forget. I never forgot you, Michael. Every day, I hoped and prayed."

"That's . . ." but I couldn't finish. What was it? Sweet, but at the same time, I felt a wave of anger about all the birthdays and Christmases she never remembered when I was here. Hell, to be honest, I was pissed about all the dinners and school events and bill deadlines she'd missed, as well.

I could tell she was biting back tears. If I was still Michael inside, I would have put my arms around her like I'd done when I was eight, crying and begging her not to go to work and leave me alone in the cold, dark house. Michael was like that.

But now it seemed like there was too much space between us, and not because we were on opposite sides of the room.

Normal sons didn't run away. I got it. But normal mothers didn't, either. A bunch of presents in the corner weren't going to give me my childhood back.

As if she knew what I was thinking, my mother sank onto the bed with a sigh. "I might as well just say it to you. I'm sorry I wasn't a better mother. It was such a hard time and I was so young. It never meant I didn't love you, though. You know that, right?"

Another surge of anger rolled through me, stronger this time, dizzying in its intensity. All the years in Barlowe that I'd had to let my anger at her dissolve and reconfigure into something like pity seemed like only a tick of the clock as my calm was eaten away. “It was a long time ago,” I spat out with only half of the bitterness I felt.

I moved toward the window to get as far away from her as I could in the small room. The way the houses were set up, I could still see straight into the Gordons’ backyard behind us. I remember spending a lot of time running through our yard to get to theirs. Their daughter, Jenny, was the same age as me and she had been the only thing I’d ever missed about Millway. Still, I hadn’t even thought about her in a long time.

My mother’s voice pulled me back. “Now that you’re older, maybe you’ll understand. I want to make it up to you.” The determined tone in her voice was something new. It wasn’t like the “I’m going to stop drinking” promises she used to make, and it wasn’t like the “When you get home from school, we’ll do something special, just the two of us” lies I’d stopped believing when I was young enough to still believe in Santa Claus and fairytales. Maybe she actually meant it this time. Too little, too late. The role of mother in my life had been filled by someone else.

“It doesn’t matter,” I said. And it was true. I’d done my best to stop wanting anything from her a long time ago. Besides, I wasn’t sure I was sorry about how things turned out.

If I was planning on staying, I’d tell her that.

If I was planning on staying, I’d make sure she knew I wasn’t the boy she wanted back.

THREE

Chief Perkins cut a path through the reporters and into the house, followed closely by a young guy who was, I guessed, in his twenties and maybe on his first case. He was looking at Perkins for permission to even walk in the door. For some reason I couldn't explain, I felt as close to comfortable with Perkins as I was going to with a cop. Having this extra witness created a strange knot in my stomach. I didn't even catch his name.

"How are you feeling?" Perkins asked as we all settled onto the floral couches and fake suede loveseats. My mother's decorative style had improved. But where Wilson and Maggie's house was a mismatched jumble of well-loved items collected during their travels or made by artistic friends, my mother's house felt like a magazine ad for a discount store. Everything matched, but nothing had any personality.

I shrugged. If I was honest and said "pissed off and homesick," it would have caused more problems. If I told them I felt like an amputee who woke up with stabbing pains in a leg that had been cut off, I was pretty sure they'd take me somewhere far more unsettling than the police station.

"We'd like to ask you a bit about what you remember," Young Guy said to me, reading off a pad. His face was so pockmarked, all I could think was how much it must have sucked to have been him in high school. I actually felt bad and wondered what he'd done in his past life to get stuck with this case. It was a hell of an unlucky break.

He stared at me, trying to look older and more experienced than he was, so I stared back and asked, "What do I remember about what?" I wasn't trying to be a dick. I just had no problem making them work for the info I was going to hand them.

Perkins coughed and gave me a stern look. "The day you went missing."

My mother inhaled sharply. Her surprise shocked me. What else was she expecting we'd talk to the police about? The weather? Last year's Red Sox season? She had to know this was coming. My "youth" and my "potentially fragile emotional state" were the only reasons we were here in the house instead of at the station.

"I was at school," I said. That much was true. I'd gone to school and aced my first English test of the year even though I'd spent most of the hour staring out the window at the fall leaves as they dropped one by one from tired trees.

"And then you walked Jenny Gordon home and went to the library?" Young Guy asked, fiddling with his pen. It turned out he was the type who drummed his pen without thinking about it. I could see him itching to do it now. Badly. And Perkins must have known, because he kept looking over and the fiddling would stop for a minute.

"Yeah," I said to Perkins. "I walked Jenny home. She lived over there." I glanced toward her house, looking through my mother's kitchen, the same kitchen that had been totally empty the day I left. On top of it, my mother had never bothered to sign me up for the lunch program. All I'd had that day was a bottle of energy water I'd managed to swipe from the locker room and half a bag of chips someone had left on their tray. I was so hungry when I got to Jenny's that when she jokingly offered to trade me a bag of homemade cookies for a kiss, I jumped at the deal.

I vaguely remembered feeling bad about leaving Jenny. But she had what I never did—a family—and I'd been sure she'd be okay without having to deal with all my drama.

Better, even.

From my mother's expression, it was clear Jenny still lived there. I felt a pang of something I hadn't in a long time. Once we'd been friends. Then I left, and Trip found me. After, it was like the memories of my whole life before I got to Barlowe played back in black and white.

Young Guy bounced his knee up and down. "The library?" he asked, sounding annoyed.

I glared at him. "Yes, then I went to the library."

I didn't bother telling them that after I walked Jenny to her house, but before I'd gone to the library, I'd stopped home to find the house cold and empty. My mother was out and had either forgotten to, or chosen not to, pay the heating bill. I didn't tell them that I'd almost sat down at the table and started my homework. I didn't tell them that I'd been overwhelmed by the idea of another night, cold and alone, and packed a bag hoping some miracle would happen.

The cops nodded in unison. Of course they were relieved by the lack of anything new in what I'd said. They figured they knew the whole story already and that this entire conversation was simply a formality.

"Do you remember anyone following you? Anything strange on the way?" Chief Perkins asked while Young Guy started taking notes. At least his transcription gave him something less annoying to do with his pen.

I told them how I walked, uneventfully, to the library. About how I tried to study, but couldn't focus. And how from there I'd gone to the park. In those days, it always felt like I was leaving. Never moving toward something, always away.

My heart beat uncomfortably hard as I told them about how I talked to Wilson at McKuen Park. I knew, from some community day, that Wilson owned Woodhouse Houses, even though, I learned later, they didn't qualify as *houses*. What he really built were cottages people used as offices or beach bungalows. He built playhouses for parks, like the one I'd slept in at McKuen, and he built the most insane tree houses ever, like the one he'd built with Trip.

"Michael?" Young Guy said.

Crap. I wasn't sure which parts I'd said out loud and which I'd only been remembering. "Can you call me Sean?" I asked, daring him to say no. How hard it could possibly be to get someone's name right?

Both officers looked at my mother. She rubbed her forehead like she was hoping to smooth the question and the stress away. Then she nodded.

"Sean, then." Young Guy scratched his head. "So Wilson Woodhouse, the contractor, was the man who took you?"

I could see their thoughts spinning. They were itching to run the name through their databases, eager to close this cold case and get credit for bringing a child abductor to justice.

I paused. There wasn't a lot of room for me to screw this up. And although what I was going to tell them was completely true, it was, without a doubt, the last thing anyone in this room wanted to hear.

"He didn't take me," I said quietly. "Not really." I took a deep breath I hoped would propel the words out of me. "I wanted to go. I didn't give him a choice."

The cops looked at each other like they thought I was lying. Or so damaged I was fooling myself. Next to me, my mother stiffened. I tried not to look at her.

"So you ran away?" Young Guy asked.

It was splitting hairs, but this was the single most important question they could ask. I knew, from the conversations I'd overheard between Wilson and Maggie, that Maine was the one state that didn't make harboring a runaway a crime. But if I committed to being a runaway, they were more than likely going to throw me in some juvie detention center or ship me off to military school, and there went the trust fund and our plans. There went Trip's chances.

To save Maggie and Wilson, I had to sacrifice myself.

Which meant sacrificing Trip.

Maggie and Wilson had saved me. Desperate as he was, even Trip wouldn't want me to throw Maggie and Wilson under the bus. After all, he loved them, too. I clutched at the boomerang, praying I was doing the right thing.

I'd been quiet, gathering my thoughts long enough that the cops must have assumed the answer was difficult for me for other reasons.

Perkins reached out a fatherly hand and held my wrist. His face had "Stockholm Syndrome" written all over it, like Wilson brainwashed me or I had to believe this story to get through the last five years with my sanity intact.

"I know this isn't easy, but we have to ask. Did Wilson Woodhouse hurt you in any way?"

It was inappropriate, I knew, but I couldn't keep from laughing. "Wilson? No." I shook my head. "He never laid a hand on me."

Wilson's face floated in front of my eyes, concerned like it had been right after I came to stay with them. His blue eyes dulled with dark circles under them from guilt and worry and other emotions the twelve-year-old me hadn't known how to name.

He wouldn't have approved of what I was doing. That knowledge sat in my stomach like a brick.

"But he took you with him?" Perkins asked.

In my head, I explained how easy it was for a twelve-year-old boy with no father and a neglectful mother to leave his shitty life to go with someone who offered him everything. Outwardly, I stayed silent.

Suddenly, my head started to pound like a jackhammer. I reached up to massage my temples, but that didn't help.

"Can I . . . I'm tired. Can we stop for now?" I was milking the situation, but that didn't mean I was lying.

Young Guy piped up first. "I think we should press on."

My mother put her arm around my shoulders, but it felt nothing like when Maggie did the same thing. "Can we give him another day to get his bearings?" she asked Perkins.

He glanced from her to me and his eyes crinkled. "Look, Amy, I know this is hard. But the longer we wait . . . memory gets funny sometimes."

"We've waited five years," she said, pulling me closer to her. This time it was easier to relax into her embrace.

"I know." Perkins reached out and patted her hand. "I know. Tell you what, Sean," he said, deliberately. "Let me grab a glass of water, and then we'll quit for the day?"

My mother started to get up, but he motioned for her to

sit and gave me a leading look. Obviously, he was after more than water. I didn't know what he was up to, but I was curious to find out. I stood and led him into the kitchen, although I got the feeling he'd been in there more than I had.

He helped himself to a glass, filled it from the tap, and leaned back against a granite counter that hadn't been there five years before. "You aren't on trial or anything, you know that, right? None of our questions . . . We know none of this is your fault."

I wasn't stupid enough to argue. "Yeah," I said, suddenly inarticulate. Wilson would never have let me get away with such a non-answer.

"Predators don't stop with one kid. You're seventeen, almost an adult. Your mom is in the other room, so if you help me, we don't need to upset her with all this. I'm going to be straight with you. With you gone, it's very possible your abductor is going to find a replacement, and we don't want to give him time to do that. You understand? We need to shut him down."

I glanced around the room. The kitchen was clean, almost too clean. It didn't even look used. I felt a stabbing pain behind my left eye and reached up to rub it.

"Sean?"

"Wilson isn't going to do that." I tried to push down the piercing ache in my head.

"How can you be so sure?"

I looked up just as the condensation dripped off the bottom of his glass. One drop. Then two.

My head screamed so badly I could barely keep my eyes open. I forced them wide and looked right at Perkins. "Because he died," I said, not even wanting my mouth to form the agonizing words. "He fell at a tree house build site. Just over two years ago."

The tree house. Everything started and ended there.

I'd been in Barlowe for a full week before the pelting rain that had been coming down almost nonstop, let up. For the first time, I could look out the window and see a wooden structure in the trees: a bunch of interwoven planks—some colored, some not—which had come together by magic to form a house that hovered over the property. I'd never seen anything like it. It was like something in a book of fairy tales drawn with colored pencils and dreams.

"What's that?" I'd asked.

Wilson's wife, Maggie, walked over to me, balancing first on a purple walking stick decorated with silver stars and then on one covered in what looked like newspaper clippings. She smiled her peculiar lopsided smile as she looked up at the trees.

"That," she said, "is Trip Marchette."

I stared at her. Maybe it was the way she said his name. Maybe it was the name, itself, or maybe I just had my one and only psychic flash, but I'd shivered as if I'd instinctively known what he was going to mean to me.

Oblivious, Maggie said, "Well, that's not really Trip. But that's what he does."

"Trip Marchette." I rolled the name over my tongue.

"He lives next door." She pointed vaguely around with her purple stick and I had to duck to keep from getting smacked in the head. "Well, what passes for next door." She thrust a shaky finger through the window at a large grouping of towering trees toward the back of the house. "His house is about three hundred yards that way. Our property line ends right after the row of birch trees in there."

I stepped outside into a yard that seemed to stretch forever. The Woodhouse property sat alongside a state park, but there were no solid markers for where one stopped and the other began. I learned later that Maggie was forever having to shoo curious hikers out of her vegetable garden. On that day, the first clear one since I'd arrived, it seemed like a paradise compared to the dull and predictable architecture of suburbia I was used to.

I looked in every direction, but didn't see anything that might have been a neighboring house. It was fall and the trees were full with leaves the shades of sunset that caught the afternoon light and reflected it back in rays of stunning color.

Later that afternoon, I met Trip for the first time.

He had his own key to the house and was carrying two heavy-looking paper bags, which he put on the knotty pine table. Trip gave Maggie a kiss on the cheek and somehow managed to keep his eyes on me the entire time.

He was around my age, with dark curly hair that seemed to be everywhere all at once, and silvery gray eyes that pinned me in place as he looked me over.

My shoulders pulled back and I stood up straight. I wasn't used to being examined like that.

I relaxed when he broke into a strange, adventurous smile that hinted at the types of mischief I was never brave enough to get into on my own.

I'd almost forgotten Maggie was there until she said, "Trip helps me out a lot here. In turn, I tutor him."

I nodded toward him. "So that's yours?" I pointed up into the tree. The way the sun was hitting, I could see the structure a little more clearly.

"Yeah, you want to see it?" he asked. The tone of his voice made it plain my answer would be important.

I nodded again. We both looked to Maggie for approval, but she'd wandered over to the table and was rummaging in one of the bags.

"One thing first." She held out a box to Trip and they exchanged a puzzling look.

He led me to the bathroom in the back of the house and started lining the box's contents up on the counter. Little bottles and vials.

"What is this stuff?" I asked.

"You'll see." He mixed the contents together. It reminded me of the chemistry set Jenny's parents had gotten her for Christmas. "Maggie says if you're gonna stay, you need to fit in. I help her with hers all the time."

I crinkled my nose at the smell. Trip handed me a towel and told me to close my eyes.

When I hesitated, he leaned right into my face, those magnetic gray eyes staring straight into mine. "No one here is going to hurt you," he whispered. It was a strange thing for a kid to say, but I believed him.

I followed his instructions and closed my eyes while he massaged something wet onto my head. It felt surprisingly good.

A few minutes later, he told me I could open my eyes and sit up.

After he washed my hair out, I moved over to the mirror. In place of my sun-kissed blond hair was a mop of black even darker than Trip's.

"Holy crap," I said and then covered my mouth. Maybe *crap* was a bad word here. I didn't want to give anyone an excuse to send me home.

I closed my eyes and then opened them again. My hair was still dark. I don't know who I looked like, but it wasn't Michael Sterling with the drunk mother who was never around.

Trip reached out and messed my hair up. "Hey, you look kinda like me now." He leaned his head down so that we filled the mirror together. I didn't think that was such a bad thing at all.

"Can I see your tree house?" I asked.

He looked at his digital watch and his face got dark. "I need to get back. How about tomorrow?" He pulled at the two braided bands on his wrist—red and blue on the left and green and yellow on the right.

"What are those for?" I asked, gesturing to them.

He let the bands go and they made snapping sounds against his wrists. "They're supposed to help me remember left from right."

I guessed it was a stupid question and he was just screwing with me.

I didn't realize until later that he was being honest.

Perkins called my mother into the kitchen and told her to get a cold compress for my headache. Since I was a minor, I needed to repeat what I'd said in front of her so it could be part of my official statement.

This time, instead of being comfortable on the couch, we sat stiff and formal around the dining room table.

"Let's take this from the top, okay?" He gave me a look that made it clear he neither expected nor wanted an answer from me. This wasn't an optional conversation.

Perkins glanced at his notes and frowned. "So, Wilson Woodhouse was finishing up the structure at the park. Was that the first time you'd spoken to him?"

I shook my head and the room shifted slightly.

"How many times before that would you say he'd talked to you?"

"How many angels can dance on the head of a pin?" I responded without thinking.

I hadn't watched a lot of TV in Barlowe, aside from some DVDs of old musicals that Maggie and Wilson had collected from somewhere. But they had a library that bled from room to room. I'd spent the last five years reading everything that wasn't nailed down. Maggie and I had a game where we'd quote something and see if the other could guess where it came from. Throwing out quotes had gotten to be a habit, particularly when I was at a loss for words.

Perkins gave my mother a confused look that I was pretty sure meant he thought I was off my rocker. I needed to salvage the situation sooner rather than later.

"I used to hang out at the library and the park a lot," I said. I wondered if my mother was going to step in and confess before I had to say it. But she simply leaned her elbows on the table, bending forward eagerly.

I took a deep breath and dove in. "I don't have a father. And my mother . . . even when she was here, she wasn't."

Perkins narrowed his eyes. Obviously, I'd crossed some sort of honor-your-mother line.

"I was a dancer," she said to Young Guy, whose eyebrows had gone up into his hairline. "Not ballroom."

I laughed and Perkins looked like he wanted to kill me.

"And I'm an alcoholic," she continued in a strong voice. "But I've been sober now for three years."

Good for her. I didn't dare try to think about how my life would have been different had she done that when she still had a kid at home.

"I had a lot of time on my hands." I skipped telling him I'd always felt scared. When I was younger, I'd been sure that someday I'd come home from school and find my mother dead on the couch. Or that my unknown father would turn out to be some psycho and show up to drag me down to the depths of hell with him. If it hadn't been for Jenny, I would have been completely and utterly alone.

I looked into Perkins's eyes and gave him the most honest truth of all: "I felt safer with Wilson than I did here."

Next to me, my mother groaned, sounding like a wounded animal. "I should have been here more," she whispered, her eyes fixed to the table. "If I'd only . . ."

"Do you need a break?" Perkins asked. She shook her head and he leaned over and put a hand on my arm. He was touchy, this one. "Sean. Did you know he was planning to take you?"

"He didn't take me," I insisted, my voice getting louder. "I hid in the back of his truck under a tarp. They didn't even know I was there until the next morning. For weeks, Wilson and Maggie sat me down every single night. Each time, they asked me if I wanted to come back to Millway and each time I said no. Finally, they asked how I felt about changing my name."

I felt compelled to try to win the cops over with the force of the truth even though there was no chance of them understanding it.

"Look, Wilson was on the road a lot for work. His wife was sick." I used past tense, which was stupid. Not like they couldn't just look Maggie up in their database. But maybe they wouldn't bother. Maybe they'd just leave her alone. "She had a muscular disease. Degenerative." I swallowed the rush of emotion that welled up when I thought of Maggie. "She hates, I mean, *hated*, doctors. She needed someone home to take care of her. Someone to talk to. She . . ."

I took a deep gulp of air that stuck in my lungs. Before I left Millway, I'd had to give up on the idea of my mother ever pulling herself together. As I got older, I'd tried everything I could think of, including stealing her keys to try to keep her home. I canvassed the house for those little bottles of booze she'd bring home from work. I stole money from her purse and hid it with the hope of keeping the lights on. Nothing ever worked.

When Wilson told me about Maggie being sick, I thought, *Here's someone I can do something for, someone I can help. Someone who would actually appreciate it.*

"Wilson loved her, but he needed to work and that meant

traveling. He . . ." The words were elusive. Slippery as wet oak. As soon as I grasped for one, it slithered away.

I tried hard not to freak out, but suddenly the thought of Maggie alone in the cottage without me or Wilson was terrifying. I knew Trip would check on her, but he was dyslexic and had always been worried he'd mess up the complex dosages of her meds. The more stressed he was, the worse the chances of that happening became. And as much as he believed my coming back was a good idea, I doubted his ability to stand up to his uncle without me giving him a hard time. Who knew what would happen to either of them without me.

The room was quiet, like sound didn't exist in any form I was used to. The weight of three sets of eyes rested heavily on me.

Perkins cleared his throat. "Jimmy, can you go out to the car and radio the station? Run the name Wilson Woodhouse."

Young Guy narrowed his eyes at being so obviously dismissed. I wondered if I was going to be the victim of some sort of police brutality. No witnesses and all that.

When the front door clicked shut, Perkins stood near the front window and glared at me. "That the story you're sticking to?"

I nodded.

"'He's a good kid,' they all said. 'He looks after his mom. He's smart.'" Perkins scowled again. "Boy, were they handing us a line of shit."

In spite of the fact that I couldn't disagree with him, I felt a rush of blood to my face.

He wagged a finger in my direction. "Get over here."

I did as he said.

He pulled the curtains apart and pointed at the news vans assembled in front of the house. "You see them?"

I nodded.

"They're like piranhas. And they aren't going to leave until they're fed something. I have a mind to throw you out there and let them devour you, but out of respect for your mother, I'm not going to. So here's the deal. You keep your mouth shut. Do you hear me? You don't say anything. Not one word. Not to anyone."

I nodded again. Suddenly, this all seemed more real than I'd been expecting.

"Amy," he said, his voice softening as he walked back to my mother who shifted in her chair. "If you don't know the caller, don't answer the phone. Or just direct them to contact the station. I'll get one of our lawyers to draft a vague release about how happy you are to have your son back. National press has enough on their plate with the kids who really *are* missing." Perkins cast a withering look in my direction. "The locals are caught up in that damned backyard chicken ordinance that's coming up for a vote next week. They'll all be camping out at the courthouse soon enough. As soon as something else shiny comes along, they'll be out of your hair."

Perkins turned back to me and pulled himself up to his

full height. I became more aware than ever of the gun in his holster, but the look in his eyes was just as brutal as any bullet.

"A runaway. This whole town has wasted five years on a *runaway*. I'm sure as hell not going to be the one to tell them that."

Maybe I should have kept my mouth shut. Maybe I should have lied. I pressed my lips together. There was a quote that I was too stressed out to remember exactly. But it was by Camus and basically said that truth can be overwhelming, while lies can be as beautiful and easy as you want. Maggie totally would have won this round of our game.

Looking at my mother's stricken face, I wondered if it wouldn't have been a better plan to let everyone believe I'd been abducted. Tortured. That was the reality they'd prepared themselves for. That was what was going to make them feel better.

No one could handle the truth. That I'd been happy.

FOUR

The few remaining members of the press who were still camped outside my mother's house wanted a sob story.

The cops wanted a hero.

The truth: I was just a boy sitting in a tree trying to figure out how to lay claim to a sum of money with his name on it in order to save the best friend he wasn't even sure he was speaking to.

The tree in question was impossible to miss. The only magnolia in the neighborhood, it looked like it had been dropped into my mother's yard by helicopter rather than planted. Huge pink flowers filled it in the summer. In the winter, its gnarled branches looked ominous, like it was protecting the back of the house from an invading army.

It had been my safe haven from my mother and the empty house and the nights when sleep was something I could only imagine.

From my perch, I watched a girl make her way across the yard. The lights from the cameras in front of the house bounced off the long threads of her fuzzy top. Her brown hair was pulled back and she had something soft bunched in her hand. My mind raced to merge the distant memory of the girl I'd known with the girl in front of me. I remembered what Jenny looked like at five, at ten. She was seventeen now, just like me. I had to let her new, more grown-up features settle into place inside my head.

Her eyes weighed heavily on me as she climbed up the trunk. I was the deer caught in her headlights. In the five years I'd been gone, I'd guess I'd spent less than twenty-four hours total around anyone my age, aside from Trip.

I was out of practice.

From the corner of my eye I watched her settle on the branch next to me before she held out what she'd been carrying—a sweatshirt.

"It's cold tonight." She offered a tiny smile along with the shirt.

I tried to smile back, but my mouth was frozen in place. I'd left all my emotions in Barlowe and just felt empty. I took the shirt anyway, shrugging it over the goose bumps on my arms. I didn't particularly want to be warm or comfortable.

Being cold was somehow the only thing that made sense to me, given how numb I felt. But I was always bad at turning my back on kindness.

Before I'd left, Jenny had been my best friend. My only friend once I'd moved up a grade. There'd been the usual middle school rumors about us being "a thing" since we were together all the time, rumors that I'd tried to stop more than she had. But the truth was, I hadn't been attracted to *any* girl, or any person, really. Not until Trip, anyhow. And while I'd liked Jenny and cared about her, I hadn't loved her. It wasn't until I left Millway that I started to understand what love was.

For all the good that did me.

"I couldn't sleep," she said carefully, pulling me out of my thoughts.

I leaned back against the tree. I had no idea how to reply. Any words I had were stuck in my throat.

"Michael," she said, and then winced. "My mom said she heard . . . I mean. What do you want me to call you?"

My fingers floated over the edges of the boomerang. "You're the only one who's asked." Whatever I said was going to feel wrong. I had to choose. She could call me Ishmael or Mary for all the difference it made. I was one giant, blinking exit sign. "Sean," I said. "I mean, Sean is fine."

I caught a surprised look on her face before she quickly wiped it away.

"That's cool," she said, pointing at the charm hanging around my neck. "What is it?"

I tucked the wood into my shirt. It felt warm against my chest, even in the cold air.

What was it? A promise I wasn't sure hadn't been broken. A deal I wasn't sure I could keep. A future I probably no longer had.

I settled on "Gift from a friend," shocked to hear my voice crack.

Jenny stared at me like I was an alien. Like I'd fallen from the stars. Like I'd grown an extra head. Questions scrolled through her eyes like that news ticker in Times Square.

"You must be—" she started and then stopped. "Are you glad to be home?"

I sighed, and heard myself sigh. Then I laughed because I sounded dramatic, like an actor in a horrible old movie. My breath turned white in the cold, and it made me think about Trip trying to teach me to blow smoke rings. I'd sucked at it, which had made him smile—a rare gift that was its own reward.

I shook my head. "This isn't . . . It's kind of . . ." I bit my lip. The thought of Millway as home made my stomach curdle.

We sat in silence. I looked around for the moon, feeling abandoned when I couldn't find it. Jenny's eyes were fixed on my profile.

Then she said, "Your mom always thought you'd be found, you know. I mean, all of us did." She reached out and squeezed my arm and the branch bounced slightly as I flinched. "Everyone at school is already wondering if you're coming back. They've been leaving me messages."

I wanted to ask who "everyone" was, but at the same time, I didn't want to know. It wasn't like I'd had a ton of friends before I left. The kids at school had been far more interested in comic books and video games than the ways I'd found to pick the locks when Mom passed out and forgot to let me in. They hadn't wanted to see my list of things I could buy from the corner grocery for dinner when I could only scrounge a buck in change from under the sofa cushions.

"Don't worry," she said. "They're all just really happy that you're okay. I am, too, Sean. I'm so happy."

"Thanks." I ran a hand through my hair. I wondered how these nameless people would define "okay." I wondered why she was so happy I was back when I hadn't been a part of her life for so long.

Jenny told me about kids I barely remembered and had no interest in. I let her talk. There was something comforting about her steady stream of words.

I zoned out until I caught her last sentence: "Do you remember all the time we used to spend out here?"

I nodded. "Yeah. I remember." Then I actually thought about it. Tried to touch the memories in my head and couldn't quite manage it. "But it's distant. Kind of like a dream."

A truck rumbled by on Marjoram. I'd forgotten, for instance, that all the streets in this part of Millway were named after herbs. When the rumbling was so far away I couldn't hear it anymore, the silence settled back around us like a shroud.

I wanted to say something to let her know I appreciated

that she even gave a damn. The most obvious place to start was to ask her about herself, but I couldn't figure out where to begin.

Eventually, she broke the quiet. "So, do you think you're coming back to school?"

I reached up and snapped a tiny, brittle branch off the tree. Then I broke it again. And again and again so it formed a series of wooden triangles. I let them go, one by one, and watched them spin as they fell.

Even when Trip and I were younger and had talked about me coming back to Millway, I hadn't thought about the specifics of going to school, to class, seeing everyone I grew up with. I'd never thought about much past showing up here and leaving again.

Jenny stared like she was trying to see inside me.

I tried to remember what it was she'd asked. School. *What's the point? I'm leaving as soon as I can,* I said in my head, even as my mouth said, "I've been homeschooled. But there are laws about going to school and stuff, right?"

Her face clouded over and she shivered. "My mom would kill me if she knew I was out here, but I couldn't wait to see you." She smiled and leaned in toward me, bumping her shoulder into mine. "I really missed you."

My cheeks grew hot and I felt my hand rising to my neck and to Trip's boomerang. I clenched my fist, forced it down, and closed my eyes. I wished I could turn back the clock, but I didn't know to what point. Definitely not to the time I used to live here, but maybe to a couple years ago, before Wilson died. Before everything with Trip got so complicated. Before Maggie got so sick. Back to when everything had seemed so much simpler.

Whatever time period I considered, I couldn't see Jenny being a part of it.

"Are you . . ." she began, then went quiet. When Trip did the same thing, it always filled me with an odd anticipation. Like I knew whatever he was going to say would be something that mattered. With Jenny, the pauses were kind of annoying. Who knew what sort of questions she'd been saving up?

Just when I thought I couldn't take the tension anymore, she said, "Sorry. This is weird, right? I shouldn't be asking you questions like I'm from the paper or something. Sorry."

I wanted to agree, but she looked so sad, and the wind was blowing through the trees, and she'd brought me a sweatshirt. So instead, I said, "It's okay. What do you want to know?"

I waited for the obvious. Where did I go? Why did I go? What am I doing back?

"Was it horrible?" she whispered.

I actually had to stop to think. Living in Barlowe was many, many things. Beautiful. Frustrating. Bizarre. Home. But the only horrible part, except for Trip's uncle, was leaving it.

"No." I blinked. "No."

She let out a short breath and folded her arms like she was trying to figure out how to get me to give her more than a one-word answer. I wasn't trying to be uncommunicative; I just had no idea what to say to her, to anyone.

"Did you have a lot of friends there?" Jenny asked.

I gave her the honest truth. "One. Just one, really."

"It must have been someone special." She looked disappointed, and I felt a little sick.

"He . . ." I stopped myself. How could I sum up Trip Marchette? So many emotions assaulted me at once, I had to reach out for the branch to steady myself. Of course, Trip was special. He'd been my only friend, and not just because I'd been so isolated. With Trip around, I never needed anyone else. But he'd also screwed me over in ways I was still trying to wrap my head around. Ways that made it hard to breathe.

Jenny waited for my answer and I threw a noncommittal "yeah" in her direction.

"How does that work?" Her face scrunched up and there was a bite to her voice that hadn't been there before. "I mean, they aren't going to let you keep in touch with anyone you knew from there, right?"

A sharp thread of panic cut through me. I hadn't even thought someone might tell me I couldn't be in touch with anyone in Barlowe. I had enough reasons not to be in touch with Trip, but they were, I was sure, temporary issues that would work themselves out when our anger faded. And when we found a time when Trip could talk without fear of his uncle's favorite brand of pissed off. And when we had something to say to each other that wouldn't feel like a knife in the heart.

My stomach lurched, and I swung myself down to the ground before looking back up at her. I was an idiot for even thinking I could have a normal conversation in this tree, with this girl. Or with anyone. Why should I even try?

I wasn't stupid. I knew she wanted to hear I'd missed her and couldn't wait to get back to Millway. But I couldn't honestly tell her that. And if I was keeping my promise to Chief Perkins, I couldn't even tell her where I'd been.

"Jenny." I stared at my shoes and forced the words out. "It isn't you, but trust me on this. I don't think it's a good idea for us to hang out."

I walked back to my mother's house without turning to look at her. I was glad no one was there to ask me how grateful I was that she didn't call me back.

FIVE

The kitchen was warm, but I was shivering. I cranked up the thermostat and pulled Jenny's sweatshirt off. The Gordon crest—a stag sitting on a crown, the word "remaining" over it's head—stared accusingly back at me. I balled the shirt up to cover the stag's smug expression and used it to wipe the freezing sweat from my face, just as the heat kicked on and the warm air blew the curtain away from the window.

Jenny was still sitting in the tree. Every once in a while, she'd look in my direction and my stomach would twist with guilt, which wasn't fair because, for once, I was certain I was doing the right thing—forfeiting her friendship to keep her from being hurt.

I was shocked when she'd asked me if being in Barlowe had been horrible. Shocked she didn't know that the official story about me being abducted by aliens or fairies or the mob or whatever, was all bull.

Condensation fogged up the window and made everything look like a dream world, distorted and out of focus. I took a step back when Jenny turned to look toward the house, but I could tell she couldn't see me. Still, I went to hide upstairs, past the phone that kept ringing and the answering machine that blinked 27 MESSAGES over and over.

The desk chair was too small, like doll furniture, so I sat cross-legged on the bed's patchwork quilt. During her tour of the house, my mother told me my grandmother had sent it without a note when I was born; only the postmark on the package had given away the identity of the sender. It has been on this bed ever since. But when I closed my eyes, all I saw was the blue duvet on my bed in Barlowe, the one I used to hide under when I was up reading and didn't want the light to show.

I'd never met my grandparents. Two letters from their lawyers—the first regarding the trust, the second informing my mother that they'd died—were the only communications my mother ever mentioned to me.

My mother wasn't a hoarder, but I remembered her habit of shoving mail—bills, cards, and junk alike—into all available drawers and boxes. However much she resented her parents, I knew she wouldn't have thrown away those two rare letters.

I needed to see the paperwork about the trust, needed to hold it in my hand and prove to myself it was real. I needed to know that it hadn't all been some trick of my mind created to give Trip hope for a better future. To give me a way to save him.

I searched the closet in my room first, pushing aside worn school clothes, some old coats, and a broom. But there was nothing else in there aside from a baseball mitt, which was hardly used because my mother had never been around to take me to practice. I stepped quietly into the hall. My mother's door was closed, and I was sure she wouldn't keep paperwork in the bathroom. That left the attic, which I was hoping to avoid, and the coat closet downstairs.

The stairs didn't squeak on the way down—my mother must have had them fixed—and neither did the coat closet door. The shelf held a jumble of fake Christmas wreaths, batteries, tins of cat food (when had my mother ever had a cat?) and, at the far left, I could see the corner of a flowered photo box. I clawed at it and, when that didn't work, used a coat hanger to drag it out into the light.

I held my breath as I lifted the lid, but I knew I was on the right track when I saw my grandparents' names on the letters on top of the stack.

I closed the lid and took the box upstairs, shutting the door of my room behind me and saying a silent wish before I opened the lid again.

One by one I pulled out the papers that made up my grandparents' lives: copies of their birth certificates, a tiny manila envelope with their wedding rings, some old black and white photos all jumbled up with stacks of envelopes and tattered bits of paper that smelled like cedar.

I began to pull stuff out randomly, ignoring any handwritten letters or anything that couldn't possibly be an official document related to my trust. My fear was that my mother had gotten so "well," so organized, that she would have done the smart thing and taken out a safe deposit box at the bank.

But no, even the sober version of my mother hadn't come that far. The letter from Morris & Morris, Attorneys at Law was ripped and stained as if someone had set a coffee cup on top of it. But it was here. It was real.

I took another deep breath when I realized my hands were shaking. I wanted to call Trip. I wanted to run to Barlowe and wave the letter in his face and force a smile out of him and make him *know* that everything was going to work out just the way we'd planned. Maybe even better than we'd planned. Who even knew what the trust might be worth?

I steadied my hands and scanned the words. Stocks were being held in the name of Michael Simon Sterling, which could be claimed at the time of divestiture. I was sure there was a way around the name thing, even if I had to admit to being Michael in order to receive the money. Next was a whole lot of legalese along the lines of "in the event of Michael Sterling's death," or whatever. And *that* was followed by a list of requirements.

The first requirement nearly stopped my heart. Michael Simon Sterling had to complete the required courses and graduate from high school with at least a C average in order to claim the money.

I started to laugh. Really laugh. Like I was about to shatter. I hadn't stepped inside a school during the past five years. I'd skipped a grade in elementary school, but I'd been in seventh when I left. Seventh-freaking-grade. How the hell was I going to convince a bunch of lawyers that I'd managed to complete the other five?

The second requirement started with my name—Michael's name—and then broke off at the end of an unfinished sentence. I rifled through the rest of the paperwork, but I knew in my heart that the other pages of the letter were missing; their absence felt like a sucker punch.

Who knew what those pages contained? Maybe I had to tame a tiger or build an igloo or dig to China. Those were about as likely as my being able to graduate high school before Trip's uncle killed him or got him arrested.

My chest tightened as I felt the sting of tears eating at the back of my eyes. There was no way I was going to pull this off. I threw the box on the bed, let my legs crumble beneath me, and forced myself to try to accept the truth.

It was a stupid, childish idea to think I could simply come back, take the money, and run. More, I didn't know why I thought it would be possible to come back to Millway without missing everything in Barlowe so much.

My tears came fast and furious and I let them. I deserved them.

I was failing everyone.

I was failing Trip.

Just like everyone else in his life had.

I was becoming as cruel and unpredictable as Leon.

"Unpredictable" was what Maggie had called Trip's uncle the first time she'd mentioned him to me.

I learned quickly that Leon Marchette was more than "unpredictable." He'd been a lightweight boxer of moderate success, known best for his dirty style and cheap shots. Since leaving the ring, he stole, bought, and resold everything from auto parts to black market drugs, and was certainly breaking the law in more ways than I could imagine. Whatever he'd expected when he found out he was guardian of his dead sister's son, it certainly wasn't the complicated and exasperating boy who would quickly become the best friend I knew I'd ever have. And for not meeting his unspoken expectations, he made Trip pay daily.

Leon exacted those payments with a boxer's flair and it didn't take long for me to understand everything about why Trip sometimes wore long sleeves in summer and disappeared when he was supposed to be coming over.

But we had a plan. There was a room in the tree house, which Trip called the map room because it had a wall-sized map made of some special paper so it wouldn't fall apart when it rained. It was one of those relief maps, where the higher elevations were raised far off the surface. Looking at it always made me feel like the whole world *was* laid out in front of me.

Over the years, Trip and I had stuck tiny star-shaped pushpins in the places we wanted to go: Stonehenge, Mount Everest, New Orleans, Venice Beach.

"I'm going to be gone for a couple days," Trip said flatly, one day, right after I turned fifteen.

I looked at him. It wasn't like Leon was taking him to Disney World. "Where?"

He shrugged and turned away. When Trip was a kid, Leon liked to make him sneak through windows to unlock the door for his "associates" to commit whatever acts of violence or theft they were planning. As Trip got older, Leon made him run "errands." I never asked their purpose and Trip never offered to tell me. All I knew, all that Trip couldn't find a way to hide from me, were the bruises he got from failing at whatever task he was assigned.

"You don't have to go," I said. "Maybe Maggie could talk to Leon or something. Or one of your teachers?"

Trip glared at me and bit his lip. "Maggie can't do anything. If I said anything to anyone . . . You know what he said."

"Maybe I . . ."

"He's threatened not letting me come over here anymore. *At all.*" Trip's eyes seared with a desperation so tangible, I felt it in the pit of my stomach. "He hates you. I can't even mention your name. He thinks . . ." Trip looked down. His cheeks flushed.

I didn't want to hear what Leon Marchette thought. "We need to get the hell out of here," I said. Leon had been spinning more and more out of control, and the plan for me to leave the life I'd come to love in Barlowe and return to Millway in order to recover my trust fund had become a constant topic of conversation.

Trip sighed. "I don't get how your grandparents could squirrel money away for you in a trust fund, but *still* let your electricity be turned off."

It was a hazy summer day. The ice in my soda had already melted and condensation was running in rivulets down the side of the glass. I raised it to my cheeks to try to get what relief I could.

"When did I say it made sense?" I asked, distracted by the idea of Trip going anywhere with Leon, the heat, and by the fact that when Trip stood, he shrugged off his T-shirt. He'd been doing a lot of work outside for Maggie and his arms were browned from the sun and muscular from chopping wood and helping with local building jobs. I struggled to look away, then gave up, closed my eyes, and stretched out with my back against the floor.

"But, you really think . . ." Trip said. "I mean, you're sure?"

I felt Trip's footsteps vibrate through the wood as he walked over to me and sat down. He took the glass from my hand, finishing my drink in one gulp. His anxiety about getting away from Leon had become an almost tangible thing.

"Yeah, I'm sure," I said with more confidence than I had

any right to feel. "I mean, the trust is in my name. I'll just go back and get the money."

"And then we'll go," he said under his breath.

"And then we'll go. Where do you want to start?"

Trip made a noncommittal noise. I sat up, suddenly irritated. "You talk about leaving *all* the time. How can you not have thought about where you want to go?"

Trip shook his head, looked at the map, and paused. "I don't care where we go."

I took a deep breath, preparing to chew him out, and then thought better of it. It was too hot to argue, and arguing with Trip always made me feel guilty and empty. "Fine. So what do you want to *do* in this unnamed place?"

Trip shrugged.

"You're joking, right?"

"Shadow, that isn't . . . that's not what I think of when I think about leaving."

My stomach twisted. Trip gave me the nickname because I'd basically followed him around my entire first year in Barlowe. I'd never had a nickname before; my mother had always insisted people call me Michael. Trip's nickname made me feel special. It was ours. And he wasn't above using it to get to me.

"What *do* you think about when you think about leaving?" I asked. I could feel my heart racing, sure it was the heat. But I was having a hard time meeting Trip's eye while I waited for his reply.

He looked at me and opened his mouth, but then shut it again. I decided to wait him out.

"I just want us to get out," he finally said. "No Leon. No worries about who recognizes you." He stood and picked up his shirt, tossing it over his shoulder.

I wanted the same thing. But where Trip's vision of our future was vague, mine was all sketched out. I pictured a place where Trip could set up his tools in a park and make charms and sculptures and shelves and whatever anyone would pay for. I thought it would be cool to find a bookstore to work in, maybe one with a cat that always slept in the biography section.

He bent down on his heels next to me and leaned his elbows on his knees, fingers knitted together. "I just want us to get out," he repeated, not taking his eyes off the floor.

I swallowed, but the lump in my throat didn't budge. I wanted to share the specifics of my vision with him. I wanted to put my arm around his shoulders and tell him I'd do whatever it took to keep anyone from ever hurting him again.

Instead, I waved my hand and said, "Well, that's all a given."

Trip turned toward me, eyes opened wide, pupils growing dark as he bit his lip. Then a smile crept up the side of his face.

Trip's smile warmed me and chilled me and made it impossible for me to do anything other than make our plan work. For my birthday, Maggie had given me a copy of *The Little Prince*, and I found it painfully difficult to read without thinking of Trip, with all its talk of being responsible for the things you've tamed. That had probably been Maggie's plan all along.

At the time, I thought I had more than a couple of years left to figure out the details. At the time, it felt like anything was possible.

I shoved the box back into the closet and grabbed my mother's phone from the living room. I hadn't thought it through before, but Trip's uncle wouldn't recognize this number. Not the first time I called from it, anyway. And it was the middle of the night. With any luck, Trip would answer. I wished Leon had a legal job with set hours outside the house.

I dialed. Each time I pushed a number, I changed my mind. This was stupid. Selfish. I couldn't risk Trip getting into trouble. But I needed to hear his voice. I promised myself if no one picked up after three rings, I'd hang up. I pushed the call button and held my breath for two-and-a-half of them.

"Yeah?" Leon's voice was gruff. One word was enough to make my stomach clench, but I didn't hang up. What the hell did I have to lose?

"I'm calling to talk to Trip," I said.

There was silence. Then, "Well, well, well. If it isn't fucking Houdini back from the dead."

I squeezed the phone, acutely aware of the fifty or so miles between Barlowe and Millway. "Let me talk to him."

Leon laughed, but there was nothing pleasant about it. "See, here's the thing, mister disappearing act. I couldn't figure out why my idiot nephew's been even more of an idiot than usual. Oh, I asked him. But he never freaking learns, you know? Eventually I beat it out of him."

Acid stung the back of my throat. I wanted to kill Leon. But I couldn't even talk.

"Anyhow, whatever. I need him to get back to work. Hopefully, without you putting crazy ideas in his head, he can focus on the shit I need him to do. So in case you're as stupid as he is and you need me to spell it out for you, don't call here again."

The phone slammed down in my ear.

SIX

I had no choice but to tell my mother I needed to register for school immediately. The sooner I got things rolling, the sooner I could leave, the sooner I could get Trip the hell out of Leon's house.

My mother nodded, probably relieved I wouldn't be in the house all the time. I'd been a good student before I left, so this was also, I guessed, in line with what she would have expected. Although she probably didn't expect the urgency in my voice when I demanded it happen "right now." One call to Chief Perkins was all that was needed to set things in motion.

I tried not to make things harder for my mother than I imagined they already were. At home, the phone wouldn't stop ringing and she jumped every time it did. Her nervousness gave me an odd sort of déjà vu. It felt familiar, only not in a comforting way. It reminded me of why I'd left, and muscle memory had me moving the air fern off the toilet tank to make sure there wasn't a bottle of vodka hiding in the water.

As we pulled up to Millway High School, I had another sort of reminder from my past. The high school and middle school shared a parking lot. When I got out of my mother's car, I caught a glimpse of a bald spot surrounded by greasy, graying hair. My old social studies teacher, Mr. Laird, hadn't changed a bit. And although a run-in with him had been the tipping point for my leaving Millway, I hadn't thought of him in years, a fact for which I was infinitely grateful.

Seeing him now gave me the same tinge of sick fear I had when I was a kid and he'd threatened to call social services on me.

My mother, oblivious to what had stopped me in my tracks, pulled me along by the sleeve. I followed her and tried to forget Laird was still around.

My mother and I entered the building near the office so we wouldn't have to walk past everyone. The school was buzzing with post-Thanksgiving energy, but that was a relief compared to the tension of the house. The halls smelled like sweat, too much aftershave, and pizza grease. There was something interesting about it all. I felt like I was watching a science experiment on a topic I never knew existed.

Martina Ward introduced herself as the assistant principal and explained she was going to oversee my evaluation. She ushered us into the waiting room and then led me into an area the size of a closet and deposited me in front of a computer. The meeting had been set up in a rush and the school had never dealt with someone in quite my situation before, so they were just going to test me on the basics and then leave it up to the teachers to figure out what to do from there.

Mrs. Ward's voice was clipped and impatient, as if she had a million other things to do. It was a relief when she finished her instructions and left so I could get on with it.

The hours went by pretty quickly, and then my mother and I waited some more before Mrs. Ward called us back into her office.

The assistant principal hadn't looked me in the eyes the entire time, and it was bugging me. She'd looked at my test scores or at my mother or at the wall, but she'd never looked at me. It was like I wasn't even there. It was entirely different feeling from trying to disappear into a crowd like I used to do when, on the rare occasion, I'd go shopping four towns over with Wilson, or when Trip and I risked sneaking out at night.

It shouldn't have gotten to me as much as it did. I'd spent so much time trying not to be noticed, it should have been second nature. But this felt wrong.

I pinched the back of my thigh to make sure I was really there.

"Your son's results are . . . extraordinary," Mrs. Ward announced to my mother, like she was telling her that Bigfoot actually existed.

"He was always very bright." My mother put her hand on

my knee. It was interesting that she was proud of me now. Before, all I remembered was her yelling at me to get my "nose out of that damned book."

I squirmed as Assistant Principal Ward's tongue darted across her teeth.

"I believe that, Mrs. Sterling. His reading and comprehension scores are well above grade level, as is his abstract thinking."

I loved how she assumed my mother was married, even though she didn't wear a ring and there couldn't have been any information about my "father" in the school's file.

"His math and science, though . . ." she continued, narrowing her eyes as she finally looked in my direction for a brief second before turning back to my mother. "What methods did you use? Classical? Unit Study?"

I could feel my mother stiffen next to me.

"I read a lot," I said, jumping in before she had to answer.

"Clearly," Mrs. Ward said, her jaw tightening.

I had very few issues with Maggie and Wilson. They were the parents I'd always dreamed of in so many ways. But their refusal to let me go to school made me nuts. I understood the risk—that I'd be found out. And I knew there would be a problem registering me because I had no identification, although Trip said every town had someone who sold stuff like that. It was typical of Maggie and Wilson that they'd take in a runaway kid, but wouldn't risk my being caught with a fake ID.

Every year, I watched Trip get ready to start school and felt a clawing in my stomach. Trip hated school. It must have been torture for him to pretend, year after year, that he was following all of the reading and assignments. Leon had forbidden him from telling anyone about his dyslexia. I have no idea why Trip's teachers didn't pick up on it or how he managed to bluff them all. Sometimes, he was too charming for his own good.

Maggie helped him with his schoolwork, and I used to read his assignments out loud to him: *Huckleberry Finn*, *The Great Gatsby*, Shakespeare. He was an attentive audience and had a great memory. I looked forward to helping him more than I probably should have. But it was a shame we couldn't change places. He would have learned way more had he stayed home with Maggie, and I would have had a lot more fun if I had gone to school.

"It wasn't really that formal," I mumbled.

A.P. Ward shook her head and looked at my mother. "I don't understand why people assume they can do everything themselves and then . . ."

I laughed because suddenly I got it. Somehow, we were sitting in front of the one person in Millway who had no idea who I was.

She squinted at me. "Something funny, Mr. Sterling?"

"That's Woodhouse," I said. "Sean Woodhouse." My attempt at being a smart-ass probably would have been funnier had she been a James Bond fan, but her expression didn't change at all.

"Well, that's not the information I have here." Her sour expression stayed static. "I'm not sure what to do with you. We can schedule you for senior AP Literature and World History, but I'd strongly recommend we place you in freshman-level science and math."

Had I stayed in Millway to begin with, I'd have graduated by now. If I didn't need to get the money from the trust as soon as possible, this would all be unnecessary.

"What if we drop the subjects I'm good in and I double up on all the rest?" I winced at the thought of a school year of nothing except science and math, but I couldn't figure out any other way of pulling this off.

"Really?" She rolled her eyes. "You want to try to fulfill all of the graduation requirements in your other subjects in one year?"

"Maybe we could find a tutor?" my mother suggested.

I shrugged. It wasn't like I had anything else to do.

"I'll work hard," I said. "I'm looking forward to it, actually. I've missed school. You know, after five years without it."

I watched the expression on Ward's face change like a stain spreading over the pants of a guy who'd just gotten the piss scared out of him.

"Oh," she said and shuffled through her papers, finally realizing she had Millway's biggest news story sitting in front of her. "I'm sorry. I didn't. . . . You're that boy in the news?"

I was about to tell her it was fine. To reassure her, but instead

I forced my lips together and stayed quiet. I'd learned from Trip how powerful silence could be when used as a weapon.

"Well," she said as her cheeks flushed. "You could start as soon as tomorrow, but maybe you need time?"

"That's right—" my mother started, and I cut her off.

"Tomorrow sounds great."

My mother turned kind of green, but she nodded anyway.

And from the way she apologized when she told me I could pick up my schedule in the morning, I was pretty sure Assistant Principal Martina Ward was going to be indebted to me for a while. There were worse things.

We were almost to the car when my mother reached out and stopped me.

"I'll take you to get some clothes and things for school, but first we need to talk. We can't pretend five years haven't passed."

I nodded. What could she want to know that I hadn't already told her? Still, I knew this had to happen sometime. Better to get it over with.

My mother's taste in radio ranged from '80s rock to NPR to a local station that touted they played more Maine rockbands than any other station. I couldn't imagine that would be difficult, given that Maine was hardly rock central.

I clicked through the presets in her completely practical beige Chevy, which had a surprisingly good sound system. She didn't tell me where we were going. I didn't ask. I warmed my hands on the vents and tried to distract myself by listening to parts of songs, a smattering of international sports scores, and the middle of news stories I knew nothing about. Thankfully, I didn't hear my name mentioned in any of them.

It wasn't until we both had our hands wrapped around matching cups of tea, in a diner I vaguely remembered passing as a kid, that she began.

"I'm hoping we can be open with each other."

"It's fine." I watched the condensation race down the window. There was no way to prepare myself for the questions I'm sure she had, so I dove in. "What do you want to know?"

She looked uncomfortable, like maybe she didn't want to know anything. It hurt that she wasn't coming out and taking responsibility for my leaving. And it bothered me even more to realize how much I cared.

"That couple you lived with," she said into her tea. "Tell me about them."

The hot liquid felt like it was burning a hole in my throat.

I fiddled with a couple of packets of sugar, even though I hated sugar in my tea, and said the first thing that came to mind. "Wilson could make anything. Out of wood, I mean." I knew this wasn't what she wanted to know, but it was what fascinated me the first time I met him, how he could take a pile of sticks and make something beautiful, something you could live in. And somehow, even though they weren't related by blood, he'd passed his skill on to Trip.

I linked my fingers around the cup and tried to push the thoughts of Trip out of my head.

"Maggie," I said to distract myself. "She was a teacher before she got sick. English," I added, although I'm sure my mother had already guessed.

She nodded. These were superficial things, and probably not what she was looking for, but I wasn't sure how to dig any deeper, what to share, and what I was allowed to keep to myself.

"If they were so good to you, why didn't you go to school?"

I chose my words carefully and jiggled my cup until waves formed. "They were afraid someone would recognize me. I didn't go out in public all that much."

Her hands trembled as she shredded a napkin. I wasn't sure she even knew she was doing it. Tiny mounds of paper snow were piling up like miniature Alps. "How," she asked, "did you escape?"

She closed her eyes. I was sure someone—the cops or a social worker—had told her not to ask that. Not to push me. I hadn't prepared any answers and wasn't sure what to tell her. I wasn't expecting to come back to a mother who gave a damn.

So like I always did under pressure, I grasped for the truth even though I didn't want to think about it. "I didn't escape . . . I hadn't planned . . . Maggie told me I should come back." I tried to swallow down the sudden heaviness in my chest. "To Millway." I didn't have the words to tell her that my best friend had screwed me over. I didn't even have an appropriate quote to illustrate how it felt.

"And you listened," she said sharply under her breath.

Suddenly, she looked tired and I could see the way the last five years were written in the lines across her face. I wanted to explain it all to her. Explain how deep my gratitude toward Maggie and Wilson went. Explain how I was the only one who could save Trip. Explain that I chose to leave, but that coming back had been chosen for me—although putting up a fight was never an option.

But I knew I wouldn't have been able to make her understand, and the opportunity was lost when she reached into her oversized bag. I wasn't sure if she'd taken up smoking, or had a handgun in there and was going to shoot me. I certainly wasn't expecting her to pull out a cell phone with a red bow around it.

"I want to give you this. I know what you said about being the one who wanted to leave. But . . ." The words caught in her throat. "I don't want to lose you again."

Guilt wrapped itself around my stomach and tugged tight. "Thank you," I whispered.

At first the phone seemed like a kind of lifeline to everything I was missing, but it wasn't. Leon had never let Trip have a cell. Once, Wilson's foreman, Carson, had given Trip his old castoff, but it had only taken a week to see what Leon thought of *that*, and much longer for those bruises to fade. Obviously, I couldn't call the landline again.

"I've programmed my number in," my mother said. "I'm

sure you can figure the rest out. You kids always seem so good at these things. I mean, well, just ask me if you need help."

I nodded.

With no warning, she said, "The police want me to press charges."

"What?" The word exploded out of me. "You can't."

My mother reached out and grabbed my wrist. "Michael. Sean. Look at me."

I raised my eyes. My neck didn't seem to want to move.

"I'm trying hard to understand. You've depended on these people for years. But you have to realize that they took you. *They took you.*" Her voice choked up.

I yanked my wrist away. "They didn't. I . . ."

"You were twelve years old." Her words were loud enough to catch the attention of the people at the tables next to us. "You weren't old enough to make that decision."

"Maybe not, but *you* made it for me."

She looked like I'd slapped her.

I lowered my voice. "You weren't there. Even when you were there, you weren't . . . That day at school, the day I left, Mr. Laird called me into his office after history class. He said he'd seen you dance. He said you were a mess, and when he asked you where I was, you said I was home alone. That I was old enough to look after myself. Only I wasn't. Not really. He threatened to tell someone from social services that you were leaving me alone at night to go to the club if he could figure out how to do it without making himself look bad."

My mother ran her hand over her face. I recognized the old gesture. It was one that set my teeth on edge. "Oh, I—"

"I tried. All those years, I tried to tell you. I begged you to stop." I sounded like a little kid. All of Michael's old emotions raged up inside me and pressed against my temples. It felt like my head was going to explode.

I closed my eyes to escape the hurt on my mother's face, but Trip's eyes—the way they looked when I left—haunted me. I dug the edge of the wooden boomerang into my thumb and took a deep breath. "If you press charges, I'm leaving," I said quietly and as calmly as I could muster. "I'll walk out right now if I have to."

I realized, as I said it, that I was playing with fire. I wasn't going to get the money from the trust without my mother's cooperation. And I wasn't going to get that by twisting the knife into the pain I was sure I'd already caused her.

I rubbed my eyes and took a deep breath, feeling the air fill my lungs. I needed to get a grip before I pushed myself into a panic attack. I couldn't keep losing it.

"I'm sorry," I said, but couldn't articulate what it was I was sorry for. I simply knew that everything felt jagged and raw. "Please tell me you won't press charges. Wilson is already . . . gone." Even now, I couldn't say it without feeling like I'd lost the only father I'd ever had. "And Maggie . . . she loves me."

My mother flinched. I hadn't meant my words to hurt her and there was no way for me to explain how hard they were for me to say. It wasn't only Trip I was angry with; Maggie had her hand in my return, too. And when it came down to it, love was still a concept I couldn't quite wrap my head around. I had no idea how it applied to me at all, anymore.

Conveniently, the waitress showed up with our food. While we ate, we talked about things that didn't matter. Songs on the radio. The people who walked by our table, trying to pretend they didn't recognize me.

Inside, I was a mass of snakes. I was still reeling from finding out I'd have to graduate high school to get the money from the trust, and now the threat of my mother actually going after Maggie for giving me a home, felt like it would push me over the edge.

I concentrated on holding it together as I followed my mother around on all of her errands and then back to the house.

She put her bags down. Clothes for me mostly. I'd only brought what I could fit in one large backpack.

She sank onto the couch. "I have a meeting in the morning. AA. I need to go before work unless you need me to take the day off and take you to school."

AA sounded like a good idea, but it was her "work" I was most curious about. I figured she wasn't dancing anymore, but I hadn't pictured her working at a real job, either, which I'm sure was written all over my face.

"I'm the office manager for a medical group. I wasn't kidding about turning my life around."

I wanted to tell her I was proud of her, but I couldn't seem to form the words. "That's cool," I managed. It sounded dull as dirt, but thankfully less embarrassing than pole dancing.

I sat on the couch fiddling with the cuffs of my shirt, while she riffled through a stack of manila folders and shoved them into a shoulder bag large enough to fit a small dog.

"We can talk about pressing charges later," she said without looking at me. "I don't know if they'd stick anyway. Not here in Maine, at least. And I want us to move on, but I'm not sure I can simply let this go."

I could feel my lunch threatening to come back up.

"Call Chief Perkins in the morning if you're worried about the media. Hopefully they'll go away soon."

I nodded. The press was the least of my problems. I knew how to keep to myself.

I shuffled up the stairs, past the smiling faces in photos that looked at once so familiar and so strange.

The room felt wrong. I picked a handful of baseball cards off the desk. When I was little and my mother had money, she'd leave a pack there before she left for work, as if they could make up for everything. Alone in the too-quiet house, I'd sort them and re-sort them until I couldn't see straight.

Now I flipped through them, wondering if any had increased in value since I'd left them stacked in perfect numerical order.

Then I dug the phone out of my pocket and stared at it. I wasn't sure what to do with it. I wasn't much for games and I had no plans to make friends in Millway when I wouldn't be sticking around past June. All I wanted to do was graduate and get back to my real life.

There was only one number I wanted to dial, anyway. I could even picture my fingers pressing the buttons. But just as clearly, I could imagine Leon's reaction.

I winced and put the phone down before I did something stupid.

And what would I say to Trip anyway?

I miss you, but I shouldn't.

I'm sorry I got so upset, but you deserved it.

I came back here to save you, but I'm not sure I can.

I could talk for an hour, and none of it would be enough. Nothing I could say would ever be enough.

SEVEN

Nights sucked.

I never slept as a kid because I was too worried about my mother not coming home or people breaking into the house or maybe my mother coming home and breaking into the house.

And I never slept in Barlowe because I was too interested in reading another chapter or discussing the possibility of time travel with Maggie or jerking off or thinking about jerking off or wondering what kind of life I was going to have, given that I pretty much never left the freaking property.

Or worrying about Trip. Always worrying about Trip.

Now that I was back, it was the noise that got to me.

Some of it was the noise I could hear: my mother clomping down to the kitchen, the boulder-sized snowflakes that sizzled against the street lights, the press vans that still hadn't gone away.

Some of it was the noise that was missing: the calls of owls, the singing of crickets, the crackling of the fireplace.

In Barlowe, on a good night, sometimes the smell of Wilson's pipe alone would knock me out.

I tried to convince myself that what was keeping me from sleeping was the buzz of the remaining television cameras and the lights from what must be Millway's entire force of police cars—three—trying to keep everyone in line.

But really it was the voice in my head that told me I was failing to save Trip like I'd failed to save my mother. The kicker was: my mother didn't need saving anymore. Or at least, she hadn't until I came back. Who knew what the future held now? What edge I might push her over.

I knew Trip's problems weren't ones that could be solved by going to meetings. He wasn't going to simply sort things out while I was gone. If I couldn't get access to the trust, couldn't get him the hell out of Leon's, I wasn't sure what would happen to him.

I tried to quiet my head by reading, but the books in the room—my room—belonged to a kid, and apparently my mother still didn't read much. Aside from some sappy chick lit and a couple of books about the twelve-step program and how to give yourself over to a higher power, I couldn't find anything in the house.

I threw on my leather jacket and headed outside to clear

my head. If nothing else, I could look at the sky and hope that maybe Trip was looking up and wondering if I was looking at the sky, too.

Which made me officially pathetic.

Without the trees in the way, the clear sky looked like some huge ocean of sparkly fish. If it weren't for the hiss of the electronics that had taken up residence on the front lawn, the crackle of wires and the hum of voices from frustrated reporters who wanted to talk to me for a minute, who wanted me to answer their questions, I could almost drown in that sky.

Through the hum, I heard the squeak of an unoiled door. Jenny took slow steps through her yard, like I was a rabid dog she didn't want to startle.

I'd told her to go away, but at the same time, I felt an odd rush when I saw her. We'd been kids together. We'd ridden our bikes and talked about school and run around our yards. When things were bad with my mom, or I hadn't spoken to anyone outside of school in days, Jenny was always there. She seemed to know when I didn't want to be alone.

Maybe she still did.

So maybe being around her couldn't fill the hole inside me; it still might take the edge off.

She leaned on the gate separating our yards, making it clear she wasn't going to come in without permission. I jumped down from the tree. Her hair was pulled back again, and as I got close I could see soft pink circles under her eyes. She shifted from one foot to the other.

"Hey."

"Hey." Her eyes wandered over to the fence between us. "Sorry, I know what you said yesterday . . ."

I cut her off. "I was being a jerk. I should be the one apologizing." It felt good to tell her something honest and true.

She nodded in agreement. "If you want a break from all of that "—she waved toward the news and police vans—" you could come over. Mom's working, and I'm going to see if I can pull something together to eat."

I didn't have a watch, but it must have been late. "It's midnight or something, right?"

She nodded. "I'm hungry. I didn't really eat much today."

I wondered if that was my fault.

I wasn't hungry. And I wasn't eager to go to her house, but some damned muscle memory must have been at work. Some instinct kept rising up through the muck that made me want to be her friend again.

"I don't know. What if my mother wakes up and I'm not there?"

She gave me a startled look, then covered her face. I didn't understand why she always tried to disguise what she felt when she was so bad at it.

"Your mom can sleep through a freight train. A couple years ago, a tree crashed into your roof during a storm and she didn't even realize it until my dad almost pounded in the door to see if she was okay. But maybe you should still leave her a note first?"

I ran back to the house and rifled through the kitchen drawers until I found a sticky pad and a pen with an ad for the Millway Police Athletic League on it. I left a note on the counter and headed toward Jenny's house, humming a selection of Wilson's favorite Frank Sinatra songs so there was no room in my head to think about how many of my own promises I was breaking.

The Gordons' house was a mirror image of my mother's, their back door opening into the kitchen just on the opposite side. I walked in and the smell of cinnamon stopped me in my tracks.

Jenny started to laugh.

"What?"

"You don't remember?" She pulled a tray of cookies out of the oven. "These were always your favorites. My dad used to call them Michael's Munchies."

I stared at her. These were the same cookies she'd given me on the day I left. It was strange to hear bits of my early life reflected back to me like they were bricks fitting themselves into places made specifically for them. Like in that old video game, *Tetris*.

She poured us glasses of milk. Then we sat at the table and dug into the cookies.

"What else do you remember?" I asked, tentatively. I was a little afraid of what she would come up with, but strangely curious.

"We did everything together." Her pink cheeks reflected the

waves of electronic light coming into the front window. "Well, I mean, we spent a ton of time together. Do you remember when my mom took us to the beach and Tim Westin dumped water on my sandcastle and you made him apologize?"

I sifted through my memories, but it felt like there was a wall between my life before and my life after the day I went with Wilson.

"You were always really nice like that." Her voice was wistful.

My hands were suddenly cold on the sides of the milk glass. I wished I remembered something more important about her I could share to prove it was me and that I was there and paying attention. I hadn't thought about those times in years.

"I may not remember everything, but—" I started. "We can make new memories, right?"

Her face lit up like this was the very last thing she expected me to say. It was actually pretty high up on the list of things I didn't expect me to say, either. I also hadn't expected that making her look so happy would make me feel better than I had since I came back.

"Of course," she said, wiping crumbs from her mouth. Then she stuck her hand out. "Hi, I'm Jenny. I'm seventeen. I love winter and hate spiders. And, um . . . I think I want to be a detective."

I felt my eyes go wide. I shoved another cookie in my mouth to buy myself some time. In spite of her game sounding like some stupid reality TV show, I went along with it. "Hi,

I'm Sean," I said, trying to match her. "I'm seventeen, too. I love to read. I might want to be a writer someday." I stopped. I'd never told anyone except Trip, and I wasn't sure how to go further, so my words kind of stalled out.

It was clear from her expression that Jenny was contemplating more than our future careers when she reached over to touch my hair.

I froze.

"I like it dark like this," she said, her eyes not leaving mine. "Are you going to keep it?"

A shiver ran up the back of my neck. She was freaking me out. I cleared my throat, but my voice came out as a whisper. "It's mine."

She pulled her hand back and the air started circulating in the room again.

She took a bite of cookie and looked far more like a high school girl and less like something about to devour me.

I looked around the kitchen for a new topic of conversation, one that didn't revolve around me.

Photos covered the door of the refrigerator, and I used them as an excuse to get up and take a closer look. There was one family shot of Jenny with her parents at a school concert. The rest of the surface was filled with tropical sunsets next to crowded exotic streets. Other pictures captured vendors holding out what looked like grilled chicken on sticks, but was probably some other sort of meat.

"Um, what's your dad up to?" I asked.

She leaned back in her chair and clenched her mouth into a tight line that reminded me of her expression when I'd namelessly mentioned Trip while we were in the tree. "Didn't you know? Dad is a TV star."

She got up, her chair squeaking on the tile, and stood beside me. She reached out and took one of the photos of the vendors, studying it like she'd never seen it before.

"I haven't watched a lot of TV," I said. "Besides, I thought he was a chef." Before that he had been a lawyer. I remembered there being a lot of talk about how he left work one day and then never went back. Everyone worried he'd had some sort of breakdown. I thought it was pretty cool.

"Apparently, they're the same thing these days. Apparently, cooking in Indonesia is more fun than cooking here. Apparently, he doesn't care if he only sees us every few months." The bitterness in her voice was inescapable.

"You must get to go to a lot of exotic places," I offered. Lucky her. Being able to travel like that would solve many of my problems.

"Yeah, except I have school. And Mom has work. And even when we're wherever it is he's filming, he's scoping out locations. Or meeting with his producer. Or trying to find someone who makes stir-fried bugs."

"Bugs?" I turned the cookie over to make sure there wasn't anything odd in it.

"Or whatever," she said dismissively.

"Sooooo." I drew out the word, looking for something

neutral to talk about. "I'm starting school tomorrow. I mean, in the morning."

Her expression shifted. "Wow, that's soon. Do you know your schedule?"

I shook my head. "I'm supposed to get it from the office. I think it's a little all over the place, though. I'm not sure Mrs. Ward really knew what to do with me."

Jenny laughed. "Don't take it personally. She's a control freak. Did you know she stands and stares out her window with binoculars between classes, trying to catch kids ditching? Of course, everyone goes out the south doors now."

I laughed and it felt good, but uncomfortable, like exercising after a long break.

"So you've never been to school?" she asked. "I mean . . . not since . . ." She put her face in her hands. "Sorry. I seem to be saying all the wrong things."

I reached out and touched her arm, lost in our sudden camaraderie. "It's okay. Benjamin Franklin said, 'A house is not a home unless it contains food and fire for the mind as well as the body.' I was kind of starving here. Before, I mean."

She cocked her head and looked at me like I'd just landed from Mars. I wasn't sure if her expression was due to my quoting a long-dead Founding Father or if she was finally starting to understand that I had no regrets about leaving.

I took the safe route and assumed the former. "I guess I have to watch that." I stopped myself before I told her Trip always said I had a quote for every occasion. The one that came to mind was “And now there is merely silence, silence, silence, saying all we did not know.” William Rose Benét.

Jenny gave me a slow smile that lit her face like the glow of a sunrise. “Actually, I think it’s cool that you can pull a quote out of thin air. Anyway, I’ll meet you at school, if you want. I have to be there early for choir rehearsal, but I’ll meet you on the steps at seven thirty?”

I nodded even though I truly believed that my rejection of her yesterday was smarter than my acceptance of her friendship today. Being friends with Jenny felt so selfish that I should’ve been beating myself up. But like the addict tendencies that flowed through my veins, I was sure I could stop before I hurt her.

But then again, wasn’t that what they all said?

When I finally fell into a fitful sleep, I didn’t dream. Instead, for some reason, my brain replayed the first time Trip showed up at the door with medicine for Maggie, and in my hazy state, I watch it play out like a movie, wishing I could slow it down and take it all in.

Of course, from the minute he’d let himself in, I’d given Trip a hard time. “Oh sure,” I said. “Bring Maggie presents and not me. I see how it is.”

I’d expected Trip to laugh, but he didn’t. Instead, he shrugged and put the box on the table. “Is she here?” he asked.

I pointed out the window to the massive garden behind the house. "It's weeding day," I explained.

He nodded. It was shortly after Wilson died and we were both still getting used to the emptiness of the house. The lack of pipe smoke. Mostly the lack of Wilson's calm wisdom that made it feel like he always had all the answers.

At the time, I couldn't have imagined missing someone as much as I did Wilson.

Trip stood still and silent, close enough for me to feel the fabric of his shirt brush against my bare arm. I shivered, but didn't pull away. I pointed to the package. "What is it, anyway?"

He looked down when he said, "Her meds. From Leon. Wilson used to pick them up."

"And you're delivering."

"Looks like it," he answered, still not meeting my eyes.

I dug my nails into my palms and took a deep breath. I wondered what else Leon had Trip delivering and who those deliveries were going to. "Trip . . ."

He spun away and stuck his hands in his pockets. "It gives me an excuse to come over more, I guess."

"Like you need an excuse to be here?" I volleyed back. I didn't want to, but I let him change the subject. It wasn't like I could say anything to make a difference.

He shrugged and gave me a half-smile that lifted up the corner of his mouth. "Next time I'll bring you something, too, Shadow." He stretched his arms over his head and I stared in both real life and in my dream, unable and unwilling to rip my eyes away from the flush of his skin.

The next time I saw Trip was in the tree house. Leon had given him a black eye and it took me an hour of pleading to get him to talk to me, an hour of swearing that I was going to find a way to rescue him, before I saw the light come back into his eyes.

The next day he came over with a delivery for Maggie and a small blue bag for me. In it was the boomerang.

EIGHT

"First day back?"

I nodded and rubbed my tired eyes. I'd been standing and staring at Millway High School for what felt like an hour, but was probably only ten minutes. I'd left home early and despite what my mother said about having to leave before I did, she'd been hovering like it was my first day of kindergarten, afraid I would get lost or show up late. Actually, I was more worried she'd start legal proceedings against Maggie or that someone would tell me this was all a joke, that they weren't going to let me back into school and that the trust was, once again, out of reach.

I shoved my hands into my pockets to warm them and wondered whether I should wait for Jenny to show up or if I should head in on my own.

"Must be a bit scary."

The woman next to me looked too well dressed to be a teacher, but what did I know? I hated the thought that my history teacher would think I was freaked out about going back to school, so I shrugged and didn't answer.

"How does it feel to be back in Millway, Michael?"

I wasn't sure a teacher would look so interested in my answer, but I was beyond ready to have the whole issue of my name sorted out once and for all.

"My name isn't Michael," I said. "It's Sean Woodhouse."

Her pretty face scrunched up and she pulled out her phone and started tapping into it. "Woodhouse? Would you mind spelling that for me?"

Looking down at her bag, I saw the logo of the *Millway Examiner*, Millway's less than trustworthy newspaper. *Crap.*

I jumped when Jenny came along my other side and tugged on my sleeve. "I thought you weren't supposed to talk to the reporters," she whispered in my ear.

"I-I didn't know," I stuttered as she pulled me away.

The reporter stood there calling, "Sean, Sean . . ."

We ran until we were inside the front doors. I wondered if the fact that Perkins was going to kill me when he found out I'd talked to a member of the press would keep my nerves away.

"It's way bigger than the junior high, isn't it?" Jenny asked.

It wasn't the size of the building that made my heart race.

"It's okay," she said. "Most of them have matured. A little bit."

There weren't many kids there yet, but that wouldn't last long.

I wanted Jenny to stop talking so I could collect my thoughts. I needed a minute, but I wasn't going to get it.

"I'll walk you to the office," Jenny said.

I nodded and let her guide me through the halls while I focused on putting one foot in front of the other. Seriously, what was I worried about? High school kids? Getting a crappy assortment of classes? The reality that I'd broken an order from a cop who was already ticked off at me? In six months, this would all be over and Trip and I would be seeing the world. Or I'd screw this all up and Trip would end up as Leon's punching bag for the rest of his life. Yeah, I guess the last one was worth worrying about.

Jenny stopped abruptly and I almost walked into a girl in the hallway. "Hey, Em," Jenny said to her.

"Hiya," the girl said to Jenny, but her eyes—her cat-like green eyes—fell on me like a magnet on true north.

I wasn't up on normal teen behavior, but I was pretty sure we stood there staring at each other longer than was socially acceptable.

She wore a white linen shirt that seemed to glow against the darkness of her long curly hair. It looked oddly formal compared to the T-shirts and gaudy colors the other kids wore as they passed us. With that and a gauzy floral skirt, she looked like a sprite who'd wandered in from an English garden, rather than a Millway high school student. My first thought, before I even knew anything about her, was how much Maggie would love her.

"Emery Whitman." She stuck her hand out in my direction. "Emery like the board. Whitman like the poet."

Whitman. *Crap, I'd read Whitman. I was on top of this*. So why was my mind suddenly a freaking blank slate?

Her hand hovered in front of me until I took it. Jenny coughed and the only thing I could come up with to say was, "Be curious, not judgmental," which had to be the stupidest quote of all time for me to pull out of the recesses of my brain.

"Walt Whitman," I said under my breath to Jenny, who was staring at me. "I mean, I'm Sean Woodhouse. But are you related to the poet?" I asked awkwardly and forced myself to let go of Emery's hand.

In a voice tinged with a ghost of an accent I later learned was from spending her first five years with her mother's family on the southern coast near Cornwall, she launched into an answer involving cousins of cousins and multiple marriages while I surfed in her green, green eyes.

I had no idea what was happening.

I didn't believe in love at first sight or even lust at first sight, not that I had much experience with either. I didn't think I wanted to sleep with her. I felt like I already had. Like she understood me intimately enough to be looking into me and sorting through everything I was, and everything I wanted to be. And from that, she was taking what she wanted and discarding the rest.

"I was just walking Sean to the office to get his schedule," Jenny said. I hadn't realized Emery was done with her explanation or, for a minute, of even where I was. "See you at lunch?"

"Of course," Emery said. She started walking away and then turned and looked back at me. "You should join us if you have lunch fourth period."

I recognized those eyes. How was that even possible?

"Sean, what is it?" Jenny sounded concerned.

I needed a crane to pull my stare off Emery's back as she walked away.

What the hell?

"Should I know her?" I asked Jenny.

"I don't think so. She transferred in after you . . ."

"She looks so familiar," I said.

"She has one of those faces," Jenny replied. But it wasn't true. Emery was more interesting than beautiful, her voice strong rather than flirtatious. That didn't seem like the norm. But then, what I knew about high school girls wouldn't fill a sheet of paper.

Jenny tugged me like a rowboat until we got to the office. The room went quiet the minute we stepped through the door. I introduced myself and took the schedule from the secretary like it was made of gold.

"I've never seen anyone look so happy to see their class schedule before," Jenny said when we got back in the hall. "Let's see what you have."

I showed her the list of senior-level AP English and world

history, freshman algebra and biology, and she shook her head. “You weren’t kidding about it being all over the place, but at least we have lunch together.”

I nodded. But all I could think about was that I had to get through three periods before I saw Emery again.

I hovered outside the door of the one English class that Mrs. Ward gave me, no doubt as an apology for being so clueless in our meeting, and watched everyone walk in, trying to figure out if I was meant to remember them or not. A couple of kids looked at me and then quickly away. I knew no one would know what to say to me, and I was in the same boat. “Hey, didn’t you used to have pigtails” or “You really got your zits cleared up” didn’t seem appropriate.

The same pattern repeated itself as English gave way to algebra and world history. I actually preferred my freshman classes because I wasn’t expected to know anyone and because the other students were too afraid to say anything to me.

I was pretty sure Perkins had intervened, anyway, after I told him I hadn’t been kidnapped. I’d seen the corner of a flyer that didn’t quite make it into the garbage can. Someone had been planning a “Welcome Home, Michael” rally, but thankfully I never heard anything more about it.

After class, I followed the crowd to the cafeteria. You could almost feel the hormones flying through the air. Nothing could have prepared me for the buzz and clanking and chatter and sheer chaos of it.

I took a deep breath and made my way through the food line, looking over my shoulder for a glimpse of Jenny. For the first time, I realized that coming to Millway High after the start of the year meant dealing with questions like *Where the hell am I going to sit at lunch?* I'd read enough to know that the political and social lines were drawn long ago and that sitting at the wrong table could doom me to a senior year of being stuck in the wrong crowd. I wasn't aiming for popularity. My goal was to fit in and stay unnoticed once the novelty wore off. The idea that this one act of sitting down at a table could define me made me want to grab a sandwich and retreat to the library.

I paid for lunch with the debit card my mom gave me and almost ran into a group of girls who each dressed like they'd coordinated their outfits and held a piece of fruit like it was all they intended to eat. I was pretty sure they were trying to whisper, but the room was too loud so even though I didn't want to, I could hear every word they said.

"Damn, he's cute. Don't you want to run your hands through his hair?"

"I heard it was dyed. Do you think the people who took him did that?"

"What do you think they did to him?"

"I know what *I'd* like to do to him."

Maybe I should have been grateful they seemed so

interested in me. I wasn't stupid. It wasn't like I hadn't looked into a mirror in the past five years. And it wasn't like I hadn't seen the effect Trip had when he turned on the charm. But they didn't know me. As far as they knew, I could be a serial killer, a compulsive liar, someone who hurt everyone he came into contact with.

I started to circle away, but one of them stepped toward me.

"I'm Shayna," she said, in a way that assumed I'd be impressed.

"Sean." I looked around for an escape route, but every direction was congested with people watching us, waiting to see what would happen.

"I know. You're the boy who went missing. Everyone knows who you are."

There was something predatory about her unrelenting stare. It no longer mattered who I sat with, it had to be a better bet than her. In fact, I wasn't even sure I still wanted to eat.

"Nice to meet you . . ." I stumbled. An arm roped around my waist and caught me. I moved to break free.

"Trust me, you'll thank me for doing this," Emery whispered in my ear as she pulled me away.

"I already want to," I answered. I could feel Shayna's eyes on the back of my head.

Emery laughed and I knew then that it was no coincidence. Her laugh was deep and its richness echoed in my head. Improbable as it was, I definitely recognized her from somewhere.

I followed her to a round table with two seats left. Jenny sat next to a guy who looked like he'd just stepped out of a wind tunnel in Ireland, all messy red hair and green eyes that were a match for Emery's. He leaned in toward Jenny, watching her reaction to everything.

"Rory, Sean. Sean, Rory, my twin brother," Emery said. "Fraternal, before you ask. You can't have mixed-gender identical twins."

"I know that." I waved in Rory's direction. He waved back, but the act looked like it took effort. I wondered what had him set on edge, but I was determined to win him over simply because he was Emery's twin.

"I just rescued him from the prom queen," Emery explained to the table.

Jenny cast a withering look over my shoulder to where the girls still stood and then gave me an apologetic smile.

Rory pulled his glance from Jenny and shuddered. "That was fast, even for Shayna. Dude, trust me, that one doesn't take no for an answer."

"My brother, the voice of experience," Emery chimed in.

I liked that Emery was acting as if I'd just transferred in from a neighboring school rather than being the "big story" in Millway.

"I had no idea she was nuts when I said I'd go to the game with her and her friends," Rory said with a sheepish grin I'd bet got him out of trouble on a regular basis. He was attractive in a way that snuck up on you when you weren't focused on it.

It was nice to listen to the table's banter. Nice not to be the center of attention for a while.

"Shayna thinks she's Millway's official welcoming committee, but unless you're looking for an excuse to end up on a course of antibiotics, I'd avoid the whole lot of them," Emery said.

I watched as she pulled a number of small plastic containers out of her bag. Scones. Blackberry jam. Clotted cream. Somehow she was transforming the school cafeteria into an English tea salon.

I bit into my tuna sandwich and nodded. I had no intention of going near those girls ever again.

"How was your morning?" Jenny asked quietly, like my answer might be something I didn't want to share with anyone aside from her.

I swallowed quickly. "It was good, actually. Although I'm not used to being around so many people."

"You're new blood." Emery said, leaning in from across the table. "And they all love a juicy story."

I pushed up my sleeves and wondered how long it took to stop being "new blood" in a place as small as Millway.

Emery asked Jenny about some assignment for their trig class, which gave me the opportunity to scan the room. I was fascinated by the cliques. I tried to figure out where Trip would fit in. Suddenly, it struck me as odd that we hadn't talked about things like who he ate lunch with or where he sat in class. It was difficult to imagine him fitting in with any of these self-determined groups of jocks or goths or drama kids.

I always thought I knew everything there was to know about Trip Marchette, but all it took was walking into a high school cafeteria to be proved wrong.

I held the charm around my neck and wondered what he'd be doing, if he was in class or at lunch. Hoping he wasn't hiding out in the tree house after one of his uncle's tirades. I missed knowing his schedule. I missed him and I wasn't sure which of us I was more pissed at for that.

Rory cleared his throat loudly enough to get my attention.

I dropped my hand, but my eyes stayed on him as his gaze shifted quickly to Jenny. I had the feeling he didn't want to look at her, but couldn't help it. It was hard to tell what their relationship was.

His phone lit up as the opening bars to "Rule, Britannia" played. "Dad wants to know if we want to meet up for dinner," he said reading off the screen.

Emery shrugged. "Sure, why not. You want to come, Jen?"

Jenny looked at me and then back to Emery. "Yeah, I'd love to. But Mom is working and you know how she is about me going out on school nights when she isn't home. Even with you guys."

"Yeah, but now that he's here . . ." Rory started and then stopped as he looked at me accusingly. "You've kind of been an excuse for everything parents haven't wanted their kids to do around here. You know, we could get abducted or something."

I felt like I should apologize to the whole high school.

Jenny put her hand on my arm and I pulled my eyes away from watching Rory type into his phone to look at her.

"I need to get something from my locker, but I'll meet you out front after school if that's okay," she said.

"Yeah," I replied. "Yeah, sure."

Rory pushed his chair away from the table with a squeak. "I'll come with you," he said to her. "I want to grab something from the choir room."

It was an obvious lie.

He leaned over Emery and broke off a bit of scone and dipped it into her jam like it was a ritual. Then he and Jenny took their trays over to the conveyer belts. She turned and gave me another apologetic smile before Rory distracted her and made her laugh at something.

"Don't ask." Emery shook her head disapprovingly.

I wasn't going to. I had a lot of questions for her. The ones that involved whatever was going on between her brother and Jenny were pretty far down the list.

She raised her eyebrows over those ridiculous green eyes and waited.

"Do I know you from somewhere?"

Her brows fell as she slathered a piece of scone with cream and jam. "I was going to ask the same thing, but . . ." She hesitated, not like how Jenny did, as if she was afraid to say something wrong, or how Trip did when he was wrestling with finding words that fit together, but like she was trying to figure it out. Figure me out. “I mean, it isn’t really likely, with you being away and all.”

Before I could think about it too long, because it wasn’t as if she was going to run to tell Perkins or shove a microphone in my face, I said, “I was in Barlowe. Well, on the border of it, actually. Near the state park.”

If she was as surprised as I was to hear me spewing out information, she did a good job of hiding it.

“The only time I’ve been in Barlowe recently . . .” Her eyes went wide. “You were at Parker and Charlotte’s party.”

I didn’t have time to process her words before she covered her mouth with her hand.

“I don’t know what you’re talking about,” I whispered, all of my fear apparent in my voice.

Trip loved parties, particularly the type where there were twenty different conversations and forty different things going on at once. Once or twice a year, on the rare occasion when we thought we could get away with it, I’d sneak out and go to one with him. Sometimes we’d make up elaborate stories about my being an exchange student, or a hitchhiker Trip found on the side of the road. Sometimes, I’d walk in on my own and crash, pretending I was a friend of a friend of “Stephanie’s” or “John’s” or someone else with a common name.

We avoided parties hosted by kids from Trip’s school, but there were three private schools in the area and Trip seemed to know people at all of them. One was for gifted kids, one was actually an expensive reform school, and the third was a boarding school for kids with so much money, it was like they formed their own gated country.

Trip inevitably ended up drinking too much. I'd stand in the corner nursing a plastic cup of cheap wine and talking philosophy with the other people who ended up standing in the corner, or sifting through the bookcases and CD racks, making up stories about the people who lived there.

Had she been in Barlowe on any of those other nights, Emery and I would have been able to laugh about it. But the party at Parker and Charlotte's played out in a totally different way. It had been less than a week ago, but it felt like it had been years. I couldn't even imagine her there.

I didn't know what I expected Emery to do, but it wasn't to reach over and take my wrist in her ice-cold hand.

The bell signaling the end of lunch sounded and Emery rose to her feet and released my wrist. "Let's get this straight. Jenny is my friend and she's been waiting for you for five years. Lead her on and you're going to end up with my boot up your backside. Do you hear me?"

I choked out a laugh, but then stopped when I realized she was totally serious.

I wiped my sweaty hands on my jeans, while her words untangled in my brain. "Wait. What do you mean she's been waiting for me five years?"

"Why do all the pretty ones turn out to be dumb?" She

shook her head and her curls bounced. "Do you think she was tying all those ribbons and writing all of those letters to the newspapers for kicks?"

"Ribbons? What letters?"

"She worked harder for your return than even the police did. You've been her raison d'être."

"Her reason for living? I didn't know."

Emery reassembled the items on her tray and gave me a look that put me in my place. "Well, now you do."

NINE

While I could still hope to avoid rocking the boat further with Emery or Jenny or even my mother, thanks to Leon I was already responsible, in a way, for making things worse for Trip.

A couple of weeks before Trip delivered me back to Millway, he'd disappeared for what felt like a year, but really it was probably only a couple of days. Still, I'd started to panic.

There were reasons why, in all the years I spent in Barlowe, I'd only been in Trip's house a handful of times, and every one of those reasons wore the name Leon Marchette. But out of desperation to make sure he was okay, I'd followed the property line to their ramshackle house. Leon's truck sat off to the side, a tarp thrown over the back, hiding its contents. Curtains in one of the side rooms blew around in the breeze. I didn't go to the house with a plan, assuming Trip would know I was there through some sort of innate awareness. I inched toward the line of birches and hid there waiting.

Then I heard the distinct sound of breaking glass. I jumped and ran toward the house as Leon's gruff voice carried out of the window. "You stupid little shit. Do you have any idea how much you cost us tonight? A five-year-old would be able to read a fucking pill bottle better than you."

I sat under the window, out of breath and sick to my stomach, straining to hear Trip's reply. Instead, I heard stomping and then a slap. "*That*," Leon growled, "is for being such a lazy son of a bitch. How hard is it to pick a bottle of oxy out of an old lady's medicine chest?"

I put my hands behind me, flat against the side of the house, willing Trip to be strong enough, pissed off enough, to fight back for once.

"I tried," he said, but he was cut off with another slap.

"And *that*," Leon said, "is for talking back."

I started to stand, to pull myself up. Tried to figure out how I could get into the house and push Leon Marchette's head through a wall without getting myself killed in the process.

Inside, something squeaked across the floor.

"I'm sick and tired of you not taking this seriously," Leon said. "Just you take a look at these and maybe you'll change your tune."

I knew I couldn't risk looking in the window, but I had to fight to restrain myself.

Trip's reply was muffled.

"Since you're stupid," Leon said, "I'm going to spell it out for you. These photos could get you locked up for a long, long time. Don't think I haven't dreamed of how much easier my life would be if I wasn't saddled with you."

Photos? My legs started to quiver when I thought about what photos Leon might have that would get Trip in trouble.

"And poor Maggie," he mocked. "Supply chains break *all the time*. 'Sorry, this month's medicine shipment didn't make it. Or next month's, either.'"

Something hit the wall. There was a strangled gasp. Trip mumbled something. Then Leon again. "You really think so? I should call the police on that brat. Or better yet, it would be damned easy to put a bullet through him. If you think for a second that I believe those hippies' story about him being their nephew, you've got another guess coming. I bet I could bury that boy in the woods and no one would ever fucking know because *Sean Woodhouse*, or whatever the hell his name really is, doesn't fucking exist."

Leon's words created a cyclone of fear in my head. What the hell was I supposed to do? Was he serious? I knew he made Trip's life hell, but I hadn't thought he'd actually be capable of murder. And if he was going to threaten me, then what kind of danger was Trip in? Or Maggie?

I started toward the front door—determined to kick it in if that's what it took to get Trip out of there—just as it burst outward. Trip almost ran past me, but I grabbed a bit of his shirt and swung him around.

He jumped, turning with a clenched fist, ready to strike.

"Stop, it's me."

His eyes were wide, pupils dark. I watched as the adrenaline settled and he realized he was safe.

He shrugged my hand away, took a deep breath, and started to walk unsteadily toward Maggie and Wilson's.

"Trip? What the hell is going on?" I was beyond relieved to have found him, but worried my worst nightmares had come true. Someday, I was certain, Leon was going to push him over the edge.

I followed, but Trip didn't say a word until we were in the tree house. We sat side by side, and even then, it felt like hours before he spoke.

"How much did you hear?" he asked, refusing to look at me.

I played every searing word of the overheard conversation back in my head. It was no less painful the second time. "Something about pills. And photos. And Maggie."

Trip bit his lip. "And you."

"Whatever." I tried to sound like Leon's words hadn't terrified me. But he was right. He *could* bury me in the yard. What could anyone really do?

Trip's hand was tapping rhythmically on his knee. I wanted to reach out and grab it, hold him until he relaxed. Instead I asked again, "What the hell is going on?"

"Don't ask me to tell you," he pleaded, softly. "If you ask, I will. But I don't want you involved. Please."

It was his final word that shredded my stomach. Trip created, assumed, and accepted, but he never asked for anything outright. *Never*.

"Involved in what?" I carefully pressed.

Trip had been staring out over the state park, but then he turned and looked right into my eyes and my heart twitched with fear at his unspoken answer.

He licked his lips. "Leon's new 'business venture.'"

I couldn't take it anymore. "What is he having you do? You have to call the cops. Trip, you can't . . ."

Trip ran his hands through his shaggy hair and waited for me to wear myself out.

"I don't have a choice, Sean," he said calmly, only the use of my name reflecting his resolve.

"Bullshit. You always have a choice. You can leave. We can leave. Right now."

His eyes flashed. "No, I can't." For the first time ever, Trip yelled at me as ferociously as Leon had been yelling at him. "You heard him. He has photos."

"Photos of what?" I demanded.

Trip paused. His hands clenched into fists. I felt totally, awfully helpless. "Photos of me." He closed his eyes. "Breaking into the school science lab."

I jumped up. "What?"

"Sean, don't start. Just. Don't. Leon has a freaking arsenal in the house. And he wasn't kidding about Maggie. Or you.

He . . ." Trip's voice faded out. "I can't fight him and I can't leave. He isn't going to let me go."

I reached out to touch Trip's arm, but he flinched and pulled away, taking all the air in my lungs with him. "We'll figure something out," I said, although I knew my words came more from desperation rather than hope. "*I'll* figure something out. Maybe if we were the ones to go to the cops . . ."

"What about Maggie?" he asked. He was right. We turn Leon in and Maggie goes without the only thing she believes is keeping her alive.

I rubbed my neck. "Fine, yeah. Well."

"Sean, I need"—he started and licked his lips again—"some time. Alone."

Trip sending me away hurt more than Leon's words had, and even though I realized how screwed up it was, that knowledge didn't change anything. For the life of me, I couldn't think of anything to say. No quotes. No words. So I gave Trip what he wanted, let myself down the elevator, and walked dejectedly into the house.

The fear I'd been feeling had been given a direction, and it churned and twisted inside me. I couldn't sit still, couldn't stop watching the tree house from the window.

Was Trip okay? What would it mean if he actually considered the way Leon treated him as normal?

What if he wasn't okay and I was making a huge mistake by not insisting he stay where I could keep an eye on him?

I'd once asked Wilson why he didn't do something to help

Trip. It was a funny question because it wasn't like anyone had done much to help me as a kid, but while my mother might have been gone more than she was there, she'd never laid a hand on me.

"What would you have me do?" Wilson had asked.

"Call the cops? Talk to his teachers? Don't schools have people who deal with this sort of thing?"

"And what do you think would happen if I did that, Sean?" He sucked on the pipe I'd never seen him light, dressed like English teachers did in movies, with patches on the elbows of his jackets. There was something about him that gave off an air of calm and patience unlike that of anyone else I'd ever met. I wished I had someone else to blame for my own frustration at not being able to save Trip.

"Yes, maybe the authorities would be able to stop Leon Marchette. But what about Trip?" And here he'd paused, a space that sounded pregnant with meaning. "And what about you? Because your identity would assuredly be found out."

"You're sacrificing Trip for me?" I'd asked. I knew the answer. Maybe I'd known it all along. But I hadn't wanted to hear Wilson say it.

Wilson's silence rang in my ears as it grew dark, and then I was too exhausted to watch for Trip's exit any longer.

I walked out of my first day at Millway High School to discover

I was getting a police escort home. I hadn't done anything wrong, but go figure, cops showing up unexpectedly freaked me out. My deepest fear was that Perkins was coming to tell me that my mother was pressing charges.

He opened the passenger's side car door and I got in without having to be told.

"Did you think I was kidding about those newspaper folks?" he asked as he sped out of the parking lot. His fingers tapped on the steering wheel. Maybe the police here were so bored they had nothing to do besides pick kids up from school for talking to the wrong people.

"I didn't know she was a reporter," I said, a little relieved. "Honest."

"Hey, I was trying to help you out by keeping this name you're using out of the papers." He took a corner sharper than he needed to, and I slid into the handle of the door. "Too late now. She's already staked out the station and is being a pain in the rear end."

"Whatever. I don't care if they know who I am."

Perkins slammed on the brakes and all of the approximately fifteen pedestrians in Millway stopped and gawked at us.

He readjusted his gun and turned sideways in his seat. "Let's get this straight, son. I don't care if you don't care. In fact I don't care if you *do* care. You made your bed, you lie in it. Just make sure your mother isn't dragged through any more shit because of you, you got that?"

Um. Wow.

I guessed asking if they'd dated or anything was probably out of the question since Perkins had his hand on the butt of his gun and was caressing it like a kid petting his favorite blanket.

"The only good thing that can come of this is now we can get them on something. They aren't allowed to walk up and talk to minors like that. But seriously, you do *not* want to have this conversation with me a second time."

"My lips are sealed." I made that stupid motion of locking my mouth. "No more reporters. But I'm not going to walk around telling people my name is Michael, got it?"

Perkins glared at me, and for a minute I thought I'd gone too far. But then his mouth settled into a hard line and he said, "Got it, Mr. Woodhouse."

I coughed and hoped telling girls with pretty eyes where I'd been wasn't going to piss him off too much more.

The next day, I sat alone at lunch. I knew the old saying about keeping your friends close and your enemies closer, but Emery wasn't my enemy. At least I hoped she wasn't. All I could say for sure was that she'd been there on the worst night of my life and, therefore, scared the crap out of me.

I buried my head in my math book and hoped everyone would forget I'd ever come back.

But algebra wasn't enough to keep me from feeling Emery's eyes focused on me from across the room. To her credit, she kept her distance. I couldn't say the same about Jenny. As she started over, I pulled my head out of my book, bracing myself.

"Have you decided we can't be friends again?" she asked.

"What? No," I mumbled.

"Oh, okay," she said, but didn't move. "That explains why you're avoiding us."

"It's got nothing to do with you." I was trying to make her feel better, but I could tell from her expression I was making it worse. "It's weird to be around people all the time." As the words came out, I realized there was a kind of truth to them.

"Emery said . . ." Jenny stopped herself. It was a good thing I hadn't eaten because my stomach dropped to my knees.

"What?" I whispered. "What did Emery say?"

I pictured the two girls, heads pressed together, discussing me.

Jenny sighed. "It doesn't matter." And then she stalked off.

But it *did* matter. It mattered more than I could ever hope to explain. I shoved my books into my backpack and followed her back to her table.

I nodded to Rory, but I couldn't bring myself to meet Emery's eyes as I pulled out the remaining free chair and sat down.

Their conversation didn't miss a beat. They were all discussing someone I didn't know named Jordan who had broken into his ex-girlfriend's house and stolen her diary and was posting it online, page by page.

I coughed and decided I had no choice but to speak up. "That's horrible. People should be allowed to keep their secrets."

As I watched, Emery pulled out a thermos, a tea bag, and too many packets of sugar. "Most people think their secrets are more interesting than they actually are," she shot back.

I blinked and wondered if that was really true when a quick flip through the reality show–filled cable channels of my mother's TV would have seemed to demonstrate otherwise. I wondered if Trip would agree.

When I looked up again, Emery winked at me over her cup of tea.

I didn't know if I should confront her about what had happened at the party or just hold out and hope for the best. I took the chicken's way out and chose the latter. If Emery had questions, she kept them to herself. Millway wasn't the most conservative of towns, but I doubted there was a high school anywhere in the world that didn't love gossip, especially the kind that brands you for life and sticks labels on you whether they're true or not.

And so, at school, I waited.

I waited at home, too. My mother still hadn't decided whether or not she was going to press charges.

In the meantime, I hung with the twins so that I didn't have to deal with anyone else. Only once did I make an effort, when I went to a party during my second week back. The invitation had come from a girl in my algebra class and the party was hosted by her college-aged brother, someone I thought I vaguely remembered.

When I got to their house, I was mortified to find I was the center of attention. The next day, Jenny showed me a photo that was making the rounds on social media of me in an armchair trying to numb myself with some horrible blend of grape juice and vodka while a group of wide-eyed girls sat on the floor around me, pelting me with questions about my "abduction."

After that, I went back to ignoring everyone.

And I studied, trying to stay on top of my mountains of classwork. Trying to keep my mind from wandering back to Barlowe and everyone I'd loved there.

My strange mix of classes meant I only saw Jenny and the twins at lunch, and then only when Rory and Jenny weren't off at choir practice. I still didn't know what was up between them. It was like some weird Mobius strip: Rory's eyes on Jenny, Jenny's eyes on me, mine on Emery and Emery . . . she just seemed self-contained, which only made me more curious.

I felt strangely drawn to her. It was like a magnet: turn it one way and it is drawn to another magnet, turn it the other and they can't even be forced together.

She was pretty in an intense way. Even the tightness of her curls seemed to be a warning to tread carefully. She was never anything other than nice to me, but she watched as if she were waiting for me to slip up. I had a strong, frustrating urge to confess my every thought to her.

When my midterm results made it painfully obvious that all the studying in the world wasn't going to pull me through algebra, I sucked up my pride and appealed to Mrs. Ward for help. She promptly set me up with a peer tutor: Rory.

There were approximately three hundred students in the senior class. I didn't want to expend the energy calculating the odds that Rory would be the person I had to pin my academic hopes on.

I'd never really been alone with him and was nervous about not having the girls there to direct the conversation.

We decided to meet in the Perk Up, a local coffee house that hadn't been there before I left. Or maybe at twelve, I didn't care enough about coffee to notice it.

I was startled to find the café right across the street from my mother's old dance club. Rory caught me staring at the brick building. It had been painted blue, which was a step up from the old dingy yellow that had covered it before. I'd never been inside, and I had no intention of changing that.

"I didn't figure you were the type," he said.

It seemed like a loaded statement. "What type is that?" I asked, looking him straight in the eyes.

He fiddled with a plastic coffee stirrer. "The kind who's curious about a strip club."

The way he said it felt like he was digging for something, so I gave him part of the truth. "My mom used to work there."

Rory stared at me. I waited for him to say something more, but he turned his attention back to my textbook.

He was a surprisingly adept tutor and, one by one, the concepts started to align themselves in my head.

As I finished off a set of problems, he started humming "White Christmas" under his breath. He was surprisingly good at that, too. According to Jenny, he was hoping to sing professionally after graduation.

"You have a nice voice," I said. "Is there anything you aren't good at?"

He paused in a way that reminded me of Trip, and then said, "Emery says I'm really bad at mincing words."

"So don't," I replied and swallowed hard. If he had something to say, I'd rather get it out of the way sooner than later.

He shrugged. "Okay. You aren't the only one whose life has been messed up by all of this, you know."

My pulse pounded. I considered bolting. Instead, I dug my nails into the wood of my chair and glanced back at the club across the street. "You don't know anything about me." I started to gather my books, hoping what I said was true.

Rory reached out and grabbed my arm tight. "No, but I'd like to. Emery and I both would. You don't exactly make it easy."

I sat back down, both surprised and not by the surge I felt in my stomach when he mentioned his sister. I couldn't exactly argue with what he'd said. I knew I'd been putting up walls. But I couldn't tell him I was planning on leaving in a matter of months. And while I could accept that Emery was a distraction, an escape from everything else I was feeling, I was terrified of getting attached to anyone here. I was terrified that I'd already crossed that line.

"Look," he said with a hint of the Whitman smile, "I'm not going to pretend to get what you've been through. I'm sure this is a lot to get used to again. But really, some people might say we're pretty cool, me and Emery. And Jenny, of course."

Like a cat, some of the stress I'd been carrying stretched, curled up, and went to sleep.

But before I could say anything, he continued. "Speaking of Jenny . . ."

"What?"

His pale cheeks wore the hint of an embarrassed blush. "She's kind of on the flip side of your coin, you know what I mean?"

I shrugged.

Rory took a deep breath and leaned forward. "You did whatever you had to when you left. But Jenny had to deal with her best friend disappearing. You made your choices, but she didn't get to make her own."

A muscle in my neck spasmed. I couldn't take on responsibility for anyone else. But it would be heard to deny that he had a point.

"Yeah, I guess I get it."

"Good," he said. And it was. Or would be as soon as I had a chance to talk to her. "Wanna grab a burger on the way home?"

TEN

I hated leaving things unresolved. I couldn't put down a book until I'd finished a chapter and never walked away from a puzzle until I'd at least done the border, so it nagged at me that there was still so much left unsaid between me and Jenny.

The other side of my coin, Rory had said. Yeah, I got it. But I still had no idea what Emery had been talking about that first day about my being Jenny's reason for living. Maybe I could wrap my head around her having a kind of crush on me when we were kids. And maybe I understood why she'd be trying to make sense of my coming back. But none of that carried the kind of importance that Emery was referring to, or explained the serious tone of Rory's voice.

The next day, the sub for our world history class got sick, and we were let out early. My options were to go to the library and study. Again. Or to try to get to the bottom of things with Jenny.

Since I was out of class early, I figured I'd beat her to her locker, but she was already there. I hadn't been avoiding her, exactly. Okay, maybe I had. It had been easier as kids to ignore the smile that lit up her face whenever I came into a room, and the lingering glances I caught when she didn't think I was looking.

If she wanted anything from me, it was probably something I didn't have to give. All I had was the truth, which was the last thing I thought she was prepared to deal with. I didn't want to hurt her, but it seemed like something I might not be able to avoid.

"I haven't seen much of you lately," I said as I walked up to her, trying to keep things light.

She startled and stared at me with round eyes.

There was a quote from Julius Caesar that fit. I was never sure if Caesar actually said it or Shakespeare said he said it, but it would have to do. "No one is so brave that he is not disturbed by something unexpected."

I wanted to get to the bottom of things, but I wanted to be the one controlling the conversation. There was too much subtext between us I didn't understand.

"I thought we could catch up," I said. "You know, if you aren't busy."

She leaned back against her locker and looked down, trying to hide a smile. "Are you doing anything now? You should come over. I mean, unless your mom wants you home right after school."

I weighed my options. The choice seemed clear. "She isn't going to be home until dinner," I said, even though I wasn't sure if that was true or not.

Jenny led me out of the building. I felt as though I'd stepped into a time machine. This, I thought, was how things would have been had I not left. This would have been my real life.

I wasn't sure how to feel about that.

Jenny's mom's car wasn't in the driveway when we got there.

"C'mon. I have to put my stuff away." She motioned me up to her bedroom, and I followed her upstairs like a puppy who didn't want to be left alone.

The room wasn't as girly as I would have imagined. There were a few posters for bands I didn't know, stacks of books everywhere, and a bunch of postcards, some of which were from countries I'd never heard of.

She pushed past me, moving like a blur as she unpinned something from a corkboard over the desk and shoved it into a drawer.

"Porn shots you don't want me to see?" I joked, and she turned red as a police siren.

"No. Of course not."

I sat on the bed and watched as she went back to the desk and opened the drawer. The newspaper clipping she pulled back out was obviously kind of old because the edges were curled. She stared at it, and then at me, like whatever it was held the key to something intensely private. I got that same feeling from her a lot. Like there was major stuff she wasn't telling me. I wondered if people felt that same way around me. Maybe Jenny and I were members of a secret club neither of us knew existed.

"It's . . ." She coughed. "I don't know if . . ."

I reached over and took the clipping out of her hand. I was pretty sure if I left it up to her, she'd keep standing there grasping for words.

My own face stared up at me.

I scanned the article, which had all of the expected information, which is to say, not a lot. It was the picture that took my breath away. I didn't remember ever being so young.

The bed dipped as she sat next to me, but I couldn't look away from the paper in my hand.

"Are you okay?" she asked.

The article quoted my mother pleading for my return. The police offered a reward. Search parties had formed. I'd assumed, after the news of my going missing hit, they'd launch a search, turn up nothing, and then write me off as what I pretty much was, a runaway. I had no idea they'd still be holding rallies or that anyone besides my mother would be thinking about me after all this time.

I looked up at Jenny. "You kept this."

"Yeah." She groaned and reached out to touch my arm. "I've kind of been in charge of all of the community events. You know, the ribbon tying, the articles in the paper, and all of that."

Oh. Now I knew what Emery had meant.

"Sorry," I mumbled. I was responsible for her wasting the past five years. There was no way I could give that time back to her. And there was no way I wanted to tell her the truth now, but I had to. "I mean . . ." I leaned over and rested my arms on my thighs. My head fell heavy into my hands. I hated that this was so difficult. I hated that I felt like I was pleading guilty for a crime. "Thanks. I know you put a lot of effort into everything." I meant it, but my voice sounded flat.

"You make it sound like I built a homecoming float or something."

I lifted my head, surprised at the frustration in her voice.

"It isn't like I asked you to do it." I knew as the words came out of my mouth that they were the wrong ones.

"What was I supposed to do? Just let everyone forget about you?"

I took a deep breath. I couldn't let her believe a lie anymore. "Jenny, I have to tell you something."

She folded her arms over her chest.

I glanced at the newspaper article again.

"Look. You knew how things were for me at home." She nodded and stood, so she was looking at me. I looked down at the carpet. “I was so afraid all the time. I couldn’t stay here. I needed . . . I don’t know. More.”

I waited for the explosion. But when she spoke her voice was soft. She was talking to herself more than to me. “You really did just leave, didn’t you? I heard some kids saying that, and I defended you. But you really did run away? Why didn’t you *tell* me?”

I shrugged.

In a louder voice, definitely directed at me, she said, “Rory said he thought you had, but I told him you were my best friend. That you never would have left without saying goodbye.”

She was pissed, that much was clear. She’d been holding onto her anger for five years along with the article.

“If I told you I was thinking about it, you would have gone to my mom or your mom. Or a teacher. Someone who would have stopped me.” I felt my blood race. “I had no choice.”

Jenny’s eyes widened. “Bullshit.” She sank down to the bed like her legs were giving out. “When did I ever give you a reason not to trust me?”

I looked over at her, trying to figure out how to avoid the truth. But, in reality, the truth was all I had.

I told her what I’d only shared with Wilson, Maggie, and, more recently, my mother. I hadn’t even told Trip. My problems never seemed much in comparison to his.

“Mr. Laird told me he saw my mom dance,” I said. Jenny’s face went pale.

"Ew. You mean he was hanging out at the . . ."

"Yeah, and he said he was going to call social services. They never would have left me here, anyway." I looked into Jenny's eyes, hoping she'd cut me a break. "I'd been thinking of leaving for so long. And Wilson was in the park and . . . I had to do something while I had the opportunity."

For a minute, I hoped she was going to let me off the hook, a hope that died when she snatched the article out of my hands, stared at it, and put it back on her desk.

"I'm sorry it was so hard for you back then." Her voice was choked up and I was afraid she was going to cry. "I really am. It's my fault. I should have told my parents. I should have told someone. I knew you didn't want me to."

That was exactly what I'd been afraid of. But being proven right didn't make me feel any better about hurting her.

"Jenny. No. Don't." I rose awkwardly, unsure what to do. She'd never been anything but a great friend to me. I tried to pull her into a hug, which had always comforted me when I was upset, but she pushed me away and swiped at the tears with the heel of her hand.

"You couldn't write me? All that time, and not even an email or something to let me know you were alive?"

"I didn't have email," I said, my voice growing louder. "Maggie and Wilson weren't big on technology."

She paced the room in small circles. "So why did you kiss me before you left? Was that just another 'goodbye'?"

I ran my hand through my hair and winced. We'd been little kids. How could she have taken it so seriously?

"My mom was such a mess," I said. "She hadn't gone shopping in weeks. All I had for lunch that day were some old carrot sticks and whatever I could scrounge in school." I took a step back, expecting the worst. "You had those damned cinnamon cookies of your dad's, remember? You were joking around and told me you'd give me the bag of them if I kissed you. I was so hungry."

She inhaled loudly, and it felt like she'd sucked up all the air in the room. Suddenly, it was hard to breathe.

"We did everything together, Michael. I mean, Sean. Shit. I don't even care what name you want to use. Don't you get it? I hung out with you when no one else did. I thought I was important to you."

"You were," I shouted. Then, realizing the damage I'd done by using past tense, I corrected myself. "You are." But it was too late.

"Get out," she whispered.

"Jenny . . ."

"I said, get *out*."

I didn't think she meant it. I mean, she couldn't have. I'd told her the truth. "I'm sorry. Really. But I never asked you to do all that stuff with the ribbons. I never wanted you to do it." I looked down to see my hand squeezing the boomerang. Had Jenny said anything to an adult, I would have been trapped in

Millway. Then I never would have gone with Wilson. Never met Maggie.

Never met Trip.

I took a deep breath and looked at her. She was still at war, caught between her tears and anger. "I'm glad I went, Jenny. I'm really, really sorry. I'm not telling you this to hurt you. But I wouldn't have done anything differently."

Then I turned around and did the only thing I could.

The only thing I was good at.

I left.

ELEVEN

I didn't recognize the anger that ran through me as I stormed back to the house. For five years in Barlowe I'd been isolated, but not lonely. *This*, I thought, *this* is why I didn't want friends here. The whole thing was pointless.

My mother smiled at me, oblivious, as I burst into the living room. She held a wooden box in her hands like it contained the Holy Grail. "Are you hungry?" she asked. "There's some cold chicken in the fridge."

My stomach grumbled, but the thought of eating made me feel sick. "No," I said. "I'm okay."

"Sean." The warmth of her hand on my arm startled me. "I keep feeling like I should have more rules about things like you going out after school. Do you want more rules?"

I laughed. "No. I'm used to . . ." I stopped myself and she

opened her eyes wide, waiting. "Maggie and Wilson were kind of relaxed about stuff. I mean, they grew a lot of their own food. Wilson made a lot of their furniture. I don't know. I didn't really go anywhere, and we always tried to be honest with one another."

She nodded, and relief washed over her face. "Honest is good. But you need to start acting like you live here, you know. Whatever is here is yours. Stop feeling like you have to be so polite."

I closed my eyes. Whatever I did seemed to disappoint someone.

"I have something for you." She held the box out to me and I wondered if it was another birthday present she'd bought years before and forgotten about.

"You don't need to give me anything," I said, which was less risky than what I was thinking: *Just promise you won't press charges against Maggie and we're all good.*

"Actually, I do." She half-smiled. "You don't need to read these now. Or ever, really. But I had to write them, and I have to give them to you. What you do with them is up to you."

And with that, she turned and walked away, petting my hair as she passed.

I took the box up to my room and set it on the desk.

I wanted conflicting things from my mother. I wanted her to stop giving me things and to treat me like a transient boarder. At the same time, I wanted her to know, without asking, that I was upset about what had happened with Jenny.

Maggie would have known. Maggie would have talked to me about *Wuthering Heights*, or the teachings of Lao Tzu, or she would have told me some story about how, before she met Wilson, she knew a boy working for a traveling circus who pledged her his love and begged her to go with him. She would have distracted me.

I threw myself facedown on the bed. The sheets smelled like Millway and my mom's detergent, everything familiar and foreign at once.

I got up again and pulled out my homework. If nothing else, all the work I had to do gave me something else to focus on. The next time I looked at the clock, it was well after midnight.

I reassembled my books into my backpack and noticed the box again. It wasn't wrapped; only a green ribbon kept it closed. I pulled the end and watched it unravel.

I wasn't sure what I was expecting, but it wasn't a stack of neatly folded letters. I dug to the bottom of the box. That's all there was.

I took out the one on top and pulled it from its envelope. The writing was shaky, not like a kid learning to write, but more like someone writing on a ship. In a hurricane.

Dear Michael,

You've been gone three weeks today.

Crap.

I flipped to the last letter and looked at the date—two months ago. It felt like one huge guilt trip, all shoved into a box.

What did she want from me?

I skimmed the rest of the first letter and learned about how my mother was writing after her first AA meeting. About how she was meant to ask forgiveness from those she'd hurt, and how I was at the top of the list.

You're all I have in the world and I've lost you.

A million quotes flew through my head, all having something to do with how being angry makes you feel worse than the person you're angry with. All of the quotes echoed in Maggie's voice.

I folded the letter and inserted it back in its proper place in the pile and tried to sleep. Normally, my relationship with sleep was like an animal stalking prey. Tonight, the prey was not only getting away, but wearing bunny ears and laughing its ass off at me.

I wondered if Jenny was outside and what I needed to do to get her to speak to me again. I wondered why I even cared, except she *had* done all this stuff to find me, even if I hadn't wanted to be found. I didn't understand why she couldn't accept that my leaving the way I did had nothing to do with her. But I didn't want to hurt her anymore. I didn't want to hurt anyone.

I looked out the window at an empty backyard. If Jenny could sense I needed her, this time she didn't care.

I reached for my phone. What was I thinking? I couldn't call her this late. I wasn't sure I could call her at all.

But I was willing to use my new phone to try Trip again. This time, I'd hang up if Leon answered.

It only took one ring for Trip to pick up. "Yeah?" His voice was groggy. Familiar. Home. It reminded me of forests and wood smoke. Apples and cedar. Quotes crowded my head. I was glad I was already sitting so my legs wouldn't give out. "It's the middle of the night, who the hell—"

"Marchette."

He exhaled loudly enough for me to hear it, and then it was quiet. Finally, he said, "Is it snowing there? It is here. It's beautiful."

I smiled and shook my head. Part of me had expected Leon to have gone over the edge by this point. And maybe he had. But Trip was there. In the house. Talking to me.

I focused on pulling myself together and believing this was real. That we could chat on the phone like old friends in spite of everything.

Since he'd asked, I glanced out at the still, dull sky. "No. It's not snowing yet."

There was a pause. "Hang on . . ."

I heard drawers open and close. Stairs creak. Wilson used to say that the monstrous house Trip lived in with his uncle was held together with spit and good intentions, although he wasn't sure the intentions actually were good. More than once, we'd offered to go over and fix things up, but Leon just closed parts of the house that were structurally questionable. After all, it was only the two of them there.

I hated that house. Even when Leon wasn't there, his anger seemed to hang in the air. And when he was, I could barely stand to see the change in Trip. He became jumpy, sullen, and frighteningly quiet.

Over the phone, I heard the porch door softly latch closed.

"Are you okay?" he asked, now awake enough to realize panic was a legitimate reaction. "Why are you calling? Nothing's wrong, is it?"

I smiled again even though he couldn't see it. "Easy, tiger. I'm fine. I mean . . ." I took a deep breath. "I don't know."

Owls hooted in the background. If I closed my eyes, I could see the woods. The trees bare in the winter night. Trip wrapped in his favorite ratty jacket, which used to be black and was now some other shade of darkness.

"It's really you?" he asked, like it was possible someone was impersonating me.

"No, you're dreaming." I leaned back against the pillows.

"Nightmare is more like it."

I smiled and heard the sound of metal against metal. A lighter. Trip lighting a cigarette. I could picture his fingers flicking the ash off the end, playing like a movie. I could smell the fragrant clove smoke, sweet and spicy.

"Sean?"

I dug deep until I got to the tiny kernel at the center of what I was feeling. "Nothing is like I was expecting it to be."

Kindness laced Trip's soft laughter. "You mean, life didn't just stop in Millway? How much could have changed?"

"My mother is sober," I said. "For the moment, anyway. She's got a real job and everything."

Pause. "That's good, right?"

I considered it. It *was* good, I couldn't deny that. It was just different. Unexpected. Unsettling, like Caesar said. A positive turn of events that I could undo if I wasn't careful.

"I guess. Tonight she gave me a box of letters she wrote me while I was gone. Like one a month for five years."

Trip whistled over the phone. "That's a hell of a lot of baggage."

"Well, yeah. All she wants me to do is to read them, I guess." The urge to stick up for my mother surprised me. Five minutes ago, I was pissed at her for dumping all of this on me, and now, when Trip said the same thing, it bugged me. "Anyhow, I'm going to school, now. I mean, I might as well, since I'm here, right?"

Trip went silent. I could picture him weaving around the trees, leaving a trail of footprints in the snow. Leon would probably be laying down bear traps in the morning, thinking hikers had wandered onto his property.

I hadn't decided whether to tell Trip about the requirement to finish school before getting the money. But a tendril of anger crept up inside, a sudden reminder that Trip was the one who sent me back here in the first place. We had few secrets from each other. But just like he'd never wanted to talk about his exploits with Leon, I didn't see any good that could come from sharing the knowledge that I was going to be here for another few months in our first, and possibly only, communication.

"How's home?" I asked to break the silence. I was fishing for easy topics, but caught this one instead. I *did* want to make sure he was okay, that the guns were still locked up, and that whatever dirt Leon had on Trip stayed between them. But we were both dancing around the subject we needed to talk about most, and I wasn't sure how to drag us into that conversation or if I even wanted to.

"I'm okay." He took a deep drag on the cigarette. He liked the smell, the taste of it on his lips, the taste of it on *my* lips. Most of all, he liked the way he looked with one, he'd told me once. He didn't usually inhale. Except now he did, and that made the hair on the back of my neck stand up. "Glad I was the one to pick up the phone."

"Are you pissed at me for calling?" The idea hadn't even occurred to me until now that Trip wouldn't want to risk talking to me.

"No, of course not. Leon can do whatever the hell he wants to me if he doesn't like it."

I had no doubt he was telling the truth. And that was the problem. "I'm just tired, I guess." It was as close to an apology as I seemed to be able to come up with, but Trip accepted it. He always did.

"Yeah, someday you'll learn nighttime is for sleeping," he said.

I stared at the ceiling, wishing it was another ceiling an hour away. In Barlowe, I filled the hours of the dusky mornings with books and stoked fireplaces and cups of tea made from herbs in Maggie's garden. I'd leave notes for Trip in the tree house filled with silly quotes I'd found or fortune cookie–like proverbs I'd made up to try to get him to laugh. Here, I was simply awake.

Barlowe felt so far away. Another state, another country, another continent. Hell, another planet.

"How's Maggie?" I asked, although what I really wanted to know was whether my leaving had done anything to prompt Leon to make good on his threat to withhold Maggie's meds.

Everything went silent. Trip had a habit of thinking through what he was going to say before he said it. His speech was always filled with agonizing moments of waiting. It had taken me a while to understand he was ordering his thoughts, not being rude. "Some days are better. You know how it is. But Leon just gave her a delivery, so there's that."

I did know. But at least his answer meant nothing had changed. "I want to call her."

"She'd only tell you all the reasons to forget her. She wouldn't even like that we're talking."

He was right. As I'd tearfully packed the few things I'd bring back to Millway, she'd told me that distance had nothing to do with love and that I'd stay forever in her heart. At the same time, she was insistent I had no choice but to leave and cut myself off for a while, if not for myself, then for Trip, who,

Maggie feared, would never take action against Leon so long as I was around. And of course, as Wilson had explained long ago, her hands were tied, given her own unlawful activities.

"But you're taking care of her, right?" I asked. "Sorting her pills and everything?"

He paused again, but it wasn't like his usual silences. I'd hit a nerve. Leon had done his best to convince Trip that there was something wrong with him, and even though he should have known better, I tried not to compound it by calling him out on things like this.

And the topic of the party hung between us like bullet-proof glass.

"Shadow?"

"Yeah?"

"It'll be okay."

"I guess." There was a time when Trip telling me things would be okay was all I needed to hear. Now, I wasn't so sure.

"Hey, you ask your mom about the trust fund yet?"

I took a sharp breath. "I'm working on it."

"Still, it's a couple of weeks closer to us leaving." I could hear the longing in his voice to get as far away from Barlowe and his uncle as possible. I'd heard what he said about things at home being okay, but I wasn't sure I bought it. I wasn't sure he'd expected me to. It was the only topic he habitually backed away from.

My free hand balled into a fist. Thinking about Leon always brought me to the boiling point.

And then I realized something. "Turn him in, Trip. He can't touch me now. I'm safe."

It was our oldest argument. The elephant in the living room every time Trip didn't come over for a few days. Every time he did, and I saw the evidence of their fights. Every time I found him strung out in the tree house, waiting for something to blow over.

Worse than the physical damage was the dullness that settled into his eyes, his reticence to speak, even to me. Rather than get angry, a part of him seemed to disappear. Every single time, I waited with the same apprehension it might not come back.

"I'm fine," he said. "Really. Got a good shot in yesterday, actually. I don't think he'll be on my case for a while." *Puff. Puff. Puff.* "My hand hurts like a bitch, though."

"Yesterday?"

"English test." I realized I didn't know Trip's exam schedule anymore. I didn't need to ask any more than that. His uncle didn't get that Trip's dyslexia hadn't sprung into existence solely to piss him off.

But for Trip, fighting back was a rare and new thing. He always told me that standing his ground made things worse. And even though Trip was strong—after all, I'd seen what he could do with an ax—Leon still had a boxer's reflexes.

I wanted to reach through the phone and shake him. "Part of why I didn't put up a fight about leaving was so you could turn him in without him turning *me* in. What are you screwing around for?"

I heard rustling, then the sound of rocks hitting a tree. I inhaled and counted to ten. "Trip?"

"Your leaving threw him. He's on edge. I just need . . . It'll settle down."

I thought of Leon's gloating about how he "beat" the information about my leaving out of Trip, about the bruises, the silence, the look in Trip's eyes when things were at their worst. The guns. "Look, do whatever it is he needs you to do." I couldn't believe I was saying that, but there was no other option. "I'll come back. I mean it. I'll leave tomorrow. Hitchhike." My mind spun, focused only on ways to get back to Barlowe. I was stupid to think that money was what Trip needed most from me.

"Shadow, no." His voice broke and then he tried to regroup. "No. I'm not . . . You can't . . ."

"Trip," I whispered, all of my anger evaporating like the smoke from Trip's cigarette. "Let me—"

"I said no."

I knew arguing was pointless, so I tried something else. "Look, about what happened at the party . . ." I let my words crawl their way through the phone, hoping he might tell me it was okay again. I heard the wind howl and I wasn't sure if it was outside my window or in Barlowe. It made me feel infinitely lonely.

There was such a long silence, I pulled the phone from my ear to make sure it still held a charge. No one had the ability to make me feel as helpless as Trip.

"There's a girl here," I said carefully, "who was there that night. Small world, huh?" I could hear the distress in my voice.

"Really?" Trip asked, but I wasn't sure if he was asking a question or if he just wanted to say *something*. I doubted knowing I'd come across someone who was there, a witness, was going to make him any happier than it made me.

"We need to talk about it, Trip."

The line went quiet again before he answered. "What's left to say? You made yourself clear." I heard him swallow. The restless crunch of leaves under his boots.

"I didn't mean . . . Things got out of control." Although I wasn't sure if that was the reason for everything that had happened that night. I was certain the horrible things we'd said and done to each other afterward owed more than a little to alcohol (on his part) and shock (on mine).

"Maybe," he said. "The thing is, I'm not sorry. Not for any of it, really. But you are. And I don't know where that leaves us."

Us. I rubbed my eyes and tried to untwist whatever things in my stomach had twisted into knots. "It's just . . . I . . ." I was lost. Trip was right and we both knew it. "Here," I said finally. "It leaves us here."

"I'm not sure where that is," he said in a breathy voice that made tears sting the back of my eyes.

I reached up for the boomerang and held the charm so tightly I could feel it cutting into my skin. *It doesn't matter how far you throw a boomerang,* Trip told me when he gave it to me. *If you throw it right, it'll always come back to you.*

Again, I made the decision we'd already made years ago. I wasn't going to abandon him, I couldn't. He wasn't going to save himself, so I had no choice, not really.

"Tomorrow," I promised him. "Tomorrow I'm going to talk to my mother about the trust fund. I promise, Trip. I'm going to make this all work out. You'll see."

The plan had been clear in my head when Trip and I were kids and we stood in the tree house, staring at the huge map on the wall. After coming back to Millway, confronting my mother and demanding access to my trust, which she would give me without question, Trip and I would buy those crazy round-the-world plane tickets that allow you to have as many layovers as you'd like. And we would leave.

I knew now nothing would be that easy. For one thing, my mother's transformation had thrown me more than it should have. It would have been easier to approach the broken version of her. I wasn't sure I was brave enough to confront Mom 2.0 and say, "Mind if I cash out that trust fund and use the money to go traveling with my friend, Trip, before his uncle kills him? I mean, if you never got around to drinking through it." Yeah. Not going to cut it. And I suspected that accusation might cause more problems than it was worth.

So instead, after an awkward day at school where I hid out in the library and did my best to avoid Jenny, Emery, Rory, and anyone else I'd be forced to speak to, I cooked dinner for my mother.

Without a car, I wasn't going to make it to the grocery store, so I had to scrounge through her kitchen for enough things I recognized: whole wheat pasta, a bag of organic vegetables, and some frozen free-range chicken. I'd spent enough time cooking for Maggie that I knew my way around a kitchen. I figured I could create something edible.

I couldn't find a tablecloth, but there were a couple of striped linen placemats shoved in the back of a drawer. I threw those in the dryer on high heat—I wasn't about to go looking for an iron—and took some dusty candles off the mantel.

I set the table, put the water on to boil, and reviewed my options. Really, I had none. Or rather I had one. There was no way for me to beat around the bush and get the information I needed from her about the trust's status. The trick was going to be presenting it in a way that didn't cause her to either kick me out or call Perkins to start legal proceedings against Maggie.

My mother hugged me for what felt like five full minutes. "I can't," she kept sputtering. "I just can't."

I tried to interrupt her exclamations with my own. "Mom . . ." The word felt strange leaving my mouth, but it was getting slightly easier with time.

Finally, I pushed her gently away and rubbed my face where it was chafed from being jammed against the wool of her jacket. "It's only dinner."

Her face flushed as she wiped the back of her hand across her face.

"I've spent years thinking I'd never see you again. This is more than I ever could have dreamed of." She motioned to the table like I'd laid out some mystical feast, and not a basket of bread and plates of salad.

"I wanted to do something nice for you." Her letters were still lined up, untouched, in their box upstairs and I felt a wave of guilt for not having read them. And then another because I could tell it had been a while since someone had gone out of their way for her and I suspected my questions were going to ruin it.

She sat down at the table with all the awkwardness of a girl on her first date, not that I'd know anything about dating. It hadn't been an option in Barlowe, given that Sean Woodhouse didn't exist.

I served dinner and listened to her talk about her day while I chased pieces of pasta around on my plate.

Halfway through dinner and without any prompting, she put her fork down and said, "I want you to know I've decided not to press charges. You're here, where you should be, and I want to focus on moving forward."

I dropped my fork. "Thank you," I whispered. *Please let it be true. Please let it be true.*

I didn't ask how she'd made her decision, and she didn't offer. In a way, this gift of my mother's made it more difficult to ask about the trust. I didn't want her to feel like I was being selfish, but it wasn't a topic that could ever sound casual.

I speared a piece of chicken, and then thought better of eating it. "So, you know how you used to say Grandma and Grandpa Sterling set up a trust fund for me?"

Her actual words played through my head: *Your damned grandparents couldn't be bothered to help me, but they made sure that you're all set for college. Don't you think it might have been better for them to make sure we could eat now instead of worrying about when you turn eighteen?* Maybe she and Trip had more in common than I'd thought.

She wrapped her hands around a sunny yellow coffee mug and said, "Mmm," like she was distracted by something else.

"Is it still there?" I tried to make it sound like curiosity instead of desperation, but I wasn't convinced I got it right.

"Sure," she said, then, "Why?"

I coughed on a piece of spaghetti. "I was wondering, I mean . . ." My brain cycled through meaningless words trying to come up with an explanation that wouldn't freak her out. "You know, being back in school, I guess I wanted to know."

"Oh, right. Well." She put the mug down and sighed. "Yes, of course. James Gordon, Jenny's father, is still the executor. Your grandparents didn't trust me." Her brows knitted. "Anyway, yes. It's still waiting. I get statements by email every quarter and it's still linked to Davidson University in California, like they wanted."

My head spun with all the new information. Jenny's father. California. "What do you mean, linked to Davidson?"

She sipped her coffee, oblivious to the fact that she'd ruined my life. "Your grandparents were alums. They were living out west. I guess they thought you could go there since I'd turned out to be such a huge disappointment to them and they'd be nearby to make sure you didn't drop out like I did. Of course, they hadn't planned on dying."

"What?" I asked, although I wasn't sure which part of her story I was asking about.

She looked up like she'd forgotten I was in the room. "Sorry, I guess I'm still angry with them."

I tried to sort out the questions I had to ask her. I'd deal with what it meant that Jenny's father was the executor later. "Do you mean it can't be used for anything except for Davidson tuition? What if I didn't get in? What if I decided not to go to college?"

She waved her hand dismissively. "You'd have to ask James. But I'm pretty sure the money gets donated to some wildlife sanctuary should you not go to DU." She raised an eyebrow.

"Something like that. Whatever cause your grandparents were supporting at the time."

I tasted salt on my tongue. Blood from where I'd been gnawing on my bottom lip. I was pretty sure I was going to be sick.

"If you want to go to school closer to home, we can sort it out somehow. I'd like that." Mom sipped her coffee and grimaced. "Cold," she said as she got up and moved toward the kitchen. "Do you want anything?"

I didn't know what to do with the information. I didn't know how I was going to tell Trip that our plans had never been more than fairy tales.

I wasn't going to be able to save him. He would have to stay with Leon, repeating his senior year until the school kicked him out or Leon killed him.

I couldn't make a sound. My head just shook from side to side. I didn't even know how to begin to list the things I wanted.

TWELVE

Rory and I were knee-deep in algebraic formulas when a flurry of catcalls blared in the cafeteria.

We turned at the same time to see what all the fuss was about, and then turned back to look at each other when we realized it was all about Jenny.

I'd gotten used to seeing her in jeans and simple shirts, her hair pulled back, wearing no noticeable make-up. But that day Jenny walked toward us in a short black skirt that hugged her hips, her hair flowing over the fuzzy green sweater she'd worn that first night in the yard. Her eyes were ringed with mascara and she teetered on heels that must have been massively uncomfortable.

She and Emery hit the table at the same time, and it was

pretty clear from the expression on her face that Emery hadn't been expecting this makeover, either.

Jenny caught my eye, then looked away and sat down. I figured she was going to pretty much ignore me for the rest of the hour, the same way she had since we'd talked.

I watched the twins have an entire conversation with one glance. "You look . . ." Rory said to Jenny.

"Nice," Emery finished. "What's the occasion?"

Rory leaned in.

Jenny smiled, but didn't say anything, and I went back to moving food that I had no intention of eating around on my plate. Given everything I had riding on graduation, the potentially failing grade should have bothered me, but I couldn't work up any real emotion about it. Whatever I tried to focus on, my mind kept coming back to my promise to Trip and the trust's being linked to Davidson. I needed to find an alternate plan.

When I tuned back into the conversation at the table, Rory was talking about some audition piece he'd chosen for the Clefs, Millway's touring a cappella choir.

"Let's hear it," Emery said, and Jenny made some sound of agreement with her red, red lips.

"You're nuts," Rory said. "I'm not singing in the cafeteria. The acoustics in here suck."

I went back to trying to figure out what I was going to do about Trip. Jenny's dad was away filming his TV show and wouldn't be back until the New Year. What would the holidays be like for Trip? Would he find someone else to spend his rare Leon-free minutes with? Would he hate me when I told him that I'd made promises I couldn't keep? It didn't matter how I turned the problem over in my head. I couldn't find a way to get the money from the trust on my own, and without that . . .

Someone coughed and I looked up. "What?"

Emery shook her head. "Glad we're so interesting. I was just saying that we should go to the Tavern to celebrate my brother finally making a decision about his audition piece."

"What's the Tavern?" I asked, trying to at least pretend to be interested.

"Emery and Rory's parents run a pub," Jenny explained.

"Pick the two of you up at seven?" Emery asked me.

I wanted nothing more than to go home and try to sleep, but I knew it would be pointless, so I simply nodded.

"Jenny?" Rory stood up and nudged her shoulder with his tray.

Just as she looked up, he slipped, and his wallet went skidding across the table and onto the floor between us. It landed open, displaying the contents of its clear plastic windows like a picture frame. Driver's license on one side, a picture of Jenny on the other.

For an awkward moment, Jenny and I both stared at the photo. Finally, I reached over to grab the wallet, closing it before handing it back to Rory, who'd turned as red as his hair. He walked away without a word.

The Tavern was just outside of town. Rory explained that the building was one of the oldest in the area, but that his parents had shipped the wood for the bar itself from the UK. The inside was dark and warmed by a real fireplace. Everywhere I looked, there was some old artifact: a mailbox, an old brass ship's bell, a clock stuck at 10 p.m.

The twins' mother had said that we could hang out in the back room unless it started getting too busy and they needed the table. We sat in a dark booth, Rory tense next to me, and Jenny staring impatiently at Emery through her newly enhanced lashes. It was pretty clear that she was looking for info about the photo in Rory's wallet. I couldn't blame her. I hadn't expected it either. It was obvious he had a thing for her, but it still struck me as a little odd that he was carrying her photo around with him like that.

Jenny kept sighing, Rory drummed on the table with his knife, and Emery ran her thumb over her nails as if she were trying to sharpen them.

I couldn't take the tension anymore and got up to get a soda from the back bar.

I examined the diamond-shaped inlays in the wood while the bartender got my drink, trying not to think about how much Trip would have loved this place. I milked the soda, trying to figure out how long I could avoid going back to the others.

"Do you play darts?" Rory asked, startling me. He was leaning on his elbows against the bar, and I caught a flash of his black Joy Division shirt printed with LOVE WILL TEAR US APART. It completely echoed my feelings. Maybe he'd let me buy it off him.

"Actually, yeah. I'm good at all those games you don't need other people to play." I said it like I was joking, but I was dead serious. Darts. Crossword puzzles. Even horseshoes. Wilson had let me put up a dartboard on the side of the old barn, and I'd gotten pretty good. It was safer than chopping wood, which was what Trip did to relieve stress.

"So you're good at playing with yourself?" Rory said, snickering. "Do you know cricket?" He jerked his head toward the dartboard.

I ignored the lame joke and nodded. Cricket revolved around being the first player to hit each number between fifteen and twenty, three times, but you could get multiple points depending on which ring the dart landed in.

Rory ducked behind the bar and grabbed a wooden box. I watched with a kind of awe as he took his own set of custom darts out of the box, threaded the flights—the feathered parts—onto the shafts, and then screwed on the metal barrels.

"Seriously? You have your own darts?"

"My parents own a pub. I've had my own set since I was a kid." He smiled and there was so much warmth in it that I finally understood why everyone seemed to like him so much. He smirked as he handed me a set of darts that looked like they'd been dipped in beer and run over by a tank. They were missing flights and the bent tips were massacred.

"Thanks," I said under my breath. I was good, but I was pretty sure I was in over my head. "How about we start with 301 so I can see what I'm up against?"

"You got it." He marked 301 on the board and motioned for me to go first.

"These darts are crap," I said, looking at the three that had hit near, but not where, I'd aimed them.

"That's what happens when you let drunk people play with sharp objects." Rory lined up and threw two double bull's-eyes and a twenty, then cracked his knuckles. "I haven't played in a while. I'm a little rusty."

I snorted my ginger ale and glanced back at the table where Jenny and Emery were having a heated discussion, making me even happier that I'd left.

I bent the tip of my dart a little to get it to resemble something approaching straight. Obviously, Rory wasn't worried about playing fair, and I wasn't going to be able to beat him on skill. I decided to try another tactic.

"So," I asked, "you and Jenny, you've dated?"

The expression on his face was a priceless combination of embarrassment and cockiness. His dart hit the outside edge.

"Not really," he admitted, playing with the remaining two expensive projectiles in his hand.

"So the photo in your wallet is what? Wishful thinking?" I was trying to be a smartass, but the look Rory gave me made me want to apologize. And truth was, I genuinely liked the guy.

He shrugged.

"But you've asked her out, right?"

He stared at me like I'd told him to recite the periodic table. "It's complicated."

"Tell me about it." I didn't mean it literally. Or maybe I did. I wasn't sure.

He lined up and threw with even less finesse than his first turn, hitting the outer edge of fifteen. "She and Emery," he started, and then thought better of it. "I've spent a lot of time with Jenny. There are a lot of girls that . . ." He stopped again and shrugged. "I have no problems getting dates. She's just . . . you know."

"No," I said, honestly.

"No? You aren't into her at all?" he asked as though I'd just told him that I breathed water instead of air or that I existed on a diet of worms in a world of chocolate.

I shook my head.

"Oh." He exhaled. "Then you need to let her go, man."

I leaned over and put my beat-up darts on the table next to his razor-straight ones. "I haven't even been here."

He hesitated and pressed himself against the wall, looking uncomfortable, his normally cheerful expression strained and awkward. "I think that's the problem. Look, had you . . . I mean, had everything . . ." He looked at me, pleading for a way out.

"Yeah, had I been here."

"Right. Had you been here." He took a deep breath. "See, she couldn't go out with me, or anyone, really, because you weren't here. Had you been, you would have just gone along with your lives. You would have been friends, and met other people." He ran one of the darts under the nail of his index finger. "Maybe even dated them."

I nodded slowly as it dawned on me where he was taking the conversation.

"Had you . . ." He got stuck again and then picked up where he left off. "Had you been here, well, would you feel any differently about her now?"

I closed my eyes and tried to picture Jenny at twelve. And how she might have looked over the past five years. Mostly what I pictured was the school photo from Rory's wallet. He had it bad.

"Probably not," I admitted. I wasn't sure what those years would have held, but I had a hard time picturing a present where I was in love with Jenny.

"See, and so you would have been friends. You would have had stupid fights and stupid make-ups and that would be that. Except that now she's built you into someone else over the past five years, someone who doesn't exist."

I rubbed the back of my neck. Everything he said made perfect sense, even though it made me feel like I was losing something I didn't think I ever had. For some strange reason, it also made me think of Trip, but I didn't know what to do with that, so I just shoved the thoughts to the side of my head.

"You realize she's barely speaking to me, right?"

He shook his head hard and his hair rearranged itself into crazy spikes. When he looked back over at the girls, the expression on his face reminded me of something someone said to me about Trip at the party. *I've seen how he looks at you.*

I sighed loudly. "How about I just tell her how awesome I think you are and you take it from there."

He smiled. "Maybe. I mean, thanks."

"Right." I plucked his darts out of his hand and threw three straight bull's-eyes.

Rory laughed and pulled them out of the board. I looked back at the table. This time Jenny was missing. She must have gone off to the bathroom or something because Emery was sitting there alone, watching us. In the dim light, I could see the resemblance to her brother.

"So, look. About you and Emery . . ."

"What are you talking about?" I swallowed and pulled my eyes back to Rory. "There is no 'me and Emery.'"

As if he did it every day, Rory walked around the bar and poured himself a half pint of beer and drank it in two gulps. "But you want there to be. You do a terrible job of hiding it."

Emery intrigued me. That she'd been there on the craziest night of my life made me feel connected to her in a way similar to the same unnamable attachment I felt to Trip. More, it linked the two of them somehow. But I didn't know how to explain that to Rory, and if he didn't know about the party, I certainly wasn't going to tell him.

I took another stab at straightening the points of the bar darts.

"Just to offer some unsolicited advice, don't go there unless you want your balls handed back to you in a sling."

I stopped fiddling with the darts, surprised that Rory didn't seem upset that I was interested in his sister.

"It's nothing personal. I love Emery." He put the sharp end of the dart into his mouth, his tongue flicking over it, snake-like until I looked away. "But she's sworn off relationships. And when her mind is made up, that's it."

When I looked at the table again, Jenny was back. Emery was shaking her head at something she'd said, her curls flying around her head like Medusa's snakes, the ones that could turn men to stone.

I knew I could trust Rory's advice. He wasn't just Emery's brother; he was her twin. And since he wanted me to talk to Jenny on his behalf, I didn't think he was going to screw me over.

But for some reason his words felt like a challenge.

THIRTEEN

My mother had a horrible artificial Christmas tree. I understood all of the ecological reasons why someone might get one, as well as all of the economic ones. Had either of those been her excuse, I would have done nothing more than look the other way every time I came in the house. But she told me that she'd bought the tree a few years before, in case I returned around Christmas. It depressed her too much to go "all out" with a live tree, but she felt like she had to do something festive. I didn't have the heart to tell her I never remembered her going "all out" when I was a kid. I barely remembered us even celebrating holidays.

Since I didn't know what to get her and since, having lived on the edge of a state forest for five years, I was used to being surrounded by nature, I recruited Rory to help me surprise her with a real tree.

On the first day of break, he picked me up and we went from lot to lot examining overpriced locally grown spruce, evergreens, and firs.

Rory reminded me of Charlie Brown, choosing trees that were slightly lopsided and looked like they needed a home.

I hadn't set out to find the perfect tree, but I couldn't seem to settle on *anything*. In Barlowe, Maggie, Wilson, and I had decorated live trees out in the back of the house and strung lit garlands off every surface inside. These trees, however fresh, just seemed dead to me with their needles dropping everywhere. And the screaming children running around the lot made my head hurt.

"Do you know someplace we could just chop one down?" I finally asked Rory.

"You mean with an ax?" he asked, looking confused.

I laughed and finally settled on a tree at the lot, but the whole interaction answered a question I'd never been able to answer with any certainty. I was never sure if maybe Trip and I had only gotten so close out of mutual isolation. He was the only one my age that I'd had anything to do with for all that time, and I wondered if I would have gotten attached to anyone else in the same situation.

But the thing is, Trip would never have considered buying a tree from a lot. Instead, we'd have driven recklessly down roads that were barely roads, traipsing through muddy fields until we found a tree that he would have deemed suitable. It would have taken hours. Then, whether it was legal or not, Trip would have felled it without a thought, while I stood guard against park rangers and pissed-off farmers, watching the muscles in his back pull with each swing.

Although I had the urge to insist that Rory and I at least give it a try, I knew we'd fail. Neither of us were cut out for physical labor, and I missed the possibility of it. I missed Trip.

I missed him more when Rory and I went to a small craft market so I could look for gifts for Emery and Jenny.

Trip didn't "do" Christmas or any holiday he found overly commercialized, which was convenient because he rarely had money. Instead, he gave gifts all year round—ones he made or came across. Maggie had once told me about a girl she'd known as a child who fed the magpies that lived in the field behind her house. After a while, the birds started bringing her presents in thanks: bits of sea glass, acorns, twisted pieces of yarn they'd collected for their nests. That story had always reminded me of Trip and his gifts: a bleached starfish, an old church key he'd found in the woods and painted, and, of course, the boomerang. My presents to him never seemed to reach the same level, no matter how hard I tried. Even the things I made for him—quotes scrawled on hidden rocks and my amateurish attempts at writing in iambic pentameter—seemed forced and impersonal in comparison.

I was glad not to have to reach those standards today. My

gift for Jenny, which I was planning to leave in her mailbox since she and her mother were leaving town on Christmas Eve, was more of a peace offering than anything else. I wanted to give her something meaningful to make up for five lost years. Nothing in the racks of scarves or figurines or boxes of candy was going to do that. Instead, I picked up a book about unsolved crimes of the twenty-first century, hoping she'd at least understand that I'd been paying attention to the things that interested her.

For Emery, I chose a necklace, a bronze sphere that chimed when it moved. It reminded me of captured fairies and mystery. It was somehow both delicate and fierce and I knew the minute I saw it that it should belong to her. I hoped that, with her most of all, I'd gotten it right.

The guy behind the register was chatty and, as he rang up my purchases, he commented on the boomerang around my neck. When I told him it had been made by a friend, he thrust a business card in my direction and told me to have Trip call him.

I didn't explain why that would never happen, why Leon would never allow it, and why I wasn't ready to share any part of Trip with the world.

As Rory and I left the store, I threw the card in the trash.

Jenny and her mom were headed to Costa Rica to spend the holidays with her dad, who was taping on location. I wished

I'd had a chance to talk to her before she left. I'd given up on trying to figure out how to repair five years' worth of regret on her part, and newly found guilt on mine, but I'd promised Rory I'd talk to her, and I didn't want to rock the fragile trust we'd built.

On New Year's Eve, my mother had plans with her support group. Since that wasn't a scene I had any desire to be a part of, I took Emery up on her offer to go with her and Rory to a party at the Sugar Bar, Millway's all-ages dance club. That meant they only served coffee and soft drinks. Technically that's all *they* were serving. But every other person, it seemed, had brought some sort of flask. In fact, there was so much booze floating around that all you had to do was hold your cup out and someone would pour something in. I wasn't even sure what I'd been drinking for the past couple of hours, but it tasted better and better as the night went on.

Rory seemed to know everyone. I was in awe of how he was able to move from group to group, always welcomed into the ranks of whoever was there.

While he was off socializing, Emery and I made slow progress around the perimeter. It was a strange feeling to be at a party with people I saw every day. I didn't have to pretend to be someone else. I couldn't. But I was also hyperaware of Trip's absence. I'd been hoping he'd find a way to call me since we'd always spent New Year's Eve together, shooting off fireworks over the ice-covered fields. As I checked my phone for the millionth time, I had to accept that my wishes were just nothing more than that.

Emery reached over, took my phone out of my hands, and put it into the pocket of her dress. "Enough."

Her steel gray dress with flecks of silver running through it reminded me, in my inebriated state, of the color of Trip's eyes. She was also wearing the necklace I'd given her for Christmas. Her gift to me, a journal of handmade paper, sat pristine on my nightstand. When she'd handed it to me, she'd told me it wasn't for collecting quotes, but making up some of my own.

She hummed along to the music and we watched the crowd. After a little while, when she caught me glancing at the pocket where she'd stowed my phone, she said, "Tell me about him. The boy from the party."

The music shifted to something old and electronic and then the dry ice machine jerked to life. I was glad for the fog because it meant she couldn't see my eyes and I could pretend that the directness of her question hadn't thrown me. I took a long drink, trying to remember to breathe. "Trip Marchette. He lived next door."

"And?" she asked in a way that felt like she had some stake in my answer.

"And?" I parroted back. I wasn't sure what she was looking for, but the question was too loaded to answer incorrectly.

She glared at me and started to walk away. "Forget it."

"Wait," I said, following her through the dancers. "What's wrong?"

She turned to face me, but took a step backward. "I hate mind games."

The crowd jostled us, and I'd had enough to drink that the unexpected motion made me nauseous. I waved for her to come with me. I should have come up with some bullshit story, but the combination of alcohol and exhaustion from trying to keep the truth hidden made me want to tell her everything.

We ended up in a back room. Black walls. Candlelit. Some sort of trance music floated out of the speakers, and people, mostly couples, sat around the edges of the room. Some were talking quietly. A few were making out.

We found a wall to lean against and then I faced her. "I'm not playing games."

She stared at me, waiting.

"He's my best friend." I paused, trying to get to put my relationship with Trip Marchette into words. "He's the only person I don't usually seem to piss off."

She took a drink of her soda. Emery was emphatic about not drinking. Before we'd gotten to the club, she'd made me promise to be responsible for tasting her drinks to make sure no one had poured anything into them.

"He looked pretty pissed off when you stormed out of that party," she said.

I closed my eyes. "Yeah, he was a lot of things that night."

"Have you spoken to him since you've been back?"

"Once."

"Why only once?"

I hesitated. Like everything with Trip, there was no clear-cut answer. I picked the one nearest to the truth. "I don't want his uncle to kill him."

She blinked hard, but didn't force the question. Not knowing what she thought had happened that night at the party was freaking me out. At some level, I wanted her to understand everything between me and Trip. Even though I didn't have the words to explain the intricacies of our relationship, I wanted her to get it.

"I didn't even know about the party until that night. Trip just sprang it on me that we were going out. It was so rare that I went anywhere. And then, to end up at that house. It felt like we were on the set of some musical. That spiral staircase and all."

She nodded.

Trip had led us straight to the elaborate and surprisingly full bar. It was hard to imagine that the party was being thrown by a bunch of high school students, even obscenely rich ones. He ordered and drank a shot of whiskey, and then ordered another for himself along with one for me. "You need to relax," he'd said.

I was taking in the opulence of the room, the six-foot-tall vases of exotic flowers, the nightclub-like lighting, when Trip was spun around by a large hand on his shoulder.

"Marchette, what dragged you out of your hole?" The kid in front of us was as big as a wall, but somehow still managed to look graceful. His long fingers wrapped around a cut crystal champagne glass that probably cost more than Maggie's entire house, and the guy looked completely comfortable holding it.

"Have to visit the slums every once in a while," Trip joked and nodded to me. "Parker Hudson the seventy-third or something, this is Sean. My cousin. Sean, this is Parker. He comes with the house."

I realized, as I shook the vise Parker held out to me, that Trip and I had never bothered to get our stories straight. Even so, cousin was an odd choice. And I was more than a little disturbed that he'd used my real name.

"Cousin, huh?" Parker looked me over the same way someone would examine a fish for freshness.

"Michigan," Trip said, just as I said, "Baltimore."

"Baltimore, Michigan. It's on the lake," I said hoping like hell that Parker knew nothing about Michigan and wasn't the kind of person to look it up.

"Cool," he said. Something in his darting eyes told me that he wasn't going to remember the conversation in five minutes, and I was able to breathe again. "How long are you visiting?"

I pushed my lips together and let Trip answer. "Just over break."

Trip and I spun at the sound of breaking glass, but Parker almost seemed to expect it. "Nice to meet you. Think I'm being paged," he said as he propelled himself in the direction of the racket.

I took a mouthful of whiskey. It felt like it was burning me from the inside out. "How can you drink this stuff?"

Trip shrugged and polished off what was left in his glass.

"Cousins?" I asked.

"Yeah, that was good, wasn't it?" he replied.

I thought of asking him why we'd ended up at a party hosted by people he actually knew, but then forced myself to look around the room. Everyone was focused on their own conversations. Not one of them was looking at me as though they were trying to figure out why my face resembled the one they'd seen in the news five years before. Maybe they'd been worried about other things at twelve? But at the same time, Michael Sterling had become the poster child for "bad things that can happen to kids."

Before I could say anything, a girl appeared at Trip's side. She was perfectly polished in a way that made me think of magazine ads depicting snow-swept hills and illegally traded fur coats. She was beautiful in the same way a diamond is beautiful—cold with hard edges—white-blonde short hair and piercing blue eyes.

"This is Charlotte," Trip said. "Parker's sister."

I smiled as she examined me much more thoroughly than her brother had.

"You have a nice house," I said, which made her laugh. It was a horrible understatement.

"My brother says you're cousins?" she asked Trip with a sly grin. Her eyes fell to my waist, where Trip's thumb was hooked into a loop on my belt. He did nothing to remove it and I couldn't figure out how to move away without causing more of a scene. "I didn't realize your family was so close."

I wasn't sure if it was an accusation, but it made the whiskey come up, burning the crap out of the back of my throat.

Trip reached up and put his arm around my shoulders and pulled me to him possessively. I was too busy trying not to puke on anyone to stop him.

"Sean's my favorite relative," Trip said. All I could do was stand there and shrug when she narrowed her eyes and tried to figure out how much was truth and how much was bluster.

"I bet," she said. "Come on, *cousin*. I need your help."

She took my hand and pulled me away to help her move some boxes of champagne because, she said, they'd given their staff the night off in order to delay knowledge of the party from their parents who were vacationing in St. Moritz, and her brother was too busy getting stoned to be of any assistance. Then she asked if Trip and I were really cousins and I played it off by talking about marriages between distant aunts and uncles.

She smoothed the sleeve of my shirt between her fingers

as if she were trying to figure out the quality of the fabric and asked, point-blank, “Are you in love with him?”

I stumbled back a step and she laughed. “He never lets anyone get close. Hell, I’ve been trying to seduce him for two years,” she said. “I guess I know now why he hasn’t given in. I see how he looks at you.”

Without a word, I picked up one of the boxes and took it back to the bar. Then I followed on shaky legs as she led me back to where Trip was standing next to the DJ. Charlotte leaned up and kissed him on the cheek, gave me a hug, and left.

“I’m done being social,” Trip said as he held my gaze. I recognized the tone of his voice—it was the one he used when he was saying something important, something he didn’t want me to miss. I wasn’t sure what he meant, but his words, on top of Charlotte’s statement, made me feel claustrophobic.

I grabbed the hand of the first girl that walked by on her own, pretty, with crystals—or, given that crowd, maybe they were diamonds—threaded into her cornrows. We danced to music that was thankfully too loud for conversation. Drinks appeared in my hand without my knowing where they came from. I hated beer and didn’t have much experience with alcohol, but I downed everything I was given. My head spun as the girl and I turned in time to the music. I never caught her name and never gave her mine.

I lost track of Trip in the crowd of expensively dressed bodies. It was well after midnight when we found our way back to each other. The hallway was filled with people talking, making out, sitting and staring into space. I pulled Trip into a doorway, grabbed the glass out of his hand, and poured its contents into a plant. Then I fixed the collar of his shirt and he leaned the side of his face into my hand.

"You're drunk," I said, stating the obvious.

"Maybe." He sighed.

"There you are," Charlotte called as she stepped over bodies to get to us. She took one look at my hand on Trip's cheek and then glanced at the door we were pushed against. "I'll have to let the maid know to change the bedding before Grandma Tilly comes to visit next week."

I fantasized about melting into the wall. I was too embarrassed to even correct her.

"I like you." She smiled at me. "Are you really only staying for break?"

Before I could answer, Trip leaned an arm on each of our shoulders. "You know what they say about absence and all that."

He was drunker than I'd seen him in a long time. He drank for the same reason most kids did. Escape. Normally Trip had more to run from than most, but I had no idea, at the time, what he was running from that night.

I looked at my watch dramatically. "Oh look, is it that time already? We should get you home before you turn into a pumpkin."

I prayed that he'd take the hint. For a minute, I thought he'd fight me, but then he nodded and cocked his head toward mine. "Obviously this boy needs his beauty sleep."

"Looks like he's doing fine to me," Charlotte said, making me blush. Then she leaned in and whispered, "Make sure we see you again before you leave town, Cousin."

Emery had wanted the truth so I intended to give her every painful bit of it. I just wasn't sure what she was going to do with my answers.

"But you didn't leave," Emery said. "The party, I mean." It wasn't a question. She knew we'd stayed.

"No, Trip stopped me on the way out and said we had to talk. I told him we could talk in the truck, but he said it couldn't wait. And besides, he wanted to see the view from the top of the staircase. I was irritated, but I wasn't sure why. I think it had something to do with Charlotte. There was always something that made people want to be indispensable to him. But I don't think it was like that with her. It bugged me that they apparently knew each other so well and I'd never even heard her name before."

"I followed him through the crowd and up the stairs. There was a break in the music and my ears were ringing. We were the only people at the top. I kept thinking that it was rude for us to go traipsing around someone's house. *That* house in particular. And I didn't want to be in the spotlight. Maggie and Wilson had done such a good job of warning me to avoid it. And then . . ."

I turned away from Emery and stared into the flashing lights.

"He kissed you."

"Yeah, he kissed me. I'd spent five years pretending I didn't exist. Trying to fade into the woodwork. Plus, we never . . . not in front of anyone . . . We were always so careful. So private. But people applauded. I think I wanted to kill him. I actually imagined pushing him over the rail."

After, the shock had worn off enough for me to disentangle myself from Trip, I panicked and flew down the stairs, pushing through the crowd, spilling drinks. We'd parked at the edge of the property. It felt like it was miles away from the house.

I ran to the truck. I thought about leaving Trip there, but I wasn't sure I was able to drive, so I climbed onto the hood and stared at the sky. The stars were so bright that it felt like my retinas were burning.

I was so freaked out I could barely breathe. By unspoken agreement, we'd kept the physical side of our friendship private, not even speaking directly about it between ourselves in case anyone overheard. I wasn't even sure that Maggie knew why I spent so much time glancing out the window, waiting for Trip to raise the flag that meant he was in the tree house and waiting for me.

When he showed up at the truck, I expected him to be

contrite and apologetic. Instead, he pulled himself up next to me and said, "It's starting. Or ending."

Usually his non sequiturs amused me, but right then, I just wanted to strangle him. "What the hell are you talking about?"

He paused so long that I glanced over to make sure he hadn't passed out. Eventually, he said, "You're going home tomorrow. Not today, because tonight is really tomorrow. But the real tomorrow."

My head was spinning and my lips felt bruised even though his kiss hadn't been particularly rough and even though something deep inside me to wanted to do it again. Trip was horrible when it came to time, so I was used to him talking around things when he wasn't focused enough to stop and sort it out, but this was bad even for him. At first, I thought he was suggesting that we spend the night at Charlotte and Parker's and not go back to Maggie's until morning. Then I thought he was just drunk and rambling.

Before I could question him, he turned to me, his eyes surprisingly clear. He linked his fingers together in front of him and leaned his cheek on them. "I called the cops. In Millway. Their tip line. I didn't give my name, but they're expecting you tomorrow. In the park. McKuen Park, right?"

The thought of him calling the police was so unexpected that I almost laughed. But I knew the look in Trip's eyes, the sincerity that turned the gray almost black. "You called the cops? Why would you do that?" The question echoed inside my head and soured on my tongue.

I waited for him to say he was kidding, but Trip was silent, just sitting there, staring at me. My stomach convulsed, the night's alcohol threatening to come up. I looked away, which only made my head spin more. When I tried to get my bearings, the silence that hung between us broke apart and reconfigured into the stark realization of what he'd done. A sudden, hot flash of tears rolled down my face.

I thought I knew Trip so well. I thought I knew what I meant to him. But here he was, throwing it all away. Throwing everything away. This wasn't how it was supposed to happen.

I shuddered.

"Shadow . . ." Trip's voice was soft and pleading. He moved to put a hand on my arm and I shrugged him off. "You going back was always the plan. And Maggie said . . ."

I knew what Maggie said. Maggie said she wanted Trip's uncle in prison and that Trip wouldn't take any steps that put me at risk. But I didn't give a shit about anything Leon Marchette could do to me and Trip knew that. I twisted around, only my grip on the roll bar keeping me from tumbling off. "I don't give a damn what Maggie said."

Trip struggled to stay upright next to me. He kept his eyes on his wrist, where he usually stenciled an ornate compass. It never totally made sense to me, but it was some sort of directional cheat sheet that seemed to work for him. It was missing tonight and he seemed disturbed by its absence. He spoke slowly. "What *do* you give a damn about, Sean? Sometimes, I'm not so sure."

My heart seized with an anger so sharp it stung. I had problems wrapping my head around his incomprehensible, drunken question. I couldn't believe he'd called the cops. That he was sending me away. "Is this all just some sort of game to you?"

He sighed and in a surprisingly sober voice, asked, "Is that really what you think?"

I wanted a fight. I was ready for one. So I spit out the first thing that echoed my injured pride. "What I think is that it's been really convenient for you to just fuck the boy next door."

Trip paused, but didn't take the bait. "I love you, Shadow. I always have."

His painfully sincere words tumbled over and over in my brain, but my rage was too intense a gatekeeper to allow them to settle anywhere.

The tears pouring down my cheeks felt like acid on my skin. I didn't know how to process *this* admission on top of everything else. I thought about his comment earlier about not wanting to be social anymore, and his kiss, which was dramatic and long and seeking, and realized that what he wanted from me was something public and permanent, something that would label us as more than just best friends messing around in a tree house.

But it was those possibilities he'd destroyed when he called the fucking cops. At that moment, I hated him and I hated myself for feeling that way. I lashed out, hitting him hard enough in the ribs that he winced. And then I did it again.

He didn't lift a hand to stop me. Trip was a practiced victim. He could take a punch better than I could throw one.

I rolled off the hood of the truck and sat in the cab, wiping away my pained tears and staring at my knuckles like they belonged to someone else, until he joined me. I barely remember driving home, but I know that we didn't say a word to each other until he came to drive me back to Millway, twenty-four hours later.

Emery took the cup out of my hand and took a sip before making a face and handing it back to me. I was grateful she didn't say anything. At the same time, I wanted confirmation that my confession hadn't scared her off. Had our situations been reversed, I wasn't sure that I wouldn't have walked out.

I was suddenly desperate to change the subject and take the focus off myself. My heart was racing uncomfortably and I took a few deep breaths and looked around the room to try to calm down.

Since we'd been in the club, I'd noticed a pattern. People would come in the door and scan the room, but every single set of eyes hesitated when they got to Emery. I didn't think that it was because she was the prettiest girl in the room, just the most striking.

"Your turn," I said. "Why aren't you involved with one of them?" I waved my cup in the direction of the guys in the room, standing there probably hoping I was just someone who was hitting on her and would soon get brushed aside like they had.

She folded her arms and surveyed the room. “Which of them do you see me with?”

I glanced around and pointed at a good-looking guy. Tall. His ripped T-shirt and jeans made him look tough, but you could tell from his watch and his shoes that he had more than enough money and was trying hard to slum it. Those small details he’d forgotten gave him away.

Emery laughed. “I’m too old for him. His last girlfriend was fourteen.”

I pointed out someone else before I had to think about that scenario for too long.

“He dated someone I used to go to school with. Forgot to tell her about the STD.”

“You’re making this up, right?” I asked, hopefully.

She tugged on my sleeve and pulled me out onto the back deck. A bunch of people were huddled around a fire pit, and as my eyes adjusted to the light, I could see couples groping in the flickering firelight. Huddled in their coats against the cold, it was impossible to tell the boys from the girls, and I envied their freedom to put aside whatever inhibitions they had and follow their urges.

Emery leaned against the deck. “Been there, done that. When we switched schools, I decided that I wasn’t going to waste my time. And I haven’t. It’s all a load of crap.”

Her words echoed a conversation I'd had with Trip. "Most love is bullshit," he had told me. He meant it, but at the same time, I knew, without a doubt, that he'd do anything for me. He'd tied our futures together in a way that I'd be hard-pressed to sever. I wasn't sure what the definition of love was, but that seemed to hit close to the mark.

"Look at Rory," she continued. "My brother could have pretty much any girl he wants, but the only one he wants is Jenny and she's hung up on you."

I swallowed my guilt and tried to ignore the weight of her eyes on mine.

"Speaking of which, what about you?" she asked.

"What about me?"

"Was Charlotte right? Are you in love with Trip?"

I shrugged and watched the fire crackle in the pit. The wood popped as it burned, making it look like fireflies were committing suicide. Someone laughed. I couldn't meet Emery's eyes.

She asked me again with the certainty in her voice of someone who already knew the answer to their question. And after what I'd just told her, I'm sure she thought she did. I wasn't half as close to being sure myself.

"He's my best friend, but . . . I don't know." I said. I went to take a swig from my cup and found it already empty.

"See," she said and reached out and grabbed hold of the fabric of my jacket. "Love makes people lie. Even to themselves."

I was pretty sure that her hand on my arm was just to give

her point emphasis. But I couldn't take my eyes off that one bit of leather she held crumpled tight in her fist.

"Love is bullshit," I mumbled. When Trip said it, he'd sounded decadent and certain. From me, it just sounded whiny.

She laughed. "You're a shitty actor. You're just like Rory. You don't believe that for a second." She looked smug. And beautiful. I wanted to prove to her that everything she thought about me was wrong.

I leaned into her so slightly, I wasn't sure she'd notice. I just wanted to close the distance between us. I was afraid that if I moved too much, she'd take her hand back and I didn't want her to. It felt like an IV line to some sort of normal life.

I thought of Rory's warning and told myself that Emery's cynicism and her knowing about Trip made her safe. Nothing that happened was going to change either of us. Still, I wanted to kiss her. I wanted to make her believe in something. I wanted to be the one to cut through her armor as naturally as I'd cut through Trip's. If I could prove her wrong, I could let myself believe that I was who I wanted to be, instead of who I really was.

She turned her head and I was drawn in. Goosebumps raced up my arms as I wrapped my free hand in her hair and pulled her into a kiss. Every nerve in my body came alive in bursts of fireworks. Then I kissed her again while the sound of applause and champagne corks celebrating the New Year echoed behind us.

When we broke apart, she brushed my neck with her hand and cupped the boomerang in her palm. My entire body trembled. The way her fingers softly rubbed the wood Trip had carved was more intimate than anything else she could have done. If she'd been looking for a way to completely disarm me, she'd found her target.

Out of breath, I waited for her to say something.

Someone threw a handful of translucent confetti at us on their way out the door and it glittered like falling stars.

"Happy New Year," Rory said, appearing out of nowhere, and pulling Emery into a hug.

My heart thumped out of time as I watched them.

Rory's phone rang and they took turns sharing wishes with their parents.

While they were talking, I put my empty cup on the table and left.

I figured that the walk home would take me about twenty minutes, and I didn't mind being out in the softly falling snow. I could hear the sound of parties winding down through open windows, music mingling with the clinking of glasses. "Don't you know that I fucking love you?" someone shouted. I didn't hear a response.

I thought of calling Rory to tell him that I'd left and that they shouldn't worry, but then realized that Emery still had my phone. As I walked, I fantasized about a scenario where Trip would call and she'd answer and the idea of them talking made me smile. But my reaction was probably because of the alcohol.

Trip would love Emery's wild hair and her floaty dresses and her dislike of bullshit. I'm sure he would have been brave enough to do more than kiss her at the stroke of midnight. I'm sure he would have stayed.

I brushed my fingers across my lips, thinking both about Emery's kiss and about Trip. Then I swallowed down a lump of drunken jealousy while I looked up at the snowy sky. The cold felt good against my face and I started to snake up and down streets. I wasn't ready to go home. I came to a gas station that hadn't been there five years before. The lights were garish, and no cars were fueling up. Only one thing caught my eye: the pay phone. I wasn't sure that it would work, but I dug around in my pockets and found two quarters.

It was a new year. A number that couldn't be traced back to me. And I was more than a little bit drunk.

"Hello?" Leon Marchette's voice was filled with New Year's cheer. I wondered if Trip was even there.

"Hello?" he said again, louder this time. I pulled the phone away from my ear and stared at it. I had nothing to say to Leon and no clue what I'd say to Trip. So I just listened to the sounds of the party until he said "damned kids" and hung up.

I followed Main for a few blocks before I noticed the police car trailing me.

"Need a ride?" Chief Perkins asked, rolling down the passenger's side window.

I licked my lips and hoped he couldn't smell the alcohol on my breath. At least I wasn't driving. "I kind of like walking in the snow."

He nodded. "Yeah, me, too. But people get all kinds of crazy tonight. Come on, let me give you a lift."

I figured that it wasn't a great idea to argue with a cop when I'd been drinking underage, so I got in and did my best to keep my face pointed toward the window so that he couldn't smell my breath. I expected him to grill me, but he just talked about crime stats on New Year's Eve. When we pulled up to my house, he cut the engine and turned to face me.

"I was pretty darned pissed at you for what you pulled. The whole running away thing, but I have to say that I'm glad you're back. Your mother is happy. She says you're doing really well in school. I guess everything has worked out in the end, right?"

It was odd to think of him keeping tabs on me.

From the outside, it looked like things had worked out. But, I'd yet to unravel the issues with my trust. I hadn't kept my promises to Trip or even come close to sorting out my tangled feelings. And then there were the possible repercussions I was going to face for kissing Emery.

"Happy New Year," I said, and slid out of the car.

FOURTEEN

I always made New Year's resolutions, and more often than not, whether out of some old superstition or lack of anything better to do, I kept them. In the past, my resolutions had to do with challenges: Read *War and Peace*; chop an entire cord of wood; devise a system that Trip could follow for the complicated regime of medicines that Maggie needed to take. I'd only failed at the last.

This year, my resolutions were less concrete. I resolved to find a way to make up with Jenny. I resolved to be nicer to my mother now that we'd gotten over the hurdle of her pressing charges. It wasn't as if I thought I could make up for the time I'd been gone, or worse, the time I was going to be gone after June. But I wanted to at least try to meet her halfway.

The last thing on my list was less a resolution and more of a flashing beacon: talk to James Gordon about my trust fund. The Gordons were due home later in the afternoon and I was hoping to kill two birds with one stone and see both him and Jenny.

I took a shower under water so hot it made me wince. When I toweled off and rearranged my hair in the mirror I noticed that the roots were coming in blond—not the whitish shade my hair had been as a kid, but a kind of dull beige that looked stark and colorless against the black that was growing out. I'd have to do something about it soon.

I wasn't hiding anymore. Still, when I thought about letting my hair grow out, I felt a little like I was betraying Wilson and Maggie. What would my mother would say if I re-dyed it? Would anyone even place as much importance on the color of my hair as me? Trip, probably. Everything I did seemed important to him.

I threw a baseball cap over my head so I didn't have to look at my hair anymore and got dressed. On the way out of my room, I grabbed the sweatshirt Jenny had given me that first night I was back, then told my mom that I was going to see James Gordon to talk about the trust. She asked if I wanted her to come with me, and I said no. It was hard to think that, after all this time, she'd turned into just who I'd always wanted her to be. But this time I would be the one letting her down.

I wove a path through the suitcases still stacked in the hall and followed Mrs. Gordon to the kitchen. It was good to see her, and I was looking forward to seeing Mr. Gordon, but I was also a little nervous about seeing Jenny. I didn't know if she'd spoken to Emery or if they'd have talked about my drunken New Year's kiss. And really, we were barely on speaking terms as it was.

Mr. Gordon almost bowled me over with a bear hug as he flew out of his office off the kitchen. He was dressed in royal blue silk pajamas, a huge difference from the lawyer suits I used to see him in.

"I heard you were home. I just . . . I guess I didn't believe it until just now. How are you? Do you want something? Steph, get him a drink."

"Oh, no thanks," I said, and laughed. "A lot has changed in five years."

Mr. Gordon laughed, too. "You aren't kidding. Are you here to see Jenny?"

"Yeah," I said. "But I was hoping I could talk to you for a minute first." He looked confused. "About my trust."

"Oh," he said. For a minute, I think he'd forgotten that he was the trust's executor. Maybe he'd forgotten that he'd ever been a lawyer. "Sure, come have a seat in my office. I have to find the files."

I thrust the sweatshirt at him. "Jenny lent this to me. I thought you might want it back." He stared at it. Maybe I'd given him the wrong idea about Jenny and me.

When we got to his office, he shut the door behind me. The room hadn't changed. It still had the wooden desk, burgundy padded chair, and diplomas on the walls. Mr. Gordon looked completely out of place, as if he'd wandered in from the street and had stopped to rest his legs.

He unlocked a drawer and rummaged around. "Sorry, Michael . . . um . . . Sean. I haven't looked at this in a long, long time. Give me a minute."

I waited while he pulled out a file, flipped papers around, and made *hmm* noises.

"Okay," he said. "What can I do for you?"

I didn't see a reason to beat around the bush. "Is there any way to unlink the money from Davidson?"

"Well . . ." He rubbed the bridge of his nose. "Did you want to go somewhere else?"

I took a deep breath. "Not really, sir. I was more hoping I could cash it out."

He stabbed the cap end of his pen into the desk a couple of times. "What do you have your eye on? A sports car? There isn't . . . I mean, you haven't . . . There isn't a girl involved or anything is there?"

I laughed and assured him that no girl was involved. He looked relieved.

"Here's the thing. Your grandparents were pretty adamant on the terms of the trust. Davidson or nothing. I'd tried to give them options to work in more flexibility. I mean, what if you'd wanted to go to Harvard? Would they actually pull the funding? But, no, it was their money, and this was what they wanted. I'm afraid it's pretty much what you're stuck with."

I swallowed. "There's nothing you can do as executor?"

"I'm happy to check with someone at my old firm to see if they can find a loophole, but I was unfortunately very good at my job. If you want to use these funds, you're going to California."

I nodded, wondering what weird fates were at work to bring me back to Millway only to have all of my plans pulled out from under me.

I thanked him and got up to leave. "Just think, though," he said with a wistful glance out the window at the frozen trees. "You won't have to put up with winter and you'll be surrounded by all of those sun-bleached blondes."

I tried to smile. I knew he was just trying to help me. But I got out of there as soon as I could. I didn't have the energy to face Jenny or even myself.

This time, even my mom noticed I was upset. "Did you want to go to a different school? Something closer?" she asked. "Maybe I could take out a loan against the house."

I shook my head and hugged her, afraid that if I began to talk, I was going to lose it.

Rain started as I trudged up the stairs—one of those cold, sleety storms that was a mix of everything at once. I didn't have the patience for homework, so I dug out the box of my mom's letters and propped myself up on the pillows of my bed.

I read them in order from the first panicked scrawls she'd written right after I'd left, up through the most recent ones.

Nothing in those pages was news to me. My mother might have kept my father's identity out of her drunken ramblings when I was a kid and wasn't giving up that secret here, but the rest of it I'd heard or at least pieced together.

She summed up my conception and her downfall in one letter:

> *My freshman year at college, I went to a frat party that ended up like so many of them do—a girl "in a bad way." Sorry, that was your grandmother's phrase. Basically, I got knocked up.*
>
> *My parents had drilled into me the importance of helping others, but surprise, surprise, that didn't extend to their own daughter. Not after my "big mistake." Oh, of course, they gave me two options. ONE: They'd pay for and support an abortion. Or, TWO: Since I obviously wasn't capable of making mature decisions, I could give them custody of my baby. Of you.*
>
> *No way was that going to happen.*
>
> *I won't make you relive the following years with me, Michael. I would have liked to have broken ties with my parents completely, but I was nineteen and*

on my own with a baby. I'd exhausted the offers I had from friends to crash in their guest rooms and frankly, and I'm sure this comes as no surprise to you, I had no idea what I was doing.

Someone I barely knew offered me a job here in Maine, but the company went bust before I even got my first paycheck. I'm ashamed to say that I broke down and asked my parents for help. They cut some sort of deal with a mortgage company (your grandfather had friends in high places) and that covered a large portion of the cost of this house. Since this was your grandparents, they were careful not to cover the entire thing. That way, I'd have to "stand on my own two feet" and make up the difference.

It wasn't that I didn't want to take responsibility. You were an easy baby, charming and engaging. But I still needed to feed you. I tried to cobble together part-time jobs that would let me pay for day care, but I ended up working just to pay someone else to look after you. I still had to come up with the rest of the mortgage and pay for food and utilities and clothes.

I took in some freelance office work and watched other kids. Then I answered an ad for dancers. On a good week, I could pay our bills. Do you remember those days, Michael? When I'd come home with baseball cards and chocolate for you?

I'm so sorry that they weren't all good weeks.

I tried, I really did. I hated dancing. Not the physicality of it, but . . . well, the rest of it. The men would buy me drinks that made it easier to forget what I was doing. But Michael, please know that I never forgot you.

In one of the later letters, she wrote that the one hope she held onto was that I was alive and being raised by someone who loved me.

I thought I'd known her story, but I realized I hadn't really. Knowing the facts was like reading a history book. You could remember names and dates and even understand why something happened. But that wasn't the same as knowing how it felt.

Reading the letter forced me to reframe my memories of my mother. She wasn't all that much older than I was now when she got pregnant. She grasped at whatever solid ground she could just so she could take care of me. Was that really any different from what I was doing trying to take care of Trip?

In another world . . . if things were different. If it weren't for Trip . . .

I let myself consider the possibility of playing by the rules for once. Using the trust to go to Davidson. Maybe I wasn't what Trip needed after all. Maybe, like my mother, my being gone would spur him to do something to get away from Leon. Maybe, like her, he'd be better off without me to worry about.

In some way I couldn't quite put my finger on, reading my mother's letters had turned my view of myself upside down. All my life, it had been easy to pin my problems on her: genetics, upbringing. I figured I'd gotten screwed on the entire package and that justified everything.

I thought about lashing out at Trip after the party. About how I'd crossed a line that had been so horrible and unlikely, I'd never known enough to draw it. If I was capable of hitting Trip after everything he'd been through, what else was lurking inside me?

When Trip deposited me and my one bag of belongings at McKuen Park, he'd looked at me with those gray eyes, daring me to look away. I was terrified he was going to let me go without a word.

Then he said, "I'm never going to hate you, Sean. Stop trying to make me."

My mother's letters, without meaning to, made it clear that anything lacking in my character was my own fault; any fear of what I was capable of was well deserved.

The only person I had to blame was myself.

FIFTEEN

On our first day back at school, Emery held out my phone. "I thought you might want this back."

It looked so natural in her hand, I considered giving it to her. It certainly wasn't doing me any good.

"I'm sorry," I said. Inside, I was freaking out a little. I thought about finishing the sentence with "for kissing you," or "for leaving the New Year's Eve party without saying goodbye" or "for saddling you with my phone, which probably didn't make a single damned sound the entire time you had it." Instead, I opted for silence.

"It's okay. It wasn't that heavy," she said with a small smile.

I was transfixed as I watched her lips and surprised to realize I was thinking about kissing her again.

She pushed the phone into my hand, and I clumsily slipped

it into my backpack. Once I had that sorted out, I stood there watching people race through the halls on their way to class.

We were both running late. I'd had one of those mornings where nothing seemed to work: the milk was spoiled; the shower head came off in my hand; and the first shirt I put on had a stain on it.

"Thanks," I said and started to turn toward East Wing.

"Sean," I heard her call.

I glanced back over my shoulder.

"The kiss was nice, too."

As she was swept away in the crowd, I stood there with a stupid smile on my face. Until I realized I was in danger of missing the second bell.

I slid into English with no time to spare and replayed Emery's words over and over again. I was pretty sure she'd meant it. But the fact that I'd spent all of New Year's Eve talking about Trip now seemed like a huge waste. My focus always seemed to be in the wrong place.

Someone knocked on the classroom door a few minutes into the lecture. A girl who worked in the office held out a yellow hall pass.

Mr. Lowe readjusted his glasses and squinted at the paper. "Sean Woodhouse, apparently you're wanted in the office. You should probably take your bag with you." His expression was strangely serious. I wondered if something had happened to my mother.

I nodded and grabbed my stuff, feeling the weight of

everyone's eyes on me as I walked to the front of the room, took the pass, and followed the girl out of the door. She was a freshman I recognized from my algebra class. "Do you know what this is about?" I asked.

Her eyes darted away. "No," she stammered. "I mean . . . I can't . . ."

"That's okay." I'd find out soon enough.

As we walked in uncomfortable silence, I resisted the urge to race past her. I didn't even have to walk into the office to know that something big was happening. I could already see Chief Perkins through the door, pacing in front of the counter.

Crap. There was no way this was a social visit.

"Sean," he said formally, his cap in his hands. "We're just going to meet in the back office."

I followed him in and sat down while he shut the door. The office had been turned into a storage space. Boxes of textbooks and test materials filled the edges of the windowless room. Chairs circled a dusty table. It smelled stale, like Wilson's barn, which had gone unused after he died.

Chief Perkins wandered over to the other side of the table. "Look, son, I don't know any easy way to say this." I could hear the blood pulsing through my head. What now? What else could go wrong?

He sat on the corner of the table, more like a friendly older brother than a cop. I watched his leg swinging back and forth and then fixed my gaze on a smudge on his black uniform shoe.

“I got a call from the Barlowe police department this morning. I have some friends over there,” Perkins said, clearing his throat before he continued. “Maggie Woodhouse was found dead yesterday morning. It looks like it could be some sort of overdose, but there was no note, so they can’t immediately rule it a suicide. It might have just been a mistake. That being said, her husband’s company was losing money at an alarming rate, and from the collection of medication in the house, she couldn’t have been well.”

A fly landed on the edge of the table. I stared at it and the bug seemed to stare back. This couldn’t really be happening.

“Sean, I’m sorry. But if you know anything at all, now would be a good time to share.” Perkins’s words seemed to come from somewhere very far away even though he was sitting right next to me. “With no next of kin and no signs of a break-in . . .”

As his words trickled out, a pressure built in my chest. I realized I hadn’t taken a breath since he’d started speaking.

“Sean?” He reached out and squeezed my arm.

I shook my head and the fly took off. “No,” I said. “I don’t know anything at all.” I hauled myself up and grabbed my bag. “Thanks, though. For telling me.”

My legs trembled. Perkins reached out and caught me, pushing me back down to the chair before walking to the door and sticking his head out. “Can we get a glass of water in here?” Turning back to me, he asked, “Do you want me to take you home?”

I didn't know what I wanted. Maggie was dead. Overdose. That meant that Leon probably wasn't to blame, but who the hell knew? Maybe he'd given her the wrong pills or something. I needed to talk to Trip. I needed to know what had happened. I needed to know that he was okay.

There was a knock on the door. Perkins answered it and then turned back and pushed a cold glass in my hands. I drank, but couldn't feel anything go down my throat.

My shoulders began to shake and Perkins handed me a cotton handkerchief, the kind that old men in movies are always offering to fainting women. I clutched it tight. I wasn't sure what else to do with it, and I needed to hold onto something. Waves of grief rolled through me, so different from the kind I'd felt when Wilson had died. I'd never had a father, so I'd never known what to expect from one. Wilson was a friend, a mentor who gave me a second chance. Maggie was the mother I'd spent most of my childhood wishing my own would turn into. And now Maggie was gone.

I wiped my face on my sleeve despite the cloth in my hand and looked at Perkins, expecting that he'd tell me what to do next.

"I'm sorry," he said. "Should I call your mother?"

I wanted him to stop asking me questions and, instead, give me directions. Calling my mother wasn't going to bring Maggie back. I couldn't imagine going home and staggering around the house alone. I took a deep breath. I had to stay calm.

"I think I need to go back to class," I said and stood again, although I had no intention of going back to English and deconstructing *Rosencrantz and Guildenstern Are Dead.*

He nodded—I think he was relieved that there was nothing more he needed to do—and handed me a card from his wallet. "Sometimes you just need to keep moving. I get it. But take this. Call me if you need anything."

I gave him back the handkerchief and took the card. I almost missed slipping it into my back pocket, my hands were shaking so badly.

Perkins squeezed my shoulder. "By the way, what do you know a boy named Trip Marchette?"

My vision blurred as totally useless facts buzzed through my head. Trip couldn't hold a tune to save his life. He usually listened to an old CD of thunderstorms to fall asleep. He had a birthmark shaped like Italy on his left hip. He loved animals so much that on Maggie's last birthday, he'd filled the living room with jars of fireflies, but then paced nervously until I almost strangled him and Maggie told him to go outside and set them free.

None of this information was what Perkins was looking for.

"I . . . We . . . He lives next door." I stumbled and caught myself on the edge of the table.

Perkins's face was impossible to read.

"His fingerprints were all over that house." Perkins squinted, waiting, I thought, for more information. When I didn't say anything else, he said, "Well, it isn't our case. Just figured I'd ask."

Before I knew it, I was alone in the hall, with only one thought replaying in my head: I needed to get my hands on a car.

The bell rang. Second period. Jenny had study hall. I charged to the library, praying she was there. I wished, suddenly, that I had talked to her when I'd gone to her house to see her father. This wasn't the topic I'd been hoping to use to break the tension between us. She hadn't acknowledged my Christmas gift and I had no way of knowing what was going through her head.

I found her sitting alone, frantically copying passages out of a French lit book.

I cleared my throat. "Can I talk to you for a minute?"

She kept writing, not even bothering to look up.

"What? You didn't like the book?" I asked.

Her hand stopped mid-stroke. She put down her pen and took a deep breath, finally looking up at me with hard eyes. "Fine," she said after a minute and got up. I followed her over to the reference stacks, farthest from the librarian's station.

"Thank you for the present. Now what do you want?" she whispered in the harshest tone I'd ever heard her use.

There was so much we needed to talk about. But I didn't have time. I had to get to Trip before he did something stupid.

"I need to borrow a car. Right now." I hoped my expression conveyed my desperation. I hoped she understood that I wouldn't be asking if it wasn't important. It wasn't like I was looking for a ride to the mall or a coffee shop.

"A car?"

"There's something—I can't explain. I have to get to Barlowe."

She squinted at me suspiciously.

My heart raced at the idea that she might not do it. "Jenny, please. I know you're pissed at me for everything, and that I deserve it, but I need your help."

She stared at me for a long time. The only thing I could hear in the quiet of the library was the racing beat of my own heart. Then she slowly nodded and ran her thumb along the spine of a book about the fall of the Roman Empire. "My dad's driving around trying to find beaver meat."

"What?"

She sighed. "Never mind. Anyway, Mom took her car to work, but maybe Emery could loan you hers."

"No." My voice was too loud and the three people sitting near us turned and gave me evil looks. I took a deep breath, realizing that Emery probably should have been my first plan of attack, but this wasn't how I wanted her and Trip to meet. This wasn't how I wanted her to see me, desperate and out of control.

"Will she loan it to you? Just for an hour?"

"Maybe," Jenny said. "But she knows how much I hate driving on highways."

"You don't need to come. You don't even have to tell her where I'm going." I was begging and I knew it. And I was going to owe her big-time. I knew that, too.

I could see Jenny considering as she settled on a price. "I'll do it if you'll tell me what's going on. But I'm going with you."

My stomach dropped at the idea, but I nodded. "Yeah, just don't tell Emery it's for me, okay?"

Jenny rolled her eyes and sighed. "Meet me back here in five minutes." Then she left.

I slumped against a section of self-help books. It seemed appropriate.

SIXTEEN

I tried to say something conciliatory as I raced to catch up with Jenny on the way to the parking lot. But I didn't know the right words.

"Don't talk until you're ready to tell me everything."

Everything. Who wants to know *everything*?

I had to jog to keep up. Emery always parked as far from the school as possible in order to keep the little red VW convertible that she and Rory shared from being damaged by the kids who hung out in the lot sitting on cars and throwing around cigarettes.

Jenny tossed the keys to me. I fumbled them and she smirked.

"You know where you're going. You can do the work."

I opened my mouth to say something stupid and then closed it again and unlocked the doors.

I'd never driven to Barlowe. Despite not having a license, I'd done my fair share of driving Wilson's old truck around the rural roads that crisscrossed the state park. But the route out of Millway and back to Barlowe felt like it was packed with too much symbolism.

We kept quiet most of the drive.

"I couldn't find Emery," Jenny said, finally. "I had to get the keys from Rory."

I thought about her words for a minute and tried to imagine their conversation. "What did you tell him?"

"That I'd gotten my period and needed to go home and lie down with a heating pad. I knew he wasn't going to ask anything else."

Yeah. That was a good bet.

"So, you're going to tell me what's going on," Jenny said. "That's the deal, right?"

I tightened my hands on the wheel and swerved sharply to avoid hitting a raccoon.

"I will," I said, trying to hold it together by ignoring the reason we were driving together in the first place. "I will. Just . . . look, I don't have my license. And these roads are a mess, so I need to be really careful."

"You don't have your *license*? Why didn't you tell me that before?"

The road narrowed as we neared the approach to the house, becoming nothing more than a muddy path. The tires spun under us. I pulled over to the side and leaned my head on the steering wheel, in an attempt to slow my breathing.

Jenny was glaring at me. *Fine.*

I looked at her boots. At least she'd gone back to dressing like a real person. Those crazy heels she'd worn for a couple of days would have been destroyed on the muddy trails leading up to the house.

"Stay in the car," I told her as I got out. "I'm going to walk."

She stuck her head out the passenger side window and said, "No way you're leaving me here."

I started wading through the mud. She'd be safe out here. It was up to her if she wanted to follow.

The ground was icy in places. I could feel the cold even through my boots. I kept my eyes on my feet because, I told myself, I was trying not to slip, but really, I wanted to delay seeing the house as long as I could.

I only looked up when Jenny ran up next to me and gasped.

Aside from the yellow police tape, the house looked like it always had. Wilson had once explained that it was technically an English Tudor, or at least it was when Maggie's parents had died and left it to them. But now it was covered in so much ivy it was difficult to see anything but green. It looked like it was being eaten by the park behind it.

It seemed impossible that I'd only been living here a couple of months before. This whole place still felt like home, but now it was too quiet, too empty. I could feel Maggie's absence, even from out here.

Jenny grabbed my arm. "Where are we?"

I didn't look at her when I answered. "This is where my . . . where I was living."

"Seriously?" she asked. "I thought you were living in some dingy basement or something. This looks like the house from *The Borrowers*."

"What?"

She said something about some fairy tale her mom used to read to her about a family of tiny people who lived under the floorboards.

Under different circumstances, I think I might have been fascinated to see the house through someone else's eyes. I'd almost forgotten how unique and magical it had looked that first morning, when I'd picked my head out from under the tarp in the back of Wilson's truck and made the terrifying walk up the drive to ring the bell to ask if I could stay.

I shook my head to pull myself out of the memories; I was afraid to get lost in them.

"Chief Perkins pulled me out of class. Maggie—this was her house—she died." My words were as choppy as my thoughts. They felt like splinters coming out of my mouth.

Jenny sighed. "Oh, Lord, Sean. I'm so sorry."

"I need to get in there," I blurted out.

"I don't think you can do that. I mean, the police tape and all."

I took a deep, shuddering breath and started walking, ducking under the bright yellow CRIME SCENE ribbons and into the house.

I expected the house to be different somehow, in mourning like I was. But aside from some black powder that I knew meant that the cops had dusted for fingerprints, there was nothing out of the ordinary. I wished I'd been clearheaded enough to have asked Perkins more questions. How was Maggie found? Who found her? Where?

I couldn't imagine that anyone would have come here besides the delivery guys from UPS and the local grocery store.

And Trip. Damn, I needed to see him.

And I had to think. Had to step back to consider what the chances were that Maggie would have actually killed herself. She'd threatened it enough, usually in romantic, literary ways, musing about poisoned wine, walking into the nearby river in a crown made of flowers and drowning like Ophelia. All sorts of odd things straight from the pages of books.

I never thought she'd actually do it, though. And it killed *me* that I couldn't shake the feeling that Trip might have been involved. He was always worried about screwing up her meds. She would have thought pills were such an unromantic way to go.

I examined the old tabletop chest that held her medication. Leon claimed to get the pills from some guy in Peru. They hadn't been approved by the FDA. I didn't even know what they were made of or how the complex calculations of the dosages had been figured out.

A couple of the bottles were empty, which didn't make sense given that it was the beginning of the month. Despite Leon's threats, Trip always brought Maggie's meds over like clockwork. I opened the drawers looking for more bottles, but found nothing. Maybe the police had taken them.

I was about to turn away when the butt of a cigarette caught my eye. I hoped it was a normal cigarette. Maggie didn't smoke, so maybe it had been left here by the cops. I leaned down and inhaled and was rewarded with the sweet smell of cloves.

Trip.

Fuck.

I could taste it on my lips.

On his.

I wrapped my palm around the butt and stuck it in my jacket pocket. He'd been here. Okay. Of course he'd been here. He'd probably been here at least twice a day since I left. Maggie was still tutoring him. He was still doing some of her shopping and helping her tend the yard.

The cops knew that. It would be okay. It would have to be.

I kept forgetting that Jenny was with me, so when I turned around, and she was holding a photo that she'd picked up from the end table next to Maggie's favorite leather armchair, I jumped. I didn't have to go over there to see which picture it was.

Wilson avoided taking photos of me. "It's a shame," he always said. "You won't be able to look back on your youth." But he was just too cautious to leave any sort of paper trail.

On my sixteenth birthday, Trip had insisted that we break into a nearby gated community to use their beach access. I wasn't a strong swimmer, but it came naturally to him. He'd gotten it into his head that he was going to teach me, but we'd wasted away the afternoon racing up and down the sand and tackling each other in the waves. My lessons never moved past floating.

When we got back, Maggie took one look at us and told us not to move. We waited outside, not wanting to drag the sand that coated our skins into the house. When she returned, she had an old Brownie Hawkeye box camera that had been her grandfather's.

We were sun-drunk—giggling like we were stoned. Maggie and her ancient camera captured us with Trip's arm around my bare, sunburnt shoulders, the compass on his wrist pointed toward the camera. In the photo, Trip's face was turned to me, his expression so intimate he might as well have been kissing me. I was laughing directly into the camera at something he'd said. I wished I remembered what it was.

Maggie had the picture printed along with the rest of the roll, which was innocuously filled with snapshots of herbs from her garden. She kept this one framed by her chair, telling Wilson he'd just have to deal with it being out in plain view. It was one of the few times I remember hearing them disagree.

"You look so happy," Jenny said.

I stared at the photo, unblinking, and then took the frame from her and disassembled it, slipping the picture into my bag and tucking it between the pages of my bio textbook. I felt like I should apologize, but wasn't sure for what.

She scanned the room, leaning to examine books and a ceramic dragon that breathed smoke when lit incense was put inside, and then asked me, "What are you looking for?"

What was I looking for? If any question summed up my time in Barlowe, that was it. I'd run away from Millway, but I'd spent my time in this house searching for something I couldn't name. I'd found and lost many things in the time I was here, but the only thing I kept coming back to was Trip.

What I hadn't told anyone, not even Emery, was that despite my outrage at Trip for kissing me so publicly, I'd been the one to start our physical relationship. As long as I'd known him, he had a thing he did when he was trying to work out a word he didn't recognize, or some math assignment, or something else he was trying to make sense of. He'd bite down so hard on his bottom lip that it would be swollen the next day. I wasn't even sure he knew he was doing it.

There was something brutally honest about that gesture that I was drawn to in an almost embarrassing way, something that made my stomach churn with a desire that was both possessive and protective. And in the days directly following Wilson's death, Trip bit his lip almost constantly.

Since I technically didn't exist as far as Wilson's coworkers were concerned, I had to keep a low profile. As usual, Leon Marchette was in denial about Trip's dyslexia being anything more than obstinance. He forced Trip to drive to the funeral specifically because he knew how much Trip hated driving with him in the car. Anxiety made everything worse and Leon was stress personified. Trip didn't have a license, and neither did I, but we'd both spent enough time driving Wilson's old truck around Barlowe to have picked up the basics. Those were joyrides, though: thirty miles per hour on open fields that barely resembled roads. The path to the funeral home involved congested city driving. Stop lights. Pedestrians. Bike riders on shoulders barely wide enough for their tires.

Trip and his uncle had sat in the front with me stuffed awkwardly in the back, all of us in our over-starched dress shirts. Trip kept looking at me in the rearview mirror, his expression teetering halfway between a shared joke and a cry for help. I sat there defenseless, clenching my fists and running quotes through my head while his uncle tossed insults at him and probably fantasized about ways to abandon me on the side of the road.

Somehow, we lived to make it to the funeral. Trip and I stood together in the back, two kids playing dress-up in black suits, trying to hold it together.

Later, back at Maggie's, she'd pulled out a dusty bottle of brandy and poured us each a glass. Trip lit a fire while I drifted between them, unsure who needed my comfort more, but sure that if I stopped moving, I'd fall apart.

When we ran out of reasons to keep occupied, we sat—Maggie on the couch, Trip and me on the floor near the fire.

"You're young," she said, breaking the silence that seemed to have hovered over us since the call first came that Wilson had broken his neck in a fall. "This is your time. Don't squander it." She pointed a finger between us and squinted, trying to choose the words that would have the most impact. "You will never be as free as you are at this moment. You'll never be as beautiful. There is no such thing as growing old gracefully. Perhaps Wilson was the lucky one."

She hauled herself off the couch, waving away our offers of help. Then she poured us each another drink, downed the brandy in her glass, and headed to her room.

"Well," said Trip to no one in particular. He removed his suit coat and I removed mine. I loosened my tie and he did the same. We sat in mirror poses, arms around our drawn-up legs, staring into the flames.

My thoughts should have been about Wilson, but it was hard to believe that he was truly gone. We were used to him being on business trips, so the funeral just felt surreal. Like it was just one more delay to him coming home.

Instead, my thoughts were on Trip. On how Wilson's loss might affect him most of all.

"Why do you stay?" I asked him.

I remembered all the things that had convinced me to leave Millway. They seemed so insignificant, compared to the relentless cruelty that Trip lived with. Somehow, the taboo subject didn't feel off-limits after the weight of the day.

Trip didn't look at me. "There's no one left."

I was confused. To me, that was more reason to leave than to stay. I knew that he was talking about his family: his dad, who left a pregnant girlfriend to join the army and then never returned; his mom, dead; now, Wilson. But I was confused about why he felt abandoned by Maggie, the closest thing he'd ever had to a mother, the one person he'd do anything for without question.

I watched the fire reflecting in his eyes and realized that he was the first person in my life to make me feel tethered in any way.

"There's me," I said and cleared my throat. "I'm left."

He paused. "I wish I'd had time to build his coffin. You could have painted one of your quotes on it." He linked his long fingers together in front of him and then turned toward me. "Is that creepy?"

His voice was quiet. He bit down on his lip and I swear I *felt* every single one of the people he'd lost, every single hit he took from Leon.

Instead of answering, I leaned over and kissed him full on the mouth. He tasted of brandy and wood smoke and we both kept our eyes open.

I could hear blood rushing through my head and even though I wanted so much more, I pulled back, unsure of what I'd done. I hadn't planned it, hadn't thought about kissing him in any concrete way. In retrospect, we'd been moving toward that moment for a long time. But sitting there, in front of the fire, my lips burning where they'd touched his, I had no way of gauging what his reaction would be or what I could do to minimize any possible damage. I held my breath as he slowly sank his teeth back into his bottom lip.

"You need to know," he started, and I closed my eyes waiting for him to punch me or tell me that he never wanted to see me again. "Even when we're old, like Maggie said . . . every time I look at you, I'm going to be thinking of doing that again."

I spoke without thinking, a quote Maggie had loved that had been incorrectly linked to Anaïs Nin that I hadn't known I'd memorized. "And the day came when the risk it took to remain closed in a bud became more painful than the risk it took to blossom."

When Trip looked back at me, tears were rolling slowly down his face. It was the first time, in all those years, I'd ever seen him cry, but he did nothing to wipe the tears away. Instead I did it for him, collecting his tears on the pads of my thumbs.

Jenny's voice cut through the images in my head. "Fine. Don't answer. But you wanted to come here for something, so can we do it? This place is kind of giving me the creeps."

I licked my lips, expecting to taste cloves and Trip.

Jenny was right. I'd put it off long enough. I needed to find him.

Just like us, Trip should have been in school. But I knew him well enough to know that, in the wake of Maggie's death, he'd never made it there.

I walked through the house until I got to the back room and looked out the window, letting my eyes wander around the perimeter of the property before they sought out their target.

The tree house's manual elevator was at the top. Trip was up there.

I shivered, more than a little afraid of what shape I was going to find him in.

"Sean?" Jenny asked.

I turned around and put my hands on her shoulders. "I need to go see someone. The guy in that photo. I think he's up there." I pointed toward the tree house. "I would literally pay you to wait down here for me."

She recoiled like I'd slapped her before she carefully composed her expression again.

"Maybe I should just take the car and leave," she said.

I shook my head. "I'm not trying to hurt you, Jenny. I'm really not." I was too tired and distracted to argue. "Do what you need to."

I yanked the door open and stalked off under the tape and to the tree. The biggest problem was going to be how to get up there. There wasn't an easy way to do it without the elevator, which was, of course, the point.

I circled around and called his name.

"Shadow." His raspy voice floated back to me like a prayer on the wind.

"Elevator?" I called up and waited. Nothing.

I'd only had to climb up there once before and I wasn't looking forward to doing it again. It didn't look like I had a choice, though, so I dragged a ladder and a rope out of the barn and started to pull myself up.

"Damn it, Marchette," I grumbled as I finally managed to loop the rope over a tall branch.

Somehow, I pulled myself high enough to haul myself over the railing without totally destroying my palms. I looked back at Jenny on the ground and shrugged.

Taking the steps two at a time, my boots slipped on the wet wood. Building the tree house might have been an act of brilliance on Wilson's part as much as a safeguard for Trip, but not for the first time, I wished that they would have made a simpler version with a layout that made sense.

Instead, I had to remind myself where the hidden doors were and which levers did something useful and which were just for show. Wilson had always brought his quirky sense of whimsy to his buildings, and the same things that fascinated me at twelve irritated me now.

Crawl space after crawl space was empty, but finally, I found Trip in an alcove that I had to get to by shimmying on my belly like a soldier in boot camp.

Trip lay on his stomach, facing away from me, his nose pressed against the opening that served as the room's window.

The last time I'd seen him was when he'd deposited me in McKuen Park. We'd both been depressed, exhausted, and angry. I hadn't known what to say to a best friend who had just made me a public spectacle and then forced me to leave. I suspected we were both still depressed, exhausted, and angry. And I wasn't any closer to knowing what to say to him now.

I sat cross-legged next to him and watched his back rise and fall with each breath.

"What the hell, Marchette?" I asked as casually as I could pull off. Trip shied away from confrontation, maybe getting enough of that from Leon, and I knew from experience that the best way to approach difficult issues was from the side.

His only response was a groan.

"Come on," I said pulling him close. "It's just me."

He turned and stared like he was seeing a ghost. Then he rolled over and groaned again. "Worse. Better someone else." He was over-articulating his words, pronouncing every single fucking consonant. I never understood why people thought they could hide their inebriation by trying so hard to come across as sober.

Trip was wearing an old black T-shirt of mine. It had an Oscar Wilde quote on it. "I can resist anything but temptation." He was shivering like he was going to crack in two, so I took my jacket off and draped it over him.

"Come on. Seriously. It's too cold for this shit. You want to tell me what you took?" I didn't expect him to fess up, or even *know*. Between Maggie's house and his uncle's, Trip had a whole pharmacy at his disposal. I doubted he'd even have taken the time needed to try to read the labels on the bottles.

"Just . . ." he said and shivered again.

He didn't look like he was dying, so I pressed forward. "What's going on?"

"Maggie," he said, struggling to sit up.

"Yeah." I took a deep breath and pulled him up until he was leaning against the wall. "What happened?"

He rubbed his red-rimmed eyes and I waited impatiently while he threaded his thoughts together.

"Last Thursday. Near the end of the month. Her meds . . ." He grabbed my arm tight with both hands and looked at me with tired gray eyes. His voice full of confession. Like a little boy admitting that he was the one to have tracked mud into the house, he said, "The last few weeks, she'd been talking about it. Being lonely. In pain. Being tired. Just wanting it to stop."

I could hear Maggie in my head. I'd heard her talk that way before I left.

"Sean?" Trip's eyes were wide and trusting as if the fight after the party had never happened. His capacity for forgiveness baffled me.

"Yeah?"

"I tried, but they were mixed up. Her meds. I was sorting them out. Twice I went through them. She kept calling me.

Asking me to go get her things. A sweater. A cup of tea. I had to start over. She sent me home. I told her I'd stay, but she said to go."

I closed my eyes and tried to figure out where to focus my anger. Maggie was dead. If she'd wanted to kill herself, she knew just how to play Trip. She'd gotten exactly what she wanted. I'd just hoped she wouldn't go to those lengths to get it.

I put my arm around Trip's shoulders. He was warm and solid and disorientingly real compared to the Trip who had been living in my head. "If Maggie wanted to do something, she would have found a way with or without you." I meant to be comforting, but my own loss made the words sounded hollow.

"How could I be so stupid?" He was strung out and looking to me for answers I wasn't sure I had. I knew he was thinking of his uncle and all those years of being told he was worthless. I was afraid that he'd started to believe those words now.

"A cop in Millway asked me about you this morning," I said, changing the subject. "Have they talked to you?"

Trip nodded slowly.

"What did you tell them?"

"Yesterday. Just . . ."

He was cut off by the sound of Jenny calling for me.

Trip's eyes went wide; his hands clenched. Jenny was going to have to wait.

"She drove me here. Long story," I explained. His shoulders relaxed a little.

He blinked quickly as though it would clear his head. "I told them that I was at the house a lot, helping her."

"It'll be okay." I hoped that I was right.

He closed his eyes and paused. "No, I don't think so. I wanted to save both of you. I fucked up."

I didn't know what he was talking about, and my confusion must have shown on my face.

"I couldn't let you stay here. Leon wasn't joking. I couldn't let you get hurt for me. I'm not worth it."

"What? You're . . . You are . . . You . . ." I couldn't knit my thoughts together. Instead, I pulled him to me, resting my chin on the top of his head. I was the one who'd been stupid. Of course, that's why Trip would have sent me back. Of course. "God, Trip why didn't you tell me?" I was so freaking tired of everyone sacrificing Trip to keep me safe. Even Trip. *Especially Trip*. I was done with it. And done with being angry at him.

His breath hitched against my arm. He was trembling and I might have been, too.

"I wanted to be . . ." He shrugged, not finding the word he was looking for. "You wouldn't have left otherwise."

"Maybe."

"He might have killed you."

"Maybe."

It was the first time since the party that anything made sense. Somehow, some way, I was going to make this right. "We'll figure it out," I said. "We will. And we'll leave."

"We could go to the moon," he said with a small smile that made my stomach flip.

"Or Pluto," I threw in; it was an old running joke from the days before we had reason to talk about Leon trying to kill anyone.

"Even though it isn't a planet anymore?" he asked.

"It'll be less crowded, now."

He threaded his fingers with mine and closed his eyes. "Sounds perfect."

For a minute, everything *was* perfect. Then I realized something. "Hey, you said something about Maggie and 'last Thursday.' What were you talking about?"

"It was getting worse." Trip pulled out of my grasp and bit down on his lip with an intensity that made my stomach tighten. "Before I left, she told me what she was going to do. She said she wrote you. She said goodbye. I thought . . ."

The tree house spun around me. The anger surged back full force. "You knew in advance?" I grabbed the fabric of his shirt—my shirt. "Why didn't you tell me what she was planning? You could have called, I would have . . ."

Trip shook his head and his eyes cleared. "You always make the world into what you want it to be. All my life . . ." He was so tired; I could hear it in his voice. "All my life, people have been trying to tell me what to be. Who I am. What I can't do. Leon . . . It wasn't the one I wanted her to make, but Maggie had the right to make her own choice."

His words were surprisingly clear, but I didn't want them

to make sense. My body tensed like he'd slapped me. I wished he would have. "You kept it from me intentionally. You knew what she was doing, and you kept it from me. You let her die."

Trip stared into my eyes, but didn't say anything. As usual, he was offering no apology. The resolve in his expression was enough to break me.

I took the elevator back and left it at the bottom. He'd have to make his own way down.

SEVENTEEN

"Are you okay to drive?"

It was a simple question. Yes or no. But I couldn't seem to answer. Couldn't seem to focus long enough to give Jenny the one word she was looking for.

Oh, Trip, what the hell have you done?

"Give me the keys." Jenny held out her hand as my eyes strayed back to the tree house. Part of me wanted to rush back up there and get Trip to a hospital or sit with him until he got the drugs and grief and the pain out of his system like I'd done in the past. Another part was afraid that I'd push him over the edge of the porch.

"Sean." My head snapped back as Jenny waved her fingers in front of my eyes. "Give me the keys or I'm going to take them."

I dug them out of my pocket.

"Get in the car and pull yourself together," she said. "You're going to have to give me directions."

I managed, more or less, to whisper out the turns before we got to the intersections, but my mind felt like it was full of spider-webs. It made me wish I'd asked Trip if there was anything left of whatever mystery drug he'd taken.

As we pulled into Jenny's driveway, the deep purple shade of the door of her house reminded me of Maggie's Japanese eggplants.

"My mom is working the night shift. Rory told me to hang on to the car until Emery can come and get it tonight. Besides, if you go back to school looking like that, they're just going to send you to the nurse."

I took a deep breath. "Just . . . come in," she ordered before turning to lead the way.

Jenny made me tea. I don't know why I found that so funny, but I did. It was what Maggie would have done. Maybe that was it. Maybe it was that I didn't know anyone else my age, aside from Emery, who drank tea, so Jenny must have paid more attention at lunch than I'd noticed. I laughed through sips that I intellectually knew were too hot. Physically, I was back to feeling numb. Emotionally, I wasn't feeling much of anything.

"Talk," Jenny said, cutting through my inappropriate laughter. "Tell me what's going on or I'm going to the cops."

Jenny looked so stern when she said it, I choked on my tea.

"What would you tell them?" I asked. Just stringing those words together exhausted me. I leaned my head back into the chair's headrest, wondering what she'd do if I just fell asleep.

She blushed. We both knew she had no idea what was going on.

"So that guy . . . Trip?" She left her question hanging in the air, and I wasn't going to help her out.

I didn't want to reach up and hold the boomerang in my hand like it was the only part of him I had left. I didn't want to picture his eyes as I'd just seen them: steely gray, red-rimmed, and too dilated from whatever he'd taken. I didn't want to think about Maggie being gone or about what part Trip might have played in her death. I didn't want to feel so pissed off at him for not calling me that I felt like I'd been drinking battery acid. And I certainly didn't want to feel guilty for just leaving him there, a broken, sitting duck for Leon.

But that's exactly what I did.

My head began to pound and I was suddenly angry at Jenny for waiting impatiently for me to tell her things she wouldn't want to hear. I had an urge to spill it all in the harshest light possible. I wanted to tell her about the things that Trip and I had done to each other in the tree house when no one was watching. About how he'd let Maggie die rather than suck up his pride and call me to stop her from making a fatal mistake. About how he was in love with me, even though I had wasted every opportunity to tell him that I felt the same way. Or used to. I couldn't untangle my emotions enough to understand how I was feeling.

The truth pushed against my lips, but something in her face stopped me. I knew she'd been angry with me. Maybe she even hated me. Now what I saw was pity, and that was even worse. Hurting her with stories about Trip might make me feel better for a minute, but it would kick me in the ass in the long run. So, instead, I answered a question she'd asked me weeks ago. I told her about Maggie and her part in my coming back.

Weeks before the party, before the most terrifying of Leon's threats, before I knew the role that Trip would play in my leaving Barlowe, I'd found Maggie sitting in her garden behind the house. She looked younger out in the sun, more like she had when I'd first come to live in Barlowe, back when I'd found her beautiful and quirky and brilliant. Ever since Wilson had died, she seemed to stay inside more and more, and had begun to look gray and wilted, like a plant that hadn't been watered. I hoped that her making the effort to visit her beloved flowers meant that she was feeling better. Her words dashed those hopes.

"You should be thinking of going home," she told me.

I knelt next to the wheelchair she was using more frequently and together we watched the dragonflies chase one another around the rhododendrons. I wondered if her mind was going and she thought that we were somewhere other than her garden. Then reality set in.

"What?"

She gave me a smile that must have taken all of her energy and reached up to smooth my hair.

"You're a good person, Sean. You don't need to spend your life trying to prove it. Everyone already knows. Everyone but you."

"I . . ." I started, and then closed my mouth. There was nothing I could say. I had no idea what she was talking about. I'd never really thought about myself that way.

"And that boy," she continued. I jerked my eyes back to her. I hadn't even realized that I'd been staring in the direction of Trip's house. "He knows most of all."

"I *am* home." I took a deep breath. "This *is* home." I hadn't realized until I gave her my delayed response how painful her suggestion was. The thought of leaving Barlowe, of leaving Trip alone with his monster of an uncle, made me want to hurl.

Maggie sighed and spun a yellow leaf between her fingers. "The easy path isn't usually the right one."

I racked my brain, trying to figure out which author she was quoting. Philosopher? Eastern? "Buddha?" I tried.

"No." She coughed, a long and painful sound.

"That was me. But that doesn't make it any less true. You need to return home. You're old enough to take care of yourself now, to make your own way in the world. And I can't have you here when I die."

I shivered even though it was a warm day. Maggie had been dying since before I met her. That didn't make the thought any easier to handle.

"Why?" I asked feebly.

She raised her hand to block her eyes from the sun and looked up at me. "Because I care about you, of course. You have to think about your future, not about me. And Trip needs to follow his own path, too. He would do anything to protect you. But now it's time for him to protect himself. He can't keep sleeping in that tree house."

I hadn't known she was aware of the nights that Trip spent up there so he could avoid run-ins with Leon. I blushed, wondering which other secrets she'd discovered. I nodded, but it felt as exhausting as trying to fell a forest. Maggie knew I couldn't argue with going home eventually, if it meant that Trip might be convinced to turn his uncle in to the police.

"It felt like a timer had begun to count down and I was terrified of what would happen when it hit zero," I tried to explain to Jenny. "Where would I be? *Who* would I be? I'd already thrown away whatever life I'd had in Millway. I'd lost Wilson, and now Maggie was asking me to turn my back on her and Trip. I wasn't sure I was strong enough to do that on my own and she knew it."

Jenny paced in front of the fireplace as I held my mug of tea tight. She stopped and started ticking things off on her fingers. "You came home so that your friend could turn his uncle in."

"Mostly."

"But he hasn't done that, right?"

My pulse raced. "No, he hasn't." It made my whole ordeal sound pointless.

"And you came home so that Maggie could . . ."

"Yeah, I guess." I put the mug on the coffee table. The whole time we'd been talking, I'd been squeezing the handle and I was afraid it was going to snap off, so I put it down. "Plus, Trip called the freaking Millway police and told them I was coming back. I had no choice. Can you imagine the questions they would have asked if they got that call and then no one showed up? They would have known where the call came from. Barlowe isn't that large."

Jenny nodded slowly. Then she cocked her head like she'd just remembered something. "I overheard my parents talking. Why did you want to dissolve your trust?"

I leaned forward and stared out the window. The wind was picking up and rocking the trees back and forth. I wondered if

Trip was still in the tree house. We used to say that it sounded like the trees were having really good sex when the wind picked up.

I wondered if he was still so cold and then remembered that I'd left my jacket with him.

I didn't want to tell Jenny the truth, but couldn't figure out a good reason to lie. I swallowed. "Trip is dyslexic and his uncle is too much of a dick to have agreed to the school giving him the right kind of help when he was a kid. Now he's screwed, and he's learned to kind of bluff it. I don't think he's ever going to graduate high school, but he's a talented builder. An artist." I caught my hand moving toward the boomerang, then pulled it back down and picked up the now-cold cup of tea. "We *were* going to travel."

Were. Were. Were.

Now I had no fucking idea if there even was a *we*. And if there was, how did Emery fit into that? Did I still want to take off to some nameless place and never look back? Could I leave my mom again? Would I even want to, now that she was actually *being* a mom?

I wanted two lives and didn't see a way to merge them together.

"You mean you would have given up college for him?" Jenny's anger radiated off her.

I shrugged. "I would have gone to college at some point." Actually, I'd never figured out how I would pull off that piece of the plan, and it was the one thing that had always bothered me. "You don't need stuffy men in suits to lecture at you, Shadow," Trip had said more than once. "You're smarter than most of them, anyway."

It may or may not have been true. But I'd always kind of wanted to find out for myself.

"Wow," she said. "You must really care about him."

I waited to see if she was going to ask the question that Charlotte and Emery had asked, about what exactly I felt for Trip. But it was clear that she had something different on her mind.

"Did you say goodbye?" Her voice shook as she formed the words through clenched teeth. "When you left Barlowe to come back here, did you say goodbye to him?"

I thought it was a stupid question until I realized what she was actually looking for. "That's not fair. I'm not twelve anymore."

We both knew it wasn't really a matter of age. It was clear to both of us that I'd never felt for Jenny what I'd felt for Trip. But I wasn't cruel enough to say that out loud.

I put the mug down again and stood up. I needed to be alone, to process everything that had happened.

I had one foot out the door when I remembered the other thing I had to take care of. "Look." The whole conversation felt heavy and important and it seemed like I'd taken so much from her that it was time to give her something in return.

She stood in the center of the room, pale, unmoving.

"You matter to me. You always have. But we were never

going to be more than just friends even had I stayed. But Rory is a good guy and he really cares about you. You should give him a chance."

The remaining blood drained from her face as she stared at me and I went home to try to sort out what was left of my own life.

EIGHTEEN

The first thing I did when I got into the house was sit on the edge of the bed and take the photo of me and Trip out from between the pages of my biology book. Next, I took off my shoes, crossed my legs on the bed, and put the photo down in front of me. Then, I took the boomerang from around my neck and placed it on top of the photo. It formed a kind of shrine to a part of my life that had moved painfully out of reach.

It wasn't just that I couldn't access the money from the trust. It was that I couldn't figure out how I would ever forgive Trip for the choices he'd made. While I understood his very Trip-like reason for calling the police, he hadn't trusted me enough to talk to me. Plus, the kiss at the party and his decision to help Maggie and not tell me about it—each action had eroded a little of the blind faith I'd had in him. It felt like little pieces of me were dying off, one by one.

I stared at the picture until I realized it was getting dark.

I reached up to my neck, shocked for a minute to find my hand empty. As I shook my head to clear it, my phone started to ring. It was Maggie's number. I was either getting a call from beyond the grave or Trip had come down both figuratively and literally.

I jiggled the phone in my hand, trying to decide whether to answer until it finally went quiet. I turned it to silent and shoved it in my nightstand drawer along with the photo and charm. The only tangible memories I had of Trip.

I'd never avoided him before. It felt awkward and wrong, but I couldn't imagine what I would say. Or what I would want to hear. Emery's words from New Year's Eve echoed in my head, telling me that love makes liars of everyone. Maybe she was right and what I was feeling wasn't just the anger that was burning a hole in my stomach, but some sort of twisted love that he'd somehow thrown back in my face.

I sat there for a while and then pulled my phone back out of the drawer before I could chicken out. There was a message and two more missed calls from Trip, but I ignored them and looked through the short list of numbers stored in the memory.

It rang twice before Emery picked up.

I closed my eyes. "When you come to get your car from Jenny, can you swing by and pick me up?"

She paused and I held my breath while I waited for her to ask all the obvious questions. But she didn't. "Anyone ever tell you you're a masochist?"

I laughed. It wasn't meant as a compliment exactly, but it was relief to know that someone understood me.

It was odd to be back in the park. Odder still to be there with Emery. The cold had kept most people inside, but under the electric lights, the skating rink was full, so we stopped at the edge to watch.

"Do you skate?" I asked.

She shook her head and the ends of her curls sticking out from under her hood bobbed from side to side. "When we were kids, my dad enrolled us in lessons. I think he was hoping that we'd end up as a figure skating team. You know, twins and all. We tried for his sake, but when we were about ten, we'd both had enough. I think it broke his heart."

I smiled at the thought of Emery and Rory in matching tights and skates. "Every winter, Wilson made a rink at the back of the house. He'd played hockey or something as a kid, but he always made the rink too small for anything like that. The only thing I ever learned to do well was spin."

She took a step away and then grabbed my icy hand with her gloved one and pulled me after her. "And you're still spinning."

"Yeah," I admitted, "I am." I'd told her everything that had happened in this new shiny year as soon as she'd picked me up. "You know, even though Maggie had been sick long before I met her, I never thought anything would actually happen to her. She was tough. Determined. I never expected her to be this . . ." I searched for a word that came close.

"Tortured?"

"Selfish. I guess I understand her not worrying about what would happen to me, but I don't understand how she could do that to Trip. He's no match for Leon."

Emery stopped and turned toward me, her expression clouded and unreadable. "What are you going to do?" she asked. "Apply to Davidson?"

"I guess. I mean, it feels like everything is pushing me in that direction."

Emery turned toward the playground. Wilson's tree house was directly in front of us, but she steered us toward a tower made of increasingly smaller painted tires. She shoved her gloves in her pockets, pushed her hood off, and started climbing to the top. I followed.

"You have to tell him about the trust sometime, you know," she said, pulling herself from tire to tire. "You can't just let him assume that things are going to work out the way you guys had planned."

I sat on top of the final tire and dangled my feet over the edge, wondering what it would feel like to jump. I expected her to tell me that I was being reckless, but instead she joined me.

"I don't know what's going to happen. I haven't even applied to Davidson. Besides, I'm not speaking to Trip. There's no right choice."

"If you don't know where you're going, any road will get you there," she said and bumped my shoulder hard with hers.

I'd heard the line before, but wasn't sure where. "*Alice in Wonderland*?"

She broke out into a broad grin. "No. Well, everyone thinks it is. That's the gist of it, anyway."

Somehow, she'd beaten me at my own game, and it made me like her even more.

"But it's true," she continued. "Whatever you do is going to have repercussions. Something is going to happen regardless, so you might as well try to make it what you want."

She was right about all of it. I had to find a way to deal with my mixed-up emotions. I wondered, by her logic, what had happened because I dared to kiss her as the year turned. Maybe we wouldn't have even been here without that one impulsive move. I thought about doing it again. What road would that would put me on?

When she broke the silence, I realized I'd hesitated too long. "That night at the Tavern. Rory tried to scare you away from me, didn't he?"

I was pretty sure that her question was rhetorical. Rory was earnest and open in a way that reminded me of Wilson. I hoped Jenny would realize the chance she had. "I like him," I said.

"I do, too." She nodded. "We went to one of those creepy twin conventions once. You know, where everyone looks alike and twins are trying to pair up with other twins? It was bizarre. I felt completely out of place. I love my brother, but it isn't like we ever had our own language or anything."

"But he knows you." I wondered what she thought he'd told me and what horrible secrets she had hidden in her past.

She nodded. "He's right. Whatever he said, he's right. Rory is a better person than I'll ever be."

"I'd kind of like to find that out for myself."

A wind blew around us and she pulled her hood back up. The fur around her face made her look like an Eskimo. She leaned toward me until the hood circled both of our faces and kissed me, her eyes open. I tried to mirror her, but the stinging wind forced me to blink.

Her mouth was soft and tasted like winter. Cold and sharp as peppermint.

I shivered, wishing we were someplace private and that I could stop time so that I could sort out everything I was feeling.

She pulled away and ran a hand over her bottom lip. "See. My brother wouldn't approve of that. He'd know it wasn't real. That I'm only a distraction from your real life—an escape."

It took me a minute to catch my breath.

"Are you always so philosophical?" I took her hand and, in spite of her kiss, I was surprised when she didn't pull it back. Our intertwined fingers looked like some long-forgotten sea creature and they fascinated me.

Part of me wanted to push things as far as she'd let me. But, in truth, I was content with her kisses and her hand in mine. I just wanted to be near her and I wasn't sure if that meant that there was something wrong with me or not.

Being with her was both similar to and different from Trip. What he and I had done in the tree house felt, not casual exactly, but like some natural part of our friendship—one of the ways I could coax a rare uninhibited smile from him.

Everyone always thinks that it's all about sex, but it never had been for me. Not with Trip, and not with Emery. I wanted so much more than that from each of them.

"What if I said that I thought you were more than a distraction?"

"I'd say that you were wasting your time." I expected her to laugh at me, but her voice was level as she looked away. For the first time since I'd met her, she seemed oddly fragile and I wondered if maybe I was still capable of helping someone.

"Who hurt you?" I asked.

She kept her face turned away when she said, "What makes you think that someone hurt me?"

"Just . . . instinct." I recognized the same thing in her that I saw in myself, something unresolved and unhealed.

"You give me too much credit." She squeezed my hand and then released it. Her eyes were hidden behind her hood. I wanted to see them, but I was afraid to move and break the mood. "I used to go to school with Charlotte, you know. That's why I was at the party that night."

I nodded. I'd already guessed that part.

"Rory and I were the poor kids at Hillmeade. Anyway, the school is tiny, and the dating pool is filled with sharks, everyone just trying to claw their way even further up the social ladder. Not like I cared about any of that."

I stayed silent, not wanting her to stop her story.

"I went out with a senator's son on a whim. He was nice enough. Smart. Ambitious. Cute." She pulled her hood down and glanced at me, looking for a reaction, but I held my face steady.

"When I realized that he was taking things more seriously than I was, I broke it off. One thing led to another, and then led to him breaking into my mom's bar and getting hammered. He hit a woman with his Lexus on his way home. A mother with two little kids. He got two years' probation and a fine that his father paid off before he even left court." She paused. "I kind of figured it wasn't worth it after that. Dating. Any of it. I'll be leaving for college, so what's the point of getting involved? It would just end badly again and I'm just not that self-destructive."

I swallowed hard, searching for the right words. "I'm sorry" didn't seem to cut it. "You can't blame yourself for what other people do."

She turned and gave me a tiny smile. "You know better than that. You can blame yourself for anything." She braced herself against the highest tire and began to climb down.

We didn't say anything as I followed her back to her car.

When we got in, she put a jazz station on the radio and hummed along as she drove me home. When we pulled up in front of the house, she turned and put her hand on my cheek like Maggie used to when she was checking to see if I had a fever.

"You *almost* make me wish that things were different. But I meant what I said." She clicked the lock on the door and it was clear that I'd been dismissed.

I walked into the house not knowing what had hit me. Then I laughed.

On the table were two envelopes, both addressed to me. One from Davidson and one from Maggie.

NINETEEN

The package from Davidson included an application, financial aid forms, and a shiny brochure filled with pictures of happy students sitting around a fountain talking, poring over books in a library, and playing Frisbee on a grassy hill.

From the photos, it would be easy to believe that in California, the sun was always shining in a blue, blue sky and that the beach was as integral to student life as coursework. In one shot, a group of almost unrealistically attractive boys, mostly blond, sat together on the grass in front of a series of red brick buildings. Each boy had a book on his lap and each gestured in animated conversation. I squinted to try to figure out what subject they were discussing, but I couldn't read the titles on the books' spines.

It was all marketing, but it was effective. The pictures

tugged at me; I wanted to be there, casually discussing books as if they were the most important thing in the world.

Maybe Davidson would be the place where I could redefine myself and forget the anger, guilt, and everything else I felt when I thought about Trip. Maybe I could become someone who could prove Emery wrong.

I stared at the pictures until my vision blurred.

I wished I'd said more to Emery. I should have hugged her and told her that it wasn't her fault. Or at least done something more than I did.

It had been easy, all the time in Barlowe, to be a source of support for Trip. He had nothing and didn't feel like he could count on anyone, including himself. Whatever I had to offer him was more than he would ask for.

Emery was a different challenge. Was I strong enough to be there for someone who seemed to have it all figured out? What did I even have to give her? I was more of a mess than she would ever be.

And one way or the other, I was leaving.

I tossed the college application onto my desk. There was no way that I was going to be able to apply through the normal process, and Mr. Gordon had already said that he was going to check with the school directly.

The other envelope had no return address. But I recognized Maggie's spidery handwriting and the expensive blue paper she used when sending condolence notes or letters to the editors of the *Barlowe Blade*, complaining about something they'd written.

I held the thin envelope up to the light, afraid to open it. I fought to remind myself that there was nothing in it that could change anything. Maggie was gone; her words wouldn't do anything but make me miss her more, and even through my anger, I wasn't sure how that was possible.

I slid my index finger under the flap, slowly shredding the glue, superstitiously trying not to tear the paper. Inside was a single blue sheet. I took a deep breath and unfolded it.

In the middle of the page was a quote:

Some of us think holding on makes us strong; but sometimes it is letting go. —Hermann Hesse.

I flipped the piece of paper over, hoping for something—anything—else. I wanted her wisdom, her guidance. I wanted to find some message that made sense of her death and maybe even made sense of Trip sending me away. Maggie had always seemed so wise, but now it was hard not to think of her as cowardly for mailing me someone else's words. For killing herself.

There wasn't even a signature.

It was so like Maggie that I burst out laughing, which turned into choking sobs I muffled in my pillow. I read the words over and over, trying to figure out what lesson she was trying to teach me. Was she saying that *she* was stronger for having let go? That *I* would be stronger if I let her go? Maybe she wasn't even talking about herself. Maybe she was agreeing that I should forget about Trip and everything that had happened over the past five years.

Fat chance.

Had my mother been home, I would have gone to her and allowed her to comfort me like she had on her rare sober nights when I was a kid. But she was at a support meeting.

I'd never felt more alone.

Two weeks later, after I saw it listed online, I asked my mom to drive me to Maggie's memorial service. I knew it was asking a lot, maybe too much. I was still worried about being the thing that disrupted her carefully constructed sober life.

She was probably thinking the same thing as she considered my request, but maybe she saw it as a bonding opportunity, or maybe she assumed that, with Wilson and Maggie both dead, we could forget I'd ever left in the first place.

It was snowing, big fat unseasonably late flakes that weren't sticking on anything other than mailboxes, decks, and the shoulders of the navy blue suit I'd had to buy the day before. The one I wore to Wilson's funeral would be too small, and even if it fit, it was being sold off along with everything else in the house to settle Maggie's estate and pay off loans against Woodhouse Houses. In the lagging economy, even the rich weren't splurging on things like tree houses, and without Wilson's artistry, sales had fallen off over the past year.

The service was held in a pretty stone chapel near the cemetery. It felt medieval with its stained glass and a high peaked arch. It was just the type of place that Maggie would have picked.

Maggie had no family. Trip and I were as close as anyone came. So aside from a local poet that Maggie knew from her teaching days who was running the service, the only people I expected to come were from Wilson's company, along with my mother and me, and Trip.

I couldn't help looking for him as we walked in, our footsteps echoing in the mostly empty room. He wasn't there, and that made me both relieved and angry. Maybe his guilt was keeping him away.

As the service started, I did my best to focus on Maggie and on my loss and even on my mother and how odd it must have been for her to stand there and watch me grieve for the person who had, in her mind, replaced her.

For her part, my mother stood stone-still, taking in the poet's words, not looking at me even when I briefly took her hand. Somehow, I thought, that was what Maggie would have wanted me to do.

Unlike at Wilson's funeral, where I'd been totally numb and more than a little worried that people would ask me who I was, this time, I felt each memory sharply. The black void of Maggie's loss seemed big enough to swallow me whole.

Trying to stop myself from tearing up, I folded and refolded the program. Anything to keep my hands busy.

The poet spoke about the never-ending circle of life, and while normally I would have loved to listen to an author read their work, I couldn't focus on her words. Thoughts of Wilson and Maggie and my mom and Trip and Leon just swirled around me like smoke.

It wasn't until the woman had finished and the chapel went quiet that I found the courage to turn around and look for Trip again. He was in the back row standing next to Carson, Wilson's foreman, nursing his wrist.

I let the few people in the chapel walk back into the snow before I led my mother down the aisle.

There was no way to avoid the confrontation, and I hadn't honestly expected to, but I was surprised at how painful it was to see Trip up close, wearing his only suit, the one that got dragged out for funerals and school assemblies. The arms of his jacket were slightly short and he kept pulling at them as if he could stretch the wool. His right wrist was wrapped in a bandage, the kind you wear after a sprain or burn. I willed myself not to stare at it. Not to acknowledge the sour feeling in my stomach that always came from seeing Trip hurt.

When my mother and I reached where he stood against the door, I stopped and focused on Trip's tie. It had a pattern of tiny brown owls against a black background. I remembered Maggie asking me if I thought he'd like it. I remembered how the soft silk felt around my wrists in the tree house.

"Does Leon know you're here?" I asked. I couldn't help myself from looking at the flash of bruising that poked out of the bandage. *Fucking asshole*.

Trip looked from my mother to me and shook his head.

"I'll deal with him later." He shoved his hands into his pockets and bit his lip. I looked away. I couldn't believe Trip's arrogance. Although I knew he'd show up, I couldn't imagine how he was rationalizing it. Maggie might still be alive if it weren't for him. "I wasn't sure you'd come," he said softly.

I couldn't look into his eyes. He reached out to hug me with his unbruised arm, but I tensed and held my ground, pissed at how much I just wanted to fall into him.

"I have every right to be here," I replied. All of the anger I'd been wrestling with over the last weeks rushed into my throat in a burst of acid.

"That isn't what I meant," he said and pulled back, digging his hands into his pockets.

"This wouldn't have been necessary if you'd . . ." I looked at the worn wooden floor and shook my head. Maggie would have hated that we were fighting at her memorial.

I forced myself to look at him. The pain I was causing him was written clearly on his face. I tried not to care. I couldn't do anything to help Trip and he wasn't asking me to. Instead, I swallowed down the sting and took my mom's arm, leading her out into the storm without another word.

"Who was that?" she asked when we got to the empty parking lot.

I turned and looked back at the chapel. The cold snow stung my eyes like pine needles.

"No one," I lied. "No one at all."

TWENTY

After the funeral, the days seemed to get colder even though the calendar said we were moving toward spring. I'd walk to school wrapped in jackets, sweaters, scarves, and gloves when everyone else seemed fine with just their coats. At night, I tossed and turned in a feverish tangle of sheets that left me damp and lightheaded.

The more I tried not to think about Trip, the harder it became to banish him from my thoughts. Instead, I tried to understand Emery's comment about "wishing things were different." I didn't know what she meant, but in my loneliness, I was determined to find out.

Over the course of the next weeks, I began pushing quotes through the vents in her locker, filling flash drives with obscure music from around the world. The internet was a new fascination for me and I enjoyed finding local bands from all the places that Trip and I had planned to visit. It was a welcome distraction from my grief, as was the fact that Jenny and Rory seemed to be growing closer daily.

"I don't know what you did," Rory said to me one day, "but I owe you."

It was good to see that someone was still capable of doing things the easy way.

Emery and I never directly discussed the gifts I was leaving her. For all I knew, she thought I was stalking her. But every so often, she'd drop a reference into a conversation, making me feel like we shared a private joke.

I still wanted to prove to her that her cynicism was unfounded. That we could mean something to each other that wasn't fleeting and shallow, or intensely self-destructive. She seemed to believe that all relationships were one or the other. Besides, I wanted to prove to myself that there was someone other than Trip who could truly know me and still give a damn.

Where my feelings for Trip bordered on obsessive—because no matter which way I turned them, they just seemed out of control—what I felt for Emery was simple. Being with her made me happy. She had a way of cutting through the surface stuff we all hide behind to get right to what truly mattered.

She made me feel a little like I used to as a kid, when I'd spin around in the yard until I fell over, dizzy and disoriented.

It didn't escape me that all of my focus on Emery helped to distract me from Trip. I started keeping my phone on silent, forgetting it for days at a time. My mother regularly reminded me to take it when I went out, although she rarely called. She just liked to know where to find me, and though I promised her again and again—and meant it at the time—I often found that I didn't know where my phone had gotten to until I found it on a bookcase or in a drawer or, once, in the refrigerator.

I knew that in some way, Maggie had manipulated both me and Trip. But I couldn't shake my anger at him for not at least giving me a chance to save her. That he hadn't let me help.

I wanted to forget him, but that was impossible. I worried about what the police might find in Maggie's house or, worse, in Trip's. My mother had both Millway papers delivered daily, and I started coming downstairs as soon as I heard them hit the door at five or six in the morning. I'd pull them apart, stacking the sports sections and the ads in a pile and speed-reading what passed for news, terrified that I'd see something about Maggie's death and Trip's possible role in it or some report about a Barlowe break-in committed by a local teen. When my mother asked about my new habit, I told her that I couldn't sleep and was embarrassed by how little I knew about current events, so I was trying to catch up.

Mom offered to take me to a doctor for sleeping pills—she didn't keep meds in the house, not even aspirin—but I lied and said that I wasn't anxious to lose the study time not sleeping gave me. Somehow, she bought it.

I was terrified that one of the missed messages on my phone was Trip calling me from prison instead of doing the smart thing and calling a lawyer. But I didn't even know if those lawyer calls happened in real life or if they were just plot points in bad TV shows.

In a moment of weakness, I sat and listened to each of his messages in order. I was relieved that none of them were from prison. But the sadness in his voice made me wonder if he was going to be able to hold himself together much longer. By the time I'd reached the last message, I couldn't take it anymore.

I punched his number in and listened to the rings, which seemed to echo in my ears. When Leon answered, I held my ground and asked for Trip.

"You *did* hear me when I said to stay away, right?" Leon said. "Maybe you *are* as stupid as my nephew. Maybe I'll have to teach you a lesson, too."

When I didn't reply, I figured he'd hang up, but instead he called Trip to the phone. I took a deep breath. I knew we wouldn't have much time before Leon pulled the plug.

"I'm coming to see you," I said, making up a plan on the spot. "Can you meet me at McGuire's at six?"

"Yeah. Sure. Shadow—"

"I'll see you there," I said and cutting him off, powering down my phone.

My mother had given me a sizable check for Christmas and we'd donated the gifts she'd bought me over the years to the local children's hospital. I was saving most of the cash in case I needed it for an emergency, but I skimmed a little off the top for cab fare to Barlowe.

On my way, I stopped at the local barbershop. It had the same striped pole I remembered from when I was a kid. Two guys were busy working with straight razors on men old enough to be my grandfather.

One of the barbers came over and introduced himself as Gus. He waved me toward a chair and wrapped a towel around my shoulders.

"You sure about this?" he asked.

I wasn't. But I had to do something, and this seemed like a rite of passage. I nodded and kept my eyes closed while he snipped away at the black hair, leaving only a couple of inches of blond.

I caught a glimpse of myself in the mirror as I was paying. I looked like a completely different person.

Gus peered over my shoulder and laughed. "You'll be a hit with the girls, no?"

McGuire's was a dump. It was a diner-slash-hamburger-joint-slash-bar frequented mostly by hunters in flannel shirts with dead animals strapped to the roofs of their trucks. It was the kind of place that Trip and I wouldn't have been caught dead in, which made it perfect. I knew we wouldn't be recognized.

I got there early and snagged a table in the back. Grabbing a day-old newspaper from the bar, I read the same paragraph about a local zoning ordinance over and over, unable to focus on anything except the conversation that was coming.

When Trip walked in wearing my leather jacket, I felt a crash of conflicting emotions. For a second, time stopped and I thought, *This is what we always wanted. To just be able to go to a public place and hang out like regular people. Like we were on a date or something normal.*

I rose in my seat to meet him and then forced myself to sink back down. That wasn't our reality, I reminded myself. Whatever we'd wished for felt like nothing more than lies.

I balled my fists at my side and waited while he made the long march over to the table.

He stared at my hair, then folded himself into the booth across from me. There was a bruise on his collarbone that looked fresh. I reached toward it without thinking, but Trip moved faster and grabbed my wrist.

For a minute, we just held each other's eyes and then he took his hand back and ran it through his own hair.

"You've been hard to reach. After the service . . ." He stopped.

I'd practiced a hundred variations of this speech in my head, but now, I couldn't seem to remember any of them. The reality of Trip sitting in front of me obliterated whatever words I'd come up with.

He wrapped his arms around himself and my eyes were

drawn to his fresh bruises and his hands, white against the dark leather of my jacket. I opened my mouth, but nothing came out.

"I'm sorry," he said, filling the silence. "After what Leon said about you . . ."

"It doesn't matter."

"And Maggie . . ."

"I didn't really come to talk about that."

He reached out and grabbed my hand, his index finger pressing hard on top of my wrist. I could feel my pulse beating against it.

I jerked back. My fingers wadded up the cloth napkin in my lap. The stark white fabric was strangely out of place in the otherwise seedy dive.

"Oh," he said and chewed on the inside of his lip. The bruise glowed purple in the garish light and I had to look away. "The cops came again. The day after the funeral. They talked to Leon."

"What?" I said, panic creeping into my throat and threatening to choke me.

"Leon was freaking out. All those drugs and stuff just lying around. I almost hoped they'd find something."

"What happened?"

Trip absentmindedly traced the compass on his wrist and shrugged. "They dragged us down to the station and took Leon's fingerprints. He let them take some blood from me and . . . that was it. Nothing happened."

"How the hell could nothing happen?" My voice was a growl containing all of the anger and frustration that had built up over the last few months. There was no possible way that the police talking to Leon could lead to nothing. My eyes landed on the bruises on Trip's neck. "You at least had the chance to tell the police about what he does to you, right?"

Trip winced and pulled back.

"All you had to do was pull up your fucking sleeve." I shook my head in disbelief. "He's a powder keg, Trip. He always has been and you're just sitting there and letting him screw with you. Is that really all you think you're worth?"

I might as well have grabbed a steak knife off the table and thrust it into his jugular.

"Sean," Trip pleaded. Whether it was a warning or a request, I wasn't sure. For as much as we'd talked about escaping Leon and running off somewhere, for all the hours I'd spent talking him down and reassuring him while holding ice packs over his bruises, I knew this topic was pretty much off limits.

"Look." I took a deep breath and refocused as if I'd never blown up. "I met with a lawyer. The guy who oversees the trust."

Trip's eyes didn't leave my face as I recapped the conversation I'd had with Jenny's father.

"Well," Trip said, chewing on his lip, when I'd finished. "I guess . . . I mean, we could . . ."

I looked at the table to avoid the flash of desperation in his eyes. I should have been surprised that he had still assumed that everything would work out, but I wasn't. He was still such a fucking optimist and I didn't know if I envied him or pitied him for it.

"Mr. Gordon is going to talk with the recruiter at Davidson, since my academic record's a little unusual." I forced a laugh, but it felt all wrong. "He said that it looked good, though. Between the trust and my 'story,' he thinks the school will be willing to work with me."

"California," Trip said.

"I . . . yeah . . . warm sun and sand. Go figure." My eyes drifted to the TV over the bar showing an old World Series game. A batter stood in the box, full count. I bargained with myself. If he hit the ball, I'd let my anger go. If he struck out, I'd just take it with me and leave.

I watched the fourth ball being called. The batter walked.

"It seems stupid not to take advantage of a free college education," I said, eyeing the deep purple marks near Trip's collar again. I pulled my wallet out of my bag and dug out Chief Perkins's card and a pre-paid calling card I'd bought in Millway. I hoped the pay phone near Trip's school still worked. "Call him," I said, sliding both across the table.

The waitress finally started toward us, but I waved her away.

Trip didn't even need to read the words. Millway's police logo took up most of the space on the card's front. "A cop?"

"He's in Millway, but he said he has friends in the force here. Once things die down, tell him who you are. He'll help you get away from Leon."

Trip kept his eyes on the card. “Leon’s not just going to let me walk out. You know that,” he said. “If the cops find out what I’ve done for him, I’ll end up . . . I can’t do that, Sean. I thought . . .”

He flicked the edge of the card with his finger a couple of times. It sounded like a playing card in bike spokes.

“I’m sorry.” I meant it, but the words sounded insincere and shallow. “I didn’t think things would happen this way.”

“You didn’t?”

The skeptical tone in his voice made my breath catch. I didn’t know how to fight him and fight *for* him at the same time. I just knew I couldn’t take hearing him sound like he was breaking apart because of me. “Trip, nothing’s changed.”

His eyes snapped up to meet mine and then narrowed. “How can you say that?”

“Because I still *want* the same things,” I said sharply. But even as I said it, my head crowded with everything else that had unexpectedly fallen into place, everything *else* I wanted now. Concepts I hadn’t even dreamed of when Trip and I were making our plans in the treehouse. A relationship with my mom. Friendship with Rory. And, for whatever it meant, Emery. “And . . .” I stopped, unsure of how to make sense of it for myself, much less Trip. “I mean, I still *want* everything we talked about. But”—I shrugged—“there are other things . . . other people . . .”

Trips eyes seared into mine. He gestured toward my hair. “So, should I call you Michael now?”

I took a deep shaky breath, trying not to react. Trip reserved his anger for Leon. I didn't know how to deal with it being directed toward me.

He crumpled the card in his hand and jammed it into the pocket of my jacket. "That girl you're hanging out with, the one you said was at the party?" He paused. I wasn't sure where he was going with his question, but I recognized the bitter tone in his voice. All of his emotional armor was in place. Everything he should have used to protect himself from Leon, but ended up just using to keep out the world. "Are you fucking her? Because that would be *really* convenient."

I flinched at hearing my own words thrown back at me. When I'd sat with Trip on top of Wilson's truck after the party and accused him of sleeping with me out of convenience, I'd still been trying to come to terms with his betrayal. I'd lashed out. Hopefully, he was just doing the same.

I looked at the table. Someone had cut into the wood of the table. *L'enfer, c'est les autres*. Who, besides me, would come into this dismal place if they knew Sartre in French? I traced the letters with my thumbnail.

I thought of telling Trip that Emery and I *were* sleeping together, just to end it all, but I couldn't bring myself to form the lie, and I was too unsure of what I wanted where she was concerned to start creating stories around it. It seemed like tempting fate.

I shook my head and tried to figure out what to do to get back on track. The combination of Trip's eyes—sober, but pained and darting—and that damned bruise just got to me. I'd spent so long trying to make things better for him that it was almost instinctive when I said, "You could just come with me, you know." Trip looked confused, the mask sliding down, his eyes washing over my face. "To California," I said, before I lost my nerve. "Come with me. Learn to surf. Make your sculptures and sell them on the beach. You could go now. Avoid all this stuff with the cops."

I certainly hadn't come to Barlowe intending to ask Trip to come with me. I wasn't even sure where the words were coming from, but suddenly I wanted him to agree so much it scared me. Maybe the answer that we'd been looking for had been right in front of us all this time. Maybe the trust really *was* going to save him.

He was silent for a long time and his eyes darkened. "I can't," he said, over-enunciating like he did when he was high. "I've waited all this time to get out so that *he* can't tell me what to do. So that *he* can't decide my life. I can't just follow and watch you live your life from the sidelines."

"I'm not Leon," I snarled loudly enough to get the attention of two guys at the bar. I lowered my voice. "Besides, that makes no sense. Where does it say that you can't do what you want in California? It's a hell of a lot closer than Pluto."

A muscle in Trip's jaw clenched and I knew he was going to fight me. "Traveling was *our* plan, Shadow," he said. "*Ours.* If I came with you, it would always be me coming with you.

Me following you around. Your decision. Not mine." Trip wrapped his arms around himself again and I could see small half-moons forming where his nails pierced the leather of my jacket.

I thought of begging him. I wasn't sure he wasn't just saying no so that I *would* beg. So that he'd know I meant it.

"What fucking difference does it make?" I asked. "It would still get you away from Leon."

Trip's eyes flashed, the gray shiny as mercury. "It was never *just* about Leon. It was . . ." He shook his head, and for a minute I thought he might cry. "And you might as well . . ."

I'd known this meeting probably wouldn't end well. But suddenly the thought of losing Trip, the one person who stood by me through everything, made me feel like I was drowning.

"Damn it, Trip. It's just college," I said, slamming my glass on the table. I was desperate. Losing. Nothing that was happening made any sense.

Trip closed his eyes and took a deep breath. "No," he said, "it's not *just* anything." When he opened his eyes, I recognized the blankness there. I'd seen it enough when he was hiding out in the tree house. "It was everything," he said softly. "Everything."

I wanted to touch him. To tell him that I'd stay here or that we'd figure something else out. I wanted to tell him it would be okay. But I was paralyzed by how openly he wore his pain, and my own helplessness to do anything about it.

He bit down on his lip and slowly slid out of the booth.

In the background, someone in 1979 hit a home run and the crowd cheered. I couldn't move. I couldn't do anything but watch him walk away.

TWENTY-ONE

Two days later, Chief Perkins showed up after school like he had on my first day at Millway High.

"We have to stop meeting like this." I leaned against the car. "You're going to ruin my reputation."

He shook his head and moved around to the driver's side. "In the car, smart ass."

"What did I do this time?" I asked as I slid in next to him.

"Nothing, I hope." He put the car into gear and pulled over to the far end of the lot and then cut the engine. "This is all unofficial. Got that?"

I nodded and tried to ignore the whole school emptying around us and the way that everyone stared at the cop car in the corner, wondering why I was in it. I was about to make a comment to that effect when he said, "It's about your friend, Trip Marchette."

My shoulders tensed and, for a brief second, I worried that Perkins was going to be telling me that Trip had died, or something equally horrible.

"Was there any bad blood between him and Maggie Woodhouse?"

I exhaled. "No, she was like a mother to him. Why?"

Perkins fiddled with the leather cover of his steering wheel. His nails were ragged and bitten down. I couldn't understand what drove anyone to want to be a cop.

"His fingerprints were all over those medicine bottles and he admits to having a key to the house. Plus, his blood report looked like a pharmacology lab. Not to mention that uncle of his . . ." Perkins stopped. "Sorry, you okay? You look pale."

I felt pale, if that was possible. It was like all the blood had drained from my face. Had they found the guns? The photos of Trip? Who knew what kind of evidence Leon had held on to in order to keep Trip scared and submissive.

"Hell," Perkins said. "I shouldn't be telling you any of this. I just thought . . ."

The radio crackled and Perkins turned it off.

I stared at it as he said, "I'm not on the clock." Then he sighed. "Look, all I know is that Marchette and his uncle were let go after questioning, but that doesn't mean they won't be brought back in. If it were me, I'd have to wonder if your friend was supplying his uncle with drugs from Maggie's stock, and that led to some sort of altercation."

I leaned my head back against the window. They had it all backward, but I didn't know if setting the record straight would make things better or worse for Trip.

"And there is the matter of some insurance money that names your friend as the beneficiary. It was the only thing in Maggie Woodhouse's name, rather than the company's."

"Money?" Maggie never cared about money. She acted like it was the root of all evil. And Trip only talked about money as a means to an end.

"Well, the insurance company won't pay out in suicide cases, anyway, if that's what it was." Perkins looked in his rear-view mirror and waved off some kids who were trying to peek into the car. "Look, son, I like you," he said. "Damned if I know why, but I do."

I nodded. None of this was making sense.

"Leon Marchette is a piece of work. He made certain . . ." Perkins sighed and stared out the front window like he was hoping the word he was looking for would magically appear. "Allegations. About you and his nephew."

I hugged my backpack closer. I couldn't imagine that Leon had known about me and Trip. If he had, he would certainly have kept me from seeing him or used the information to embarrass us somehow. Unless he'd been saving it for an occasion like this.

Perkins reached out and grabbed my arm. "I didn't say that

I believed it. I mean, you did some damned stupid things, but I don't think you're the kind of person who would kill someone for the insurance money."

"Kill someone?" I shook my head and laughed. "Is that what Leon thinks? That Trip and I killed Maggie?"

"I don't know what he thinks," Perkins said. "But what *I* think is that he's grasping at straws. Anything to take the focus off himself."

"I never would have hurt Maggie. And you can take my word that neither would Trip." I made my statement as emphatic as I could, but the words still tasted sour in my mouth. Trip might not have hurt Maggie, but he hadn't done anything to stop Maggie from hurting herself. It was a fine line.

Chief Perkins put a hand on my arm. "I'm not saying you have to, but you might want to keep your distance while this all gets sorted out. There are good people on the force in Barlowe. They'll get to the bottom of all this."

Although I doubted the police department's ability to resolve things in any positive way, it felt good to have this official recommendation to stay away from Trip. I was desperate for someone to tell me what to do.

I got out of the car and walked back to the driver's side. "Thanks," I said, readjusting my backpack.

"You know where to find me," Perkins said. I started to walk away when he said, "And one more thing." I braced myself for more bad news. "Send my best to your mother."

I tried to tell myself that everything would be okay. The Barlowe police would figure out what I was sure was the truth—that Maggie had killed herself and Trip had just been caught in the crossfire. Maybe they'd find the photos and realize what Leon was doing to Trip and at least he would be okay.

But I hadn't heard from Trip since I'd seen him at McGuire's. And when I tossed and turned in bed at night, I couldn't get that bruise of his out of my mind. My only choice was to do something. I didn't know what that something was, but I knew it probably involved my new best friend, Chief Perkins.

And so, after school, with no real plan in mind, I walked to the police station and asked to see him. The station was quiet. There was a TV in the corner playing one of those police and court shows. Probably some officer's twisted sense of humor.

Perkins buzzed me in and I followed him to a conference room. I was kind of happy to see Young Guy from my interrogation sitting in front of a desk covered with files. He looked bored enough to fall over.

"What's up?" Perkins said once he'd shut the door.

I didn't know where to begin. "You said I should tell you if I thought of anything. About Maggie. About Trip."

Perkins's eyes narrowed. "Is this the kind of thing we need your mom here for? If you're confessing to anything, I'd rather she were here."

I had no idea whether he was kidding or not.

"I'm not confessing to anything. I just wanted to know what's going on. I've done what you suggested. I haven't talked to Trip, but I'm worried about him."

Perkins looked at me and sighed as if he could tell that I was lying. Then he closed the curtain on the window that separated this room from the rest of the station and sat next to me.

"I don't know what to tell you, son. I shouldn't be telling you *anything*." But he didn't have to. His face said it all for him.

I put my head in my hands. "Trip wouldn't really be good in an interrogation. And Leon is a total prick. He'll sell him out without a second thought."

Perkins's hand fell heavily on my shoulder and when I looked up, he was staring out the window.

"Did you work my case?" I asked. "When I was gone?"

He looked back uneasily and nodded. "Why?"

"I just wanted to apologize. I'm sorry." And I was. I just hadn't realized it until that moment. "Not for going, really. Just. I'm sorry that it caused you so much trouble."

Perkins stared at me for a few minutes and I drew in a sharp breath and held it until my lungs ached.

"I was just doing my job," he said and squeezed my shoulder again. "Save your apologies for the people who need to hear them."

I thought of who that would be. My mom. Jenny. Wilson and Maggie, but they were dead. Trip, who might as well be if I couldn't do something quickly.

Then I had an idea. "Can you take me home?" I asked. "I have something to show you."

Chief Perkins's forehead wrinkled as he stared at the blue piece of stationery in his hand. "I don't get it," he said.

"It's her"— I fumbled around for the words—"suicide note. Maggie's. She mailed it to me the day she died."

Perkins flipped it over as I had, and found the back blank. "Sean," he said slowly like I'd totally lost my mind.

I stomped over to the trashcan and rifled through some orange peels to get to the envelope.

"Look. The postmark is from Barlowe the day she died," I said handing it to him.

He squinted at the paper.

"We had this thing about quotes, I told you before . . ."

"Yeah, I remember."

"I know it's unusual, but you have to trust me." I heard the desperate rise in my voice and tried to calm down. "That's Maggie saying goodbye."

I sat on the side of the bed and watched Perkins's eyes sweep the room. He seemed much larger in my small bedroom than he had in his car or the station. His gun was terrifying and out of place.

I took a deep breath and explained how complex Maggie's medications were. How they came in random colors, in unmarked bags and boxes, and needed to be sorted. How her daily dosages were calculated based on her weight and temperature and the time of the month and the phase of the moon.

Then I dug my nails into my palms and closed my eyes. "Trip has problems with math and keeping things like that straight. I mean *real* problems." I opened my eyes to make sure that Perkins was listening.

"Go on."

I told Perkins what Trip had said about Maggie deliberately distracting him. "Plus, I can promise you that he wasn't voluntarily helping Leon with anything. He hates that son-of-a-bitch."

I half-expected Perkins to call me on my language, but he just cleared his throat.

"I lied to you before. I saw Trip earlier this week." I couldn't believe that I'd just admitted lying to a cop, but since I was in the process of sharing Trip's secrets, it seemed like a good idea to come clean about my own. I looked at Chief Perkins and tried to imagine him out of uniform, in civilian clothes. It would be easier to talk to him in the park or the back of the Tavern.

Sitting in my childhood bedroom and laying Trip bare felt like a betrayal. But it also felt like my last chance. I closed my eyes again as if that could protect me from my own words. "Look at the bruises on Trip's collarbone if you want to know all there is to know about Leon Marchette."

Perkins let out a long breath. There had to be some legal term for lying to a cop, and probably an associated jail sentence, but I wasn't sure I cared anymore. Maybe Trip and I could share a cell.

I could tell Perkins was considering calling me on it, but he didn't. Instead, he nodded like he understood and said, "I'm sorry, Sean. Like I told you before, this isn't our case, but if it's okay with you, I'm going to share this information with my colleagues in Barlowe."

I wasn't sure which information he was talking about: the letter or what I'd told him. I watched in frustration as he left Maggie's message folded on my desk and stood staring at me from the doorway.

"You know," he said, "I don't usually go in for a lot of that psychology mumbo jumbo, but you might want to find someone to talk to."

After Perkins left, I sat on my bed and watched as the sky got dark. I felt drugged. Drained.

I thought about calling him back and asking if he could be the one I talked to, and I probably would have, had he been anything other than a cop. I wanted to ask him to keep Trip safe. I wanted to call Trip, but everything seemed out of the question.

When my mother came home, I told her that I was feeling

sick, my second lie of the day, only this one wasn't stretching the truth very much. I went to bed early, knowing that sleep was another thing that was going to be elusive.

I kept the lights off and opened the window, lying on the bed fully dressed, aside from my shoes. The breeze blew in cold and sharp, but not bracing enough. I wanted to feel something more intense that could pull me out of my head and stop my thoughts from spinning in circles.

I wondered what would happen now. When Perkins would contact the Barlowe police. What their investigation would entail. If finally, *finally*, I could actually succeed in doing something that would help someone.

I was tense and couldn't sit still. I went to my closet and dug up the old blanket I'd brought from Barlowe—the one that had lived on the floor of the map room. I shook out the dirt it had picked up from the park and held it to my nose. The smell of cedar pulled me like a bungee cord back to the tree house in Maggie's backyard.

There was an old air mattress in one of the rooms, but I'd never trusted that it would support both of us. Trip could be gentle, but he had a fondness for wrestling and biting. The floor had always seemed like a safer bet, this blanket the only thing between us and the knotty wood.

I stripped to my boxers and took the blanket into bed with me, like a kid would. I stared unblinking at the ceiling fan above me and lost myself in memories, holding Trip's eyes in my mind like a guilty pleasure, like a drug I was trying to kick, while I stroked myself faster and then faster still, not wanting to come, not wanting to want to.

I forced myself to think of Emery, wondering what she was doing and what it would be like to feel her hands on me, to be inside a girl, to be able to do something as normal as jerk off without Trip-freaking-Marchette in my head.

I pictured the way Emery had looked on New Year's Eve in my drunken haze, her lips on mine, the corks popping around us, and the way her dress—that gunmetal dress that was the color of Trip's eyes—hugged her breasts and I came in an angry, frustrated spasm. Then I closed my eyes and tried, uselessly, to sleep.

TWENTY-TWO

My days blurred together in a haze of exams, meetings with the school, meetings with trust lawyers, more exams, and lots of waiting to hear back about other meetings, all of which were dedicated to getting me into a college I wasn't sure I actually wanted to attend.

James Gordon was right when he said that the admissions people at Davidson would be willing to work with me. I didn't know what he or Mrs. Ward told them about why I'd missed five years of school, but when I spoke to the dean's office on the phone, my mother pacing nervously in front of me, they never asked. We discussed the courses I was taking and the ones I'd need to fit in during my first year in order to catch up, and that was all. Davidson didn't require SATs or ACTs, but I'd done well enough on the ACTs to at least prove to them that I knew something. Or maybe they just felt like they had a sure bet for tuition, and that if I couldn't hack it, I'd flunk out anyway, so I was low risk.

"You won't be upset with me for going?" I asked my mom as I hung up the phone. It was clear that this was the path I was being pushed down, but there was a small voice in my head that kept asking if I would stay in Millway if my mother asked me to. I felt like I owed her something. And honestly, I almost thought I'd be relieved to stay.

She sat next to me and I thought for a minute that she was going to start crying. Instead, she tilted her head up and said, "How could I be upset with my son for going to college?"

I wanted to point out all of the obvious reasons—the *most* obvious of which was that really, I'd just gotten back. Instead I muttered, "I'll be home for Thanksgiving. And Christmas."

She nodded. "You know, it isn't at the depressing times that I miss drinking. It's in moments like this one when I want to celebrate with you, but I'm not sure I know how."

My mother might have wanted to celebrate, but I didn't have the time or energy. I studied late into the night, afraid to be left alone with my thoughts.

The weather broke without my noticing and I seemed to be the only one who didn't welcome the full onset of spring.

I still hadn't heard from Trip, but then I hadn't reached out to him either. I was pretty sure I could stay away forever if I needed to. One day at a time, like my mother's sobriety. But without Trip, it felt like the blooming flowers and the softly falling rains were mocking me. What should have been happy just felt dismal.

I ran into Chief Perkins more than could be accidental. He was clearly checking up on me, and I kind of appreciated it. I kept hoping to see his car sitting outside in the school parking lot, so that he could tell me what was going on, but he was never there. I'd see him patrolling the park, or in the grocery store examining grapefruits, or in Perk Up, where he'd offer to buy me a cup of tea. His visits were friendly and casual. He asked about school, my mother, my plans for college. He didn't bring up Trip and neither did I. I assumed that if something horrible happened, he'd let me know.

Finally, I ran out of things to keep my mind busy. I'd woken from a dream in which Trip and I'd replayed our fight after Charlotte's party and I'd pushed him over the railing of the grand balcony, his words of affection echoing on his way down.

That day, I walked into the police station and asked Perkins point-blank if he'd heard anything. He'd pulled me into an office, sat me down, and told me that he couldn't tell me anything. It was all out of his hands. I needed to "trust in the system."

I'm sure he could tell from my face what I thought of that idea.

In school, everyone came back from spring break buzzing with plans for the future. Rory had been accepted as a junior member of the Clefs. Jenny had an internship lined up at the

Portland Police Department as part of a gap year program, which would also give her the chance to spend time with Rory between tours.

I was heading to college without a major, without a direction. I'd spent years, it seemed, doing nothing but studying the words of others, and now I realized I had none of my own. I prepared for college because it was what the rules of the trust demanded, because I had no other ideas, and because all the plans I'd made for my future had gone up in smoke.

I decided that I needed to start over. There had been a time in Barlowe when I'd been happy. Now, I was detached from those emotions, couldn't recognize myself even in my own memories, but I knew in my gut that they were real.

Ultimately, there was something ironic in the fact that the place that was killing Trip was the only place I'd been truly at peace.

Wilson had tried, more than once, to explain telecommunications technology to me and Maggie, but it had never sunk in. Sometimes I still caught myself staring at a phone thinking it was all some sort of magic that allowed you to speak to anyone anywhere in the world, just by pressing a couple of buttons.

The phone in my hand was small, too small to contain all of the wishes that I was asking for it to make come true.

5

The first number was the hardest to press. What would happen if Leon answered?

5

Screw Leon. Trip dealt with him day in, day out. I could certainly hold it together on a phone call from an hour away.

5

I'd keep my calm. Ask for Trip. Wouldn't show fear.

6

And then when Trip came to the phone, we'd talk. Clear the air. There was still time to make everything right.

5

I would tell him . . .

5

Tell him . . .

3

Everything.

I held my breath. Pressed the phone against my ear. A woman's voice. Metallic. *The number you have dialed has been disconnected. No further information is available.*

I hung up. Dialed again. Same message. No. It wasn't possible. I clenched the phone in my palm to keep from throwing it across the room.

It wasn't fucking true. It couldn't be. Trip wouldn't just disappear without reaching out to me. But then that thought slid away and what was left was the fear that Leon finally made good on all his threats and Trip was hurt or missing or dead and before I knew it, I was pacing around my room, looking for something to break, to shatter. Something that wasn't me.

The guilt of having made the choice to contact him, only to find that it wasn't an option and that I'd waited too long, was killing me. My stomach felt shredded to the point that I thought I was going to be sick. My heart raced all out of time. Maybe I was dying. *This*, I thought, *this is what a broken heart feels like. Not like something that's cracked under pressure, but like something that's been shattered against its will.*

I wanted to cry, to let go of everything except this fucking pain that I knew I'd earned. I wanted to let go until I was nothing more than an empty shell. But I didn't deserve that. I deserved everything I was feeling.

I picked up the pillow and slammed it against the wall hard and long enough to bring my mother running.

It only took one sympathetic look from her before I fell apart. She put her arm around me and held me close like I'd always wanted her to do when I was a kid. Once I caught my breath, I decided to take a chance and tell her why I was having a breakdown and why I still refused to put the phone down.

I choked out a confession, telling her everything I'd never told Trip and never admitted to myself. The word "love" tore its way out of my mouth like a sharpened ax, but tasted like the truth. I raised my wet eyes to my Mom expecting to see some sort of disapproval, but she just listened, nodded, and rubbed small circles between my shoulder blades as I talked, never altering or slowing her pattern. When I thought about it later, having a former stripper as a mother might have worked to my advantage. She was probably more open-minded about sex and attraction than most parents, and she'd faced her own issues with my grandparents, who she was determined not to become. She was less likely than many to get bent out of shape about her son declaring his love for another boy.

When I stopped talking, she pried the phone out of my hand and pulled at my sleeve. "Come on, let's take a drive."

I recognized the determined expression on her face. It was one I'd worn often enough when I was convincing myself I was right about something when actually, I was just grasping at straws.

"Where?" I managed to ask as I dried my face on my T-shirt and pulled it off to replace it with one that hadn't mopped up an hour's worth of pain.

She just smiled and led me to the car, buckling me into the passenger's seat like a little kid.

Suddenly it dawned on me what she meant to do. "Mom, we can't. His uncle . . ." I didn't even mention what Chief Perkins would think of her idea.

"You let me worry about his uncle," she said.

I reached out and put a hand on her arm, trying to sort out my tangled thoughts. "Everything I promised Trip," I started, grasping for words. "I screwed it all up."

She took a deep breath. "Sean, I spent years feeling guilty for not being the mother you needed. Years wallowing in my pain and talking to my sponsor and anyone else who would listen. But then, one day, I woke up and realized that I was carrying around that pain for *myself* and not for you. I don't know if that makes any sense to you right now. Or if it ever will. But I do know that Trip must consider you very special if he's placed so much faith in you. And if that's how he feels, maybe there's a reason. Maybe you earned his confidence without even trying. Maybe it's just because of who you are and who you are *to him*. And that isn't just going to go away because things get difficult." She paused, but I could tell she wasn't expecting an answer.

Then she started to back out of the driveway. "Now, which way?"

I directed her to Barlowe. The closer we got, the harder my heart beat at the thought of having these two parts of my life crashing into each other. I wasn't sure how I'd survive the impact.

My hands clenched in my lap as I tried to mouth the words that answered Trip's announcement that he loved me. I'd never realized how much braver he was than me.

As it turned out, I didn't have to worry. If the disconnected phone number hadn't been enough, the FOR SALE sign in front of Trip's empty house finished me off.

Emily Dickinson wrote, "Parting is all we know of heaven and all we need to know of hell."

She was wrong, though. Hell wasn't when you left something. It was when you realized, too late, what it meant to you.

This time I didn't throw anything. I didn't cry. I just gave up.

TWENTY-THREE

"Why don't you look for him?"

Emery, Rory, and Jenny had all asked me the same question. Each asked it hesitantly, as if no one had made the suggestion before, worried that their very words would make me bolt.

Even my mother had asked the question. But the truth was Trip had made his decision. Or the decision had been made for him. Either way, the result was the same.

In moments of weakness, I trolled the internet looking for a sign, a photo, an obituary. I joined social media sites, searched through them, and then deleted my accounts. I found nothing, and that didn't surprise me. Aside from his very public statement at Charlotte's party, Trip embraced the type of private life that Wilson had always been after me to mirror.

One evening my phone rang, an occurrence that had become uncommon enough that I had to stop to figure out where the noise was coming from. Like someone who had never answered a phone before, I picked it up and held it to my ear. I hadn't looked at the screen. I didn't say a word.

"I'm coming over in an hour. Wear something that doesn't look like you've slept in it," Emery ordered.

I looked down at the same pair of jeans I'd been wearing for a week and at the ratty T-shirt that I'd been swapping out with one other for . . . a while.

"Why?" I asked. My brain was foggy from not having been used for much aside from scientific formulas and math equations. My final semester classes were killing me.

"It's prom night," she said. "My parents are hosting a party for Rory and Jenny. I need to get out of here."

I pulled on a loose thread at the bottom of my shirt, then glanced at the calendar. How had time moved so quickly when I felt stuck in the quicksand of my past?

"Sean?"

"Yeah." Even the one word seemed to take all my available energy.

"Did you hear me? I'm picking you up."

Somewhere in my head, her words linked together and made me laugh. "You aren't suggesting we go to prom, are you?"

Emery laughed. “Of course not. I’d sooner stick forks in my eyes. But I want you to take me somewhere.”

“Where?”

“We’ll talk about it later. One hour.”

The phone went dead. As usual, Emery made it easy for me by giving me strict instructions. I opened my closet door and stared at shirts I hadn’t worn in a couple of months. I was overwhelmed by options and just grabbed at something, which turned out to be the shirt I’d worn to Maggie’s memorial service. It figured.

I managed a half-hearted shower and then threw the shirt on over a pair of cleanish jeans. It was the best I was going to do.

Fifty-five minutes after Emery called, I wandered downstairs. My mom looked up from her crossword puzzle. The lack of surprise on her face made it clear that she knew where I was going. That had been happening a lot lately—my friends colluding with my mother.

Emery pulled up and waved at me from the driver’s seat. “I won’t be long,” I said to my mom, although I had no idea if that was true or not.

“Have fun,” Mom replied. But, as usual, she looked concerned not that I was going to have too much fun and cause trouble, but that I wouldn’t even be able to manage to work up to enjoying myself at all.

Emery got out of her car and threw me her keys. I stared at them like they were going to bite me. "Where are we going?"

She leaned against the red VW, looking far more beautiful in her crocheted dress and slip than I imagined the other girls did in their overworked prom dresses. "Take me to the tree house. I want to see it."

I didn't have to ask which tree house she meant. "Emery, I don't think . . ." Then I stopped myself. Why the hell not? What was it really except for a pretty pile of wood?

Discarded bits of police tape littered the bushes in front of Maggie and Wilson's house. The plastic had been bright yellow when I'd been here with Jenny, but now it was faded like dried hay. Next to the plastic strips, the ivy was lush and green and looked rcady to consume the building. The house had a kind of beauty that was at once peaceful and feral.

I sighed and took Emery's hand. "Come on. You wanted to see the tree house. Let's get this over with."

I led her to the back of the house and down the path I knew too well. When we got to the tree house, the full moon was just visible over the top and it seemed like I could smell every fireplace in Barlowe, burning through the last of the season's wood. My stomach jumped at the familiar scent and a million memories flooded my head.

The view from the top of the elevator froze me in place. I

don't know what I thought I'd find. Maybe I expected everything to be the way I'd left it. I hadn't been prepared for the vast emptiness. All that was left really *was* just a bunch of wood. No blankets, no books, no goodbye notes. I thought about Jenny avoiding the magnolia tree after I'd left Millway and wished I'd had that same foresight.

While Emery wandered from deck to deck, I made my way to the map room and stood in front of the huge blank wall. I ran my hands over it, touching the places that Trip and I had planned to go.

"Are you looking for a secret door in the wall?" Emery teased.

I explained about the map. One more thing that had been lost when I wasn't paying attention.

She sat on the dusty floor, the fringe of her skirt wrapped around her legs like a cat. As I settled next to her, I asked, "Why are we here?"

"I wanted to meet the part of you that got left behind," she said. It was strange, her choice of words, because that's just how I felt. Like a part of me had been cut off and was entombed in the walls like a confused spirit, never able to move on.

I changed the subject. "I wish we weren't going to be so far away from each other." After sorting through offers and packages from various schools, including one in California that I prayed she'd accept, Emery was preparing to go to Yale.

She shook her head. "Yale is pretty advanced, you know. They have phones and email and everything."

"I know," I admitted. "I guess I'm just crap at saying goodbye."

"And yet, you seem pretty good at leaving."

I looked around the tree house and thought of everything that had happened here. "Actually, it's probably the thing I'm worst at." I thought of the letter that Maggie had sent me. My inability to move on was my weakness. I'd pinned the Hesse quote up over my desk and, after a lot of thought, came to the conclusion that my childhood taught me to cling to any port in a storm. Jenny. Wilson. Maggie. Even Trip. I was doing it again with Emery, but I wasn't sure I wanted to stop. The harder I tried to name my feelings for her, the more difficult it got.

I stared at the map. "I thought I'd forgiven Trip when I saw him at McGuire's. I felt something I thought was forgiveness. I thought that was the reason I asked him to come with me, but maybe I was just trying to hurt him. I don't know anymore. But I think I understand why he didn't try to stop Maggie. He can't stand to see anyone in pain."

Emery stared at me in a way that reminded me of Trip's long pauses. Then she reached into a pocket I hadn't noticed among the knots and twists of her skirt, took out the flask I'd seen Rory use on New Year's Eve, twisted off the top, and took a sip. I wondered if he had given it to her or if she'd lifted it. Probably the latter. When she offered it to me, I shook my head out of confusion as much as anything. Emery didn't usually drink. I had no idea why she was starting now.

"Everything is changing," she said, looking off into the

distance. "Don't you feel it? Soon we'll graduate. Everyone is going to go off and do their own thing. Hell, you and I'll be on opposite ends of the country."

I nodded slowly. "Well, like you said. There are phones and email." I reached over and squeezed her hand and then wrapped my arms around my legs. I craved things from her that I was never going to get. Maybe I wanted her because I couldn't have Trip, and because I wasn't sure I should want him to begin with. Those reasons didn't make my longing for her any less intense.

She turned and put her hand on my cheek. Then she leaned in and kissed me so lightly it felt as if she was whispering against my lips.

I looked out through the wooden slats at the moon hanging desperately in the sky. "What do you think it means?" I asked shuffling words in my head like a deck of cards. "I mean, Trip and then you . . . what does that make me?"

"It makes you lucky," she answered without hesitation, "to love people who love you back. Not everyone gets that."

Suddenly, tears stung my eyes and I rubbed them away. I put my hand out for the flask and took a deep burning swig of brown liquor that reminded me of the taste of Trip's lips when he kissed me at the party. "Fuck," I said as I spat it out. I was never going to be able to escape these ghosts.

That's all that Trip was to me now, a ghost. That entire part of my life was fading like an old photograph. Emery wrapped her arms around me. I ran my hands over her skin, warmth surging through me. Her hair circled my neck like a cave I could crawl into. I kissed her again, hard and urgent and hungry. She leaned over and pushed me slowly to the wooden floor. I could feel her shaking as she kissed me. I wondered if it was from fear or the whiskey, but I was feeling shaky, too. The smell of cedar and clove and all of the glimmers of my nights with Trip swirled around, making me dizzy.

As we kissed, she undid the bottom buttons of my shirt. Her nails grazed my stomach. The room kept spinning and spinning. I wondered if Trip had smoked something or taken something or pissed something that had permeated the room and was making its way into my bloodstream.

A tack in the wall caught my eye. Dublin. It had been on our list. Trip had tried for what felt like hours to locate it and ended up pinning the tag somewhere in the Scottish Highlands.

"I really need to teach you to read a map," I'd said.

He'd come up behind me, taller because of the angled floor. I could still smell his clove cigarettes, feel his hand on my shoulder, his breath in my ear. "I have some things I could teach you," he'd said. And so I let him teach me. And then I let him again.

With Emery's tongue in my mouth and the memory of Trip's "lessons" in my mind, I was scared I was going to be sick. I broke away and rushed to the window, gasping for air and trying not to puke into Maggie's tomato plants.

Resting my head in my hands, I stood there until Emery

came up beside me, still breathing hard. There were no right words to apologize.

I expected her to, I don't know, push me over the railing like I'd dreamed of doing to Trip at the party? Chew me out? Instead, she turned my face toward her own.

I squeezed her hand and looked into her green eyes like I had that first day in school. My heart beat hard in my chest and I was overcome with the desire to beg her not to leave. Just like Trip, I couldn't have her, but I had no idea how I was going to manage without her.

"I'm really going to miss you." I leaned my head on her shoulder. "And I'm sorry," I said to her. To all of them.

And maybe she knew that. "I know," she said. "Sometimes, I think that's your most redeeming quality."

She kissed me lightly on the cheek, the type of kiss you'd give your great-aunt or a family friend you hadn't seen in a while, and beckoned me into the tree house's elevator, I turned and glanced around one final time, and then tried to turn my back on my memories.

I tossed and turned and then dragged myself up the next day in a cold sweat, afraid that I'd ruined everything with Emery and that, in the light of day, she'd decide that even friendship was out of the question. I thought about calling, but I still wasn't much of a phone person, and those calls I'd made to

Trip, only to hear that the line had been disconnected, had scarred me deeply.

And so I started to walk to her house on the other side of town, not even knowing if she'd be there.

I ambled from one side of the street to the other, telling myself that I wanted to look in a store window or check out a type of tree I wasn't sure I could identify or even that I just wanted to avoid other morning walkers. But really, I was stalling for time.

I cut through McKuen Park and was glad to see that the small gardens were deserted. Without a lot of thought, I hopped the fence and randomly picked a bunch of tulips, doing my best to make sure that the flowers were chosen sporadically and that my stolen makeshift bouquet wouldn't leave a noticeable bare spot.

As I bent down for the last one, something shiny caught my eye. A small stack of perfectly polished pennies. I thought of the only rhyme my mom had taught me as a child: "Find a penny, pick it up. Then all day you'll have good luck." I always thought it singsong-y and sickeningly sweet. But now I needed all the luck I could get, so I took one off the top and slipped it in my pocket.

Emery stood in the doorway with my gifted tulips in her hand.

"Red tulips?" A smile played along the edges of her mouth. "Really?"

I tried to figure out if I'd done something wrong. If she'd mentioned hating red or being allergic to tulips.

"I want to apologize," I said.

"You already have." She turned and walked through the living room and into the kitchen. "Have you done something else I should know about?" Her question was garbled like she was speaking into a box. When I heard the sound of a door closing and then water running, I guessed, correctly, that she had been reaching for a vase under the sink.

She placed the flowers on a table and then folded her legs up under her on the couch, gesturing for me to sit beside her.

I did as she wanted and then shifted uncomfortably. It was a warm day and Emery had her hair pinned up, but a few strands had escaped and were draped against her white tank top like shadows. I wanted to reach out and tuck them back behind her ears. I wanted to be a different person from the one who'd so badly freaked out last night.

"I'm sorry," I said. "I didn't think things would happen this way." Then I instantly regretted it because it was exactly the same thing I'd said to Trip. And look how that turned out.

I waited for her to say something that would guide our conversation and make it easier to figure out if we'd stay friends, but she just reached up and twirled one of the escaped strands of hair around her finger.

I closed my eyes and took a deep breath. "I care about you," I said.

The couch squeaked next to me and when I opened my

eyes Emery was holding one of the tulips by the stem and running her fingers over the blood red petals.

"You guys missed one hell of a party." Rory swept in the door with two cups of coffee in his hands. "Had I known you'd be here, I would have gotten you something, too," he said to me as he handed one off to Emery.

"That's okay." I saw him glance at the flowers and then at Emery. I stood and walked toward the door. I'd gotten what I'd come for.

Emery left Rory standing there and saw me to the door. I could only imagine the questions that would be asked after I left.

I started down the porch stairs, hesitated, then turned back. "What's wrong with red tulips? Do you hate them or something?"

Emery laughed. "Funny, flowers' meanings are the kind of obscure thing I thought you'd know. Red tulips stand for 'perfect love.'"

I opened my mouth but had nothing to say.

"Well, if you believe that sort of thing, anyway."

Then she closed the door and left me standing alone on the porch.

TWENTY-FOUR

The day before graduation, I came home to find Rory crumpled over on my doorstep. I was used to Rory being upbeat. Steady. But now he looked off-kilter. His eyes were red and his favorite English cricket team T-shirt was stained with what looked like a mix of coffee and blood.

"I should probably hate you," he said.

It seemed to be a general theme these days, but for once, I wasn't sure what I'd done, so I unlocked the door and gestured for him to follow.

"You get into a fight or something?" I asked.

He sat down hard on my mom's floral couch, leaned over, and put his head in his hands. I waited because I had no idea what else to do.

Finally, he looked up and said quietly, "Jenny and I broke up."

I looked for signs that he was joking, but saw none. "Oh."

He got up and walked to the mantel and picked up a figurine of a ballerina in a complicated blue dress that my mother could never quite get all the dust off of. He turned it over and over in his hands and pressed his lips closed like he wasn't going to tell me anything more.

"I'm sorry," I said to break the silence. The way he'd said straight out that they had broken up made it sound mutual, but it was pretty clear from looking at him, that it wasn't what he'd wanted. "What happened?"

"She said your name," he said not looking at me. "I mean . . . we . . . and she said your name."

I wanted to pretend that I had no idea what he was talking about. But even I wasn't that clueless.

"She said my name?"

Rory's shoulders fell. "I rented a room at the Blakemore Inn. A suite. To celebrate graduating, you know?" He closed his eyes and his fingers were white around that stupid porcelain dancer. "Anyway . . . We were lying there after, and well, she called me Michael."

Michael. Fuck.

I was afraid that Rory thought that I'd done something to undermine their relationship. Afraid that the least complicated friendship I'd ever had would be jeopardized by whatever was still running through Jenny's mind.

"I didn't—" I began.

"God, Sean," he said, slamming the dancer back on the

mantel. "Not everything is about you. Can you please just try to understand that for once?"

It felt like he was reading my mind. He was right. Of course, he was right. Not that my realization changed anything. "What can I do?"

Rory shook his head on the verge of tears. "Nothing. There's nothing you can do. There's nothing Emery can do. There's just nothing. It's over."

"Maybe it was just some stupid, in-the-moment thing," I offered. "Maybe she's just embarrassed. You can fix things, right?"

Rory looked at me with a curiously blank expression. "Some things are just broken. I mean, sometimes things just fall apart and can't be put back together."

His words hit me sharply. "You don't know that," I said. Acid ate at the back of my throat. "Have you talked to her? Maybe there is something you can do," I said again. Suddenly, I felt like I had a lot riding on Jenny and Rory staying together.

"Don't be an ass, Sean. Of course I've talked to her. We talked all night. It doesn't matter. It's just over and we both have to move on."

"Move on to what?" I asked. I knew I was being a shitty friend for thinking about myself instead of their breakup. But I couldn't ignore that moving on was the one thing that I couldn't seem to do.

"Life, man. Just move on to whatever comes next."

Looking at the unmistakable pain on Rory's face, I choked

down the question that was on my lips—*how?*—and simply nodded.

Parapraxis. Slip of the tongue. Freudian slip. Whatever you call it, it ends up the same. Michael Sterling, the one person in my life I *was* able to move on from, was living in Jenny's subconscious.

I wanted to kill him.

I hadn't seen a lot of Jenny during my self-imposed exile. As time went on, we just seemed to have less and less to say to each other. But I didn't hesitate to circle the block to her house as soon as Rory left.

I had a brief and innocuous conversation about graduation with her parents and then moved on to the kitchen.

Jenny looked up from the table when I walked in. "I don't want to discuss it."

I stood in front of the sink. "I don't really want to either, but I think we have to, right?"

Her left eye twitched. "Fine. You want to talk about it. Let's talk. You were my best friend. You left and didn't even tell me you were going. Then you came back. Only you aren't the same person. As far as I'm concerned, my best friend is dead. Your turn."

I swallowed hard. "You're pissed at me. I get it. I'm sorry. But it isn't Rory's fault." I tried to keep my voice low so that her parents wouldn't hear us.

"You aren't his mother. Why do you care so much?"

"Someone deserves to be happy."

"Oh, grow up, *Sean*. This is high school. It wouldn't have lasted anyway. Rory is going on tour, I'm . . ." She stopped. "You know, it doesn't matter what I'm doing. What I'm doing is no longer any of your business."

I wandered over to stand in front of the refrigerator. All of the photos of her father smiling in exotic locales were missing. It didn't seem to be the right time to ask why.

I turned around and spoke to Jenny's back. "I can't apologize for not being who you want me to be. But that doesn't mean that I don't care about you."

Jenny spun in her chair. "You just don't get it, and you never will. It doesn't matter how you feel if you never show it." She stood up and glared at me. "I don't have the energy for this anymore. I'd really like it if you'd leave."

"Jenny," I called, but she was walking out of the room. I figured she'd come around. That her anger at both me and Rory would fade eventually like my anger at Trip had. And so I left.

A week later, my mother told me that Jenny had cancelled her internship and was taking a year off to figure out what she wanted to do. A few days after that, Emery told me that Jenny had moved in with a cousin of hers in Seattle. She was selling coffee and dating a street artist. I wondered how someone could pick up and leave without looking back.

TWENTY-FIVE

The air was sticky, hot for Maine, even in June. It took all of my strength to pry the window open. Rory's car pulled into the drive and I could hear the improbable sound of bagpipes seeping out of his windows. Who the hell listened to bagpipes for fun?

"Sean," my mother yelled from the base of the stairs. I stared at the stacks of bags I'd packed. It felt odd to be moving and taking things with me. It was completely different from just going. That realization made me feel homesick, even though, for the first time, I was leaving somewhere I was also planning to come back to.

Davidson had asked me to come to California early, which was fine. I was desperate for a change, a distraction. Anything that would break the cycle of resignation I'd come to accept as normal.

"One second." I took one last look around and opened the drawer of my nightstand. My hand wrapped around Trip's boomerang. The wood felt warm in my hand. Heavier than I remembered. I slipped the cord over my head and tucked the familiar shape into my shirt.

Next, I took out the photo. I hadn't looked at it in a long time. Trip's expression—open, unashamed, clearly loving—made me wonder how it had been possible for him at sixteen to be so sure, so comfortable with something I'd had to wrestle with for years.

It had taken me so long to go such a short distance. And, of course, I'd arrived too late.

I stuck the photo in the corner of the mirror. It would give me something else to come back to, even if it only represented everything I'd thrown away. I didn't have the heart to bring it with me.

"Hurry up or I'm going to finish off the spread your mom made for us to take," Rory said, leaning against the doorframe. "That woman can cook."

He moved toward my stack of bags.

"Rory?"

"Yeah?"

I wanted to tell him that I was glad we were still friends. I wanted to quote something Aristotle wrote about friendship being "a slow ripening of fruit," but I'd been trying hard to stop relying on the words of old dead philosophers.

"Thanks," I said, feeling suddenly tongue-tied. "Just thanks."

Rory smiled, but I saw in his eyes that he understood. "Your mom is tearing up enough for all of us. Don't you get all emotional, too."

I smiled back. "Wouldn't think of it. Besides, we're coming back for Thanksgiving, right?"

Rory ducked his head a little. Ever since his breakup with Jenny, he'd been more subdued and a little self-conscious, as if he didn't know how to act without her.

"Yeah. I just wish I didn't have to wait another few weeks to leave, myself."

It was odd to see my own feelings reflected in Rory. We were both running away. I was looking forward to going to California, if for no other reason than that I wanted a clean start. I wouldn't be the boy who'd gone missing, but I also wouldn't be the sad friend. I looked forward to losing myself in a sea of college freshmen on their own for the first time, their only expectations being attendance at both a lot of decent parties and a few required classes.

Rory squeezed my shoulder. He grabbed one of my bags and said, "Man, what do you have in here, rocks?" as he carried it down the stairs.

I'd packed enough to fill my dorm room. The only concession I'd asked from the admissions board due to my "unique circumstances" was a single room, which they granted without question. Despite advice to the contrary from James Gordon about bonding opportunities and boozy late-night study sessions, I couldn't imagine sharing my room with anyone else, another boy in particular. In the back of my mind was a kernel of worry that what had happened with Trip would happen with someone else, and I wasn't willing to chance it.

I checked a couple of drawers to make sure that I'd grabbed everything, then ducked down under the bed to pull out the case for the new laptop my mother bought me. Someone coughed behind me.

"Rory, you don't need to get them all," I said as I pulled myself off the floor.

And stopped.

The case slipped to the floor as my heart leapt into my throat, threatening to choke me. I'd finally lost my mind. "You're really here," I said.

"You're really going." Trip looked surprisingly at ease, happy to have caught me off guard after all this time.

"Yeah." I took a step closer to him. It felt like I was being visited by a clove-scented ghost. I was afraid to reach out my hand and find that he was just a trick of the light. "I think there'd be trouble if I don't show up now."

He came up to me and hugged me quickly, just long enough to leave a searing heat on my arms. I'd been cold for months—although the doctors couldn't find anything wrong with me. Suddenly, my blood was moving again.

I stood there in shock, watching Trip walk around my room, picking things up and putting them back. He paused in front of the mirror and reached over to pull the photo of us out of the frame.

"I wondered what happened to this," he said, still looking down. "I tore the place up. I was afraid the police had it."

He spun to face me and his gray eyes held mine. There was so much I wanted to say to him and I wasn't sure I remembered how to speak.

"Did you know that the Pacific Ocean is shaped like a triangle?" he asked.

I shook my head, having no idea what he was talking about. If this was a hallucination, it was a doozy.

He bit his lip and paused. "I think it would be cool to see it."

What was he doing in my mom's house? I had to replay his words in my head, afraid to get my hopes up that I'd heard right. "You're coming to California?" I whispered.

He put the photo on the nightstand and sat down heavily on my bed. "Soon. I mean, if I can find a place to crash."

His eyes were fixed on some point on the opposite wall. I couldn't take mine off his profile.

I forced myself to blink and let myself fall backward on the bed next to him, watching the fan rotating on the ceiling. It made me think of Emery telling me to talk to Trip or I'd just be spinning. She'd been right.

"I don't get it," I said carefully. "What changed?"

He leaned back and draped his left ankle over my right one. "Your cop friend."

I jolted up onto my elbows. "Perkins?"

"I asked him not to tell you. In case it didn't work out. In case I screwed it up. I thought it would be easier if you just forgot me."

I licked my lips, which had suddenly become bone-dry. "I could never . . ."

"I know what you told him, and it's okay. They closed the case, you know. Maggie's. Ruled it a suicide. And Leon's gone. They got him on tax fraud of all things. I've been living with a foster family. They're going to let me stay since I'm repeating senior year. The school knows everything now." He reached over and squeezed my arm. "I'm turning into you. All I do is study."

I wasn't sure whether to smile or cry with relief.

"I've been working," he continued. "I have Wilson's old tools. I've sold some stuff."

His words circled around me like fireflies. And like fireflies, I was hopeless at holding on to them long enough to make sense of them.

"I missed you, Shadow."

"I missed you, too," I whispered, before I lost my nerve. I looked at my hands, unsure what to do with them. "Why are you here?"

He laughed so genuinely that I believed he couldn't possibly be real. He plucked at tufts of my blond hair and I shivered as his hand moved down the side of my face, and then around my neck. He pulled me toward him and kissed me hard and forcefully, his solid arms pinning me in place.

"So many questions," I said dizzily when we broke apart.

"Is that a quote?"

"No," I said, my mouth settling into a smile. "I actually do have a ton of questions."

He held my eyes and then took my hand and brought it to his mouth, biting down on the soft skin under my thumb.

I gasped.

"Five minutes, Sean," my mom said from the doorway. I closed my eyes and waited for her to say something else. Who knew how long she'd been standing there.

I took a deep breath in the quiet of the room.

"Mom, this is Trip Marchette."

Trip looked at me and lowered our hands, but didn't let go. My mom barely hesitated before she came over and put a hand on his shoulder. "It's nice to meet you, Trip," she said, as casually as if she'd just walked in to see us playing checkers. "I'm sorry that you boys don't have more time. But James Gordon is nothing if not punctual, and you have a long drive ahead of you."

I had offered to take a plane to make it easier on everyone. But Jenny's dad had insisted on driving me. The official story was that he was heading to California for a new TV show. But Emery told me that really, Jenny's parents were having a "trial separation." I couldn't even imagine how that worked.

Mom walked out and I exhaled while Trip stood up. I panicked at the idea of him leaving as quickly and mysteriously as he'd appeared.

"Guess your questions are going to have to wait," he said offering his hand to pull me up.

I looked at him, desperate to find a way to make him stay. It was only then that I noticed that he was wearing my shirt, my favorite shirt—the one I'd worn to Charlotte and Parker's party, white with tiny bloodred pinstripes that were wavering in front of my eyes.

I reached out and caught some of the fabric in my hand. "No. Wait. How did you even know how to find me? Was that Perkins, too?"

He paused long enough that I wasn't sure he was going to respond. My heart raced at the thought that my mother was going to tell him to leave before I even knew the answer to this one question.

His eyes roamed my room and settled on the remaining suitcases. "I just needed time," he said, not answering my question. "And so did you." He walked over to my desk and grabbed a Sharpie, then reached for my arm. He pushed my sleeve up and slowly wrote a number on my skin. When he was done studying it, he drew a small compass next to it. "I have a cell now, Shadow. Call me."

I nodded and swallowed hard.

We stared at each other for what felt like hours. Trip had offered everything he could. The ball was back in my court.

I took a deep breath and started to speak, although I had no idea what I was supposed to say. "Trip, I . . ."

"Sean," my mother called. "James Gordon is here."

I groaned. That figured. "Be down in a second."

Trip hadn't moved a muscle. I stretched up and kissed him, slowly and deliberately. His sigh made me wish we were back in the tree house, thinking we had all the time in the world.

"I have to go," he said, but made no move to do so.

"I'll call you," I promised. I meant it, but it felt like I'd just wasted an opportunity to make things right between us once and for all. "Probably twenty times before I even get to California." There were things we'd need to talk about. Maggie. The party. Where he was living. Why I'd pushed him away so hard. But I was pretty sure that none of the twenty calls would answer those questions.

And honestly, I didn't care.

I wanted to tell him that I loved him. That was, I thought, what was expected of me. But *everyone* said those words all the time and they didn't feel like enough. There were a million things to say, but we were out of time. And somehow, I knew he understood.

TWENTY-SIX

The fog was rolling over the quad outside of my dorm window. It was early morning, my favorite time at Davidson. It seemed like all of California was quiet, everyone still too hungover from the previous night to have started stirring.

I'd been given a room overlooking the chapel, which sat on a hill in the middle of campus. If I timed it right, I could watch the sun hit the top of the bell tower and shoot in blinding streaks over the quad. I found it a calming way to begin the day, and it made me feel less guilty about my insomniac tendencies.

"Come back to bed," Trip mumbled.

"In a minute," I said.

I slid off the windowsill and stretched. A piece of white notebook paper wedged halfway under my door caught my eye.

Joe Cole, the junior who was assistant editor of the *Davidson Index*, lived next door to me and we'd become friendly due to his ever-creative attempts to get me to write for the paper. So far, I'd managed to evade them, but we both knew it was only a matter of time. I'd stopped avoiding friendships the minute Trip walked into my room in Millway, and Joe had been the first person I'd worked up the courage to open up to. The note was beautifully written in the almost calligraphic style he had, and contained an invitation to brunch before we all left for Thanksgiving.

In three days, Trip and I would be heading to Maine. He'd go back to the Andersons—the family he'd been living with—and I'd head back to my mom's. His visit here was largely due to her commissioning a sculpture from him as a thank-you gift for Chief Perkins. She'd generously paid Trip enough to buy at least three roundtrip Maine–California plane tickets.

The twins were coming back to Millway as well, and I was both excited and nervous for us to all be together again. Although I hadn't heard from Jenny, Rory had. He'd told me that they'd decided to try to stay friends. I wondered if they'd be able to pull it off.

My bare feet were cold against the wooden floor as I made my way past my desk. I'd hung a bulletin board on the wall. Maggie's Hesse quote was the centerpiece.

I'd come to realize that Maggie had been wrong all along. Wrong for giving up. Wrong for making Trip live with the guilt of what she'd pushed him into helping her to do. And wrong for thinking that there's more strength in letting go than in holding on and fighting for something that mattered. It had taken me eighteen years and a lot of pain to learn that, but I wasn't going to make the same mistakes she had.

For years, I'd thought she was the perfect mother, teacher, and guru rolled into one. It was Wilson I'd followed to Barlowe, but it was Maggie I stayed for. In the months since she'd died I'd made peace with both my grief over her death and the anger I felt toward her for taking me in, and then casting me off when she'd thought better of it.

But I couldn't reconcile myself with what she'd done to Trip, who would have done, and ultimately did, everything for her. I was pretty sure I'd never understand why she didn't just swallow a handful of pills and leave him out of it if she was so committed to seeing her plan through.

Shortly after I came to school, I'd dreamt that I was standing with Maggie, Wilson, and Trip, watching as the house's new family explored the tree house. Two angelic looking children, a boy and a girl, were racing around it and their father was saying something about dismantling the elevator. I'd looked at Trip, concerned that this would bother him, but he was smiling and said, "It's good that they don't need it."

In my dream, I turned to Maggie and asked, "Why did you do it?"

"Because I couldn't think of a reason not to," she replied. "Living should have a reason."

The smoke alarm in the hallway had gone off before I

could press for more of an answer, and no matter how hard I tried, I couldn't get back to the place where she might give me one.

I wandered back to bed and slid under the covers.

"Go to sleep, Shadow," Trip murmured with a sleepy smile that I knew not to take for granted.

I sat and listened to his breathing and tried again to figure out what that dream had meant.

"You aren't sleeping, are you?" Trip asked.

"I'm thinking about sleeping," I said, only I wasn't. Really, I was thinking about staying in one place and everyone knowing where to find me. I was thinking about Trip moving out here next year and us getting an apartment and a dog or a plant or something else that would assume we'd be back at the end of the day. Something that would wait for us and that we'd love too much to let down.

He sighed and sat up suddenly, rubbing his hands through his dark hair.

"What?" he asked.

"Nothing."

"You're never thinking nothing."

I shrugged.

Trip paused and his serious expression made my breath catch.

"I wanted them to see. I kissed you at the party because I knew you were leaving. And because I wanted to. And because I wanted them to see."

I tried not to smile, but failed. "Do you like dogs?" I asked.

He smiled back. It was one of those smiles I used to wait weeks for in Barlowe.

"I like *you*," he said.

Maggie's quote caught the corner of my eye, like it seemed to do more often than not. Maybe, I thought, everything in my life from now on was going to be judged by whether I was holding on too tightly or letting go too quickly. Maybe that was an important question and Maggie's last gift to me.

"I like you, too," I said. "You know that, right? I mean, I more than like you, I . . ."

Just then, the phone vibrated on my nightstand. Given how rarely that happened I felt like I had to answer it.

"Sean Woodhouse."

"Emery Whitman."

Emery. We'd emailed daily, but I hadn't heard her voice since she'd left for Yale, and it made my heart leap.

"You do know that I'm on Pacific time?" I asked lightly. The clock read 6 a.m.

"Yeah. Sorry about that. I wanted to catch you unprepared and I just have one question."

"Shoot."

"Trip's there, right?"

"Yeah. That's your question?"

"No, my question is: are you happy?"

"What?"

"Come on, Sean. College couldn't have wiped out your brain that fast. Are you happy?"

I looked around the room. My desk had a stack of books on it taller than I was. Literature. French. Fine art. Next to that was my plane ticket home for Thanksgiving.

Trip was looking at me with a puzzled, bemused expression. On the phone, Emery started humming the *Jeopardy* theme song, trying to rush my answer, although I sensed she'd wait for a while if she needed to.

"Yeah," I said. "I'm definitely happy."

"Good. That's all I wanted you to know. See you next week." And then she hung up.

Only Emery would call me, not so that I could tell *her* that I was happy, but so that I could tell myself.

I put the phone back and looked at Trip, who was uncharacteristically relaxed. "I'm happy, too." He laughed. "Not that anyone's asking."

"You are?" I was pretty sure it was the first time I'd ever heard him say those words. "I mean, I'm asking."

Trip gave me his no longer rare smile and dunked me under the duvet. I opened my mouth to quote something about happiness being just one in a series of choices we make every day and then shut it, closed my eyes, and for the first time in ages, fell blissfully asleep.

ACKNOWLEDGMENTS

Boomerang took a circuitous route to publication that involved tears, joy, and more than one very long trail of breadcrumbs.

All along, I knew that I'd first want to thank Brent Taylor. Aside from being a dear friend, Brent has been a part of this book's journey since he was barely older than Sean and I asked him to read a manuscript that had been torn apart and sewn back together in dramatic fashion. I know exactly which scenes came from conversations with him, because they're some of my favorites. He continues to champion and support me and this story, and has become both an inspiration and a gift to the publishing community. My gratitude to him knows no bounds.

To Beth Hull, my long-suffering writing partner. *Boomerang* wouldn't be a book without you, nor would I still be writing at all, to be honest. How do I even begin to thank you for your tolerance, your calm friendship, your humor, your brainstorming, and your patience when I go into battle with all forms of punctuation? I have learned so much from you about writing and life and I'm so grateful that you put up with me. You deserve ALL the ponies and more than one magnum of wine. This book was always yours as much as mine and now that your name is up front, it's official.

Alison Weiss was the perfect editor for this book. She understood Sean and Trip from the beginning, and pushed me to make them even more Sean-like and more Trip-like. Thank you for taking on these messy, messy characters who love quoting books that are still within copyright. We got there in the end! Also, gratitude to all at Sky Pony, particularly Joshua Barnaby, Kat Enright, and Kate Gartner.

My agent, Lauren MacLeod, proves every day that perseverance wins out. It took me a while to find you, but boy, it was worth the wait. Your intuition, transparency, and sense of humor make the publishing journey a million times smoother and I'm eternally grateful to have you in my corner.

So many truly wonderful writers and others have given me feedback and shared their insight. I'm very grateful to Rachel Solomon, Brigid Kemmerer, and Emery Lord, in particular, for the kind words and support. Many thanks, as well, go to: Shawn Barnes, AdriAnne Strickland, Lisa Maxwell, Dana Alison Levy, Stephanie Cardel, Carmen Erikson, Stephanie Scott, Susan Gray Foster, Suzanne Kamata, Lynn Lindquist,

Michael Waters, Molly Jaffa, Beth Phelan, SCBWI-MidSouth, Levi Buchanan, and whoever else might be inadvertently missing from this list. Thank you for walking this journey with me.

Additional thanks to Peter Knapp and Michael Strother, who each, in their own way, gave me the encouragement I needed to keep going when things were difficult. Publishing can be tough and you both shone a much-needed light into an otherwise dark tunnel.

Last, but never least, love and gratitude to my father, Harold Baker, who remains my most vocal fan and my husband, John, who makes it all worthwhile. (See, now you're my favorite, as well!) And to Keira: may the people you love always love you back.